A FRUSTRATING START

Winston took out the wooden strips from his coat pocket. After a little more arguing with Katie this morning, he'd won the right to carry them around today to show to Mr. Penrose. Now he held them out to his friends for inspection. "These were in a secret compartment."

"A secret compartment!" Mal said. "Awesome."

"But that box was like . . . this big," said Jake, placing his hands lightly apart.

"It had a false bottom. These were underneath."

They looked at the words. BALL. LINE. WAY. PLACE. "All right," said Jake. "So what does it mean?"

"I have no idea."

"You think it's a message or something?"

Winston shrugged. "I wish I knew. My whole family stared at this for hours yesterday. We didn't get anywhere."

Mal finished the last of his banana as the bus pulled over to the curb. More kids got on board. "What's with those extra letters?" said Mal.

"You tell me. I give up."

Jake was floored. "I cannot believe what I just heard. Winston Breen is giving up on a puzzle?"

OTHER BOOKS YOU MAY ENJOY

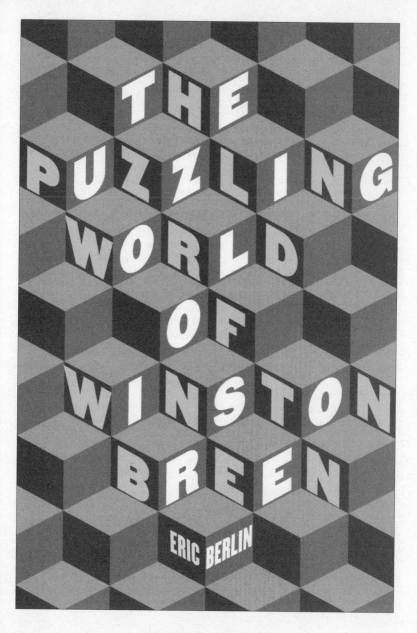

THE
PUZZLING
WORLD
OF
WINSTON
BREEN

ERIC BERLIN

PUFFIN BOOKS
An Imprint of Penguin Group (USA) Inc.

PUFFIN BOOKS

Published by the Penguin Group

Penguin Young Readers Group, 345 Hudson Street, New York, New York 10014, U.S.A.

Penguin Group (Canada), 90 Eglinton Avenue East, Suite 700, Toronto, Ontario, Canada M4P 2Y3
(a division of Pearson Penguin Canada Inc.)

Penguin Books Ltd, 80 Strand, London WC2R 0RL, England

Penguin Ireland, 25 St Stephen's Green, Dublin 2, Ireland (a division of Penguin Books Ltd)

Penguin Group (Australia), 250 Camberwell Road, Camberwell, Victoria 3124, Australia
(a division of Pearson Australia Group Pty Ltd)

Penguin Books India Pvt Ltd, 11 Community Centre, Panchsheel Park, New Delhi - 110 017, India

Penguin Group (NZ), 67 Apollo Drive, Rosedale, North Shore 0632, New Zealand
(a division of Pearson New Zealand Ltd.)

Penguin Books (South Africa) (Pty) Ltd, 24 Sturdee Avenue,
Rosebank, Johannesburg 2196, South Africa

Penguin Books Ltd, Registered Offices: 80 Strand, London WC2R 0RL, England

First published in the United States of America by G. P. Putnam's Sons,
a division of Penguin Young Readers Group, 2007

This edition published by Puffin Books, a division of Penguin Young Readers Group, 2009

13   11   10   12   14

THE LIBRARY OF CONGRESS HAS CATALOGED THE G. P. PUTNAM'S SONS EDITION AS FOLLOWS:

Berlin, Eric.

The puzzling world of Winston Breen / Eric Berlin.

p. cm.

Summary: Puzzle-crazy, twelve-year-old Winston and his ten-year-old sister Katie find themselves
involved in a dangerous mystery involving a hidden ring. Puzzles for the reader to solve are
included throughout the text.

ISBN 978-0-399-24693-7 (hc)

[1. Brothers and sisters—Fiction. 2. Puzzles—Fiction. 3. Mystery and detective stories.] I. Title.

PZ7.B45335Puz 2007   [Fic]—dc22   2006020531

Puffin Books ISBN 978-0-14-241388-3

Design by Katrina Damkoehler
Text set in ITC Century

Printed in the United States of America

For Janinne.

I mean, *obviously*.

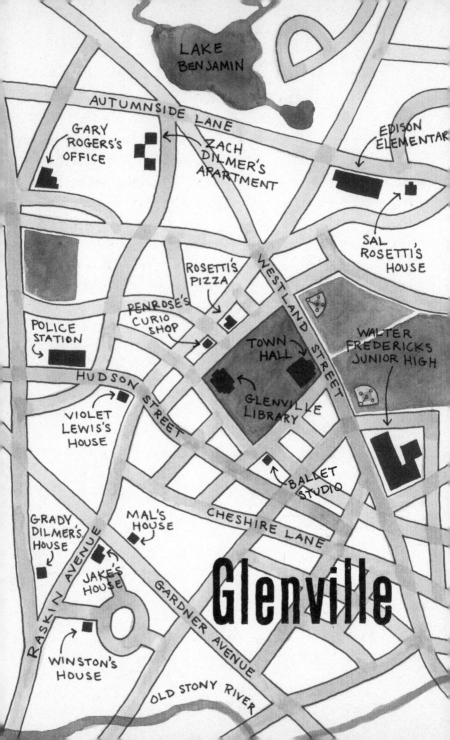

ABOUT THE PUZZLES IN THIS BOOK

This book contains quite a few puzzles. You can solve them if you want, although you don't have to solve them to enjoy the story. Most of the answers can be found in the back of the book. Some of the puzzles are so important to the story, however, that the answer will be revealed as you keep reading. You'll know those puzzles when you get to them. Note that you can't really skip these and come back to them later, because you'll learn the answer almost immediately. Take a few minutes to try them, and then continue the story.

And if you don't want to write in this book, just head over to **www.winstonbreen.com**. You can download and print out all the puzzles that require you to write or cut things up. Happy solving!

WINSTON BREEN WAS solving a puzzle, but then Winston Breen was *always* solving a puzzle.

The living room was filled with friends and relatives, all celebrating the tenth birthday of his little sister, Katie. Helium balloons bobbed about, pretending to be party guests. It was bright and sunny, and Katie and her numerous girlfriends had spent the day shrieking like crazy and running around the backyard. Winston talked to his relatives, ate hot dogs, and busied himself with the large message board his parents had placed in the front hall, rearranging the letters HAPPY BIRTHDAY KATIE into HIPPIE HAD BRATTY YAK.

Now, Katie sat cross-legged on the floor, smiling in anticipation: It was time to open the presents. Sitting that way in her new party dress, she looked like the child princess of some faraway country, surrounded by admirers and, most especially, the gifts they had brought. Winston tried to remember if he had taken birthdays so seriously just two years ago. He guessed that he had. Certainly when it came time for the presents, anyway.

Winston's present was at the bottom of the pile, so it would be a while before she got to it. He thought she would like it, even though he had bought it just yesterday. Panicked that he had forgotten about the party, he had bicycled through the chilly late-afternoon air to Penrose's Curio Shop. After spending his usual long time exploring the crammed, rickety shelves and chatting with Mr. Penrose, he had come across a small wooden box, just big enough to hold with two hands. It was carved with a pattern of diamonds, and Winston envisioned his sister keeping . . . well, *girl stuff* in it. He didn't know what. She could figure that out. Anyway, the box seemed like just the thing, and now it was sitting here with the other gifts, wrapped in the same red wrapping paper his parents had used.

While Katie opened her new toys and clothes, Winston picked up a stray scrap of wrapping paper, printed with a pattern of different shapes. His first thought, as usual, was to wonder if there was a puzzle buried among the circles and squares and triangles. Even if there wasn't, looking for a puzzle was a lot more fun than watching his sister ooh and ahh over a new pair of pants. He sat back and furrowed his eyebrows while the party continued on around him.

It took some time, but he saw it: A puzzle! Good! As he smiled with satisfaction, however, he became aware that someone was staring at him. He glanced to his left and saw Mrs. Rooney, a fairly new neighbor from down the block. Her eyeglasses were on the tip of her nose, and she was staring openly at Winston like he was a newly discovered and perplexing kind of insect.

Winston knew what she was going to say before she said it. He'd had this conversation, in one form or another, a thousand times before. And sure enough, she said, "That's a piece of wrapping paper."

"Yes . . . it is." He glanced at his mother, who smiled sympathetically. She'd had this conversation herself, many times, on behalf of her son.

Mrs. Rooney said, "You were staring at that piece of wrapping paper. For a long time."

"I was looking for a puzzle," Winston said simply.

Mrs. Rooney glanced at the bit of paper. All she saw, of course, was a scrap of garbage. "A puzzle?"

"I like puzzles," said Winston. Sometimes he thought he should just make up a sign, so that when people asked him why he was staring so intently at that billboard, or that road sign, or the plaque on that statue, he could just wave the sign at them: *Don't mind me. Everything is fine. I'm looking for a puzzle.*

Mrs. Rooney seemed to decide that Winston was probably not insane. Now she just looked curious. "Did you find a puzzle?" she asked.

"Oh, yes. See?" He handed her the paper.

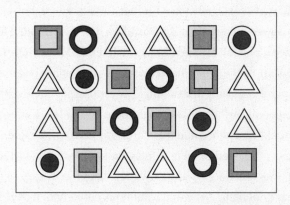

"You can draw a line that touches every shape exactly once and ends up back where it started. The line can't cross itself and has to touch the shapes in this order: circle-square-triangle, circle-square-triangle. Can you see it?"

And soon, while the party continued on around her, Mrs. Rooney was frowning intently at that same scrap of wrapping paper. Winston sat back, smiling. The only thing better than discovering a puzzle was stumping somebody else with it.

(Answer, page 211.)

Katie had finally gotten to Winston's gift—the last present in the pile. Winston leaned forward. She tore off the red wrapping paper, revealing the box. Eyes gleaming, she opened the lid. There was nothing in it. Katie looked blankly up at Winston.

"You bought me an empty box?" she said.

"A *nice* empty box," said Winston, a little offended. When Katie continued staring at him, he added, "You can keep things in it." Although that, he thought, should have been obvious.

"It's lovely," said their mother, Claire, who was sitting next to Katie on the floor. "It's a lovely keepsake box. Say thank you, Katie."

She didn't. She stared at her brother for a moment more and then closed one eye and peered at the box like a detective looking for clues. She opened it and felt around its smooth interior. Meanwhile, the party began to shift to the next phase. Winston's two aunts began clearing away paper plates and plastic cups. Several other relatives thought another slice of birthday cake might be a good idea. Katie's friends, fueled by cake and punch and then forced to sit still while Katie opened her gifts, now blasted outside to play on the lawn. The birthday girl, however, was oblivious to all of this. She held the box up to the light and felt its underside, frowning a studious detective's frown.

Winston watched this with a frown of his own. "Katie," he said, "the box is the gift. There's nothing in the box."

"You're up to something," said Katie.

"I'm not!" Winston protested. He wasn't sure how to defend himself—so many times in the past, he *had* been up to something. Last year, Winston had hidden Katie's birthday gift in the toolshed and had

4

given her clue after clue until finally, sweaty and exhausted, she found the thing two hours later. Katie tried getting revenge on his birthday, but he had marched through her clues in less than ten minutes, and she was so angry she wouldn't talk to him for the rest of the day.

So it was certainly possible that Winston was playing some kind of puzzly trick with this empty box. Nonetheless, their father said, "Katie, just say thank you. It's a very nice gift."

"I just want to know what the trick is with this box!" she said, lifting the lid again and poking around inside.

"There's no trick! I promise!" said Winston.

There was a faint snap—the sound of a tiny piece of wood breaking. "Aha!" said Katie, with triumph. And she lifted out a part of the box.

"What did you do?" said Winston, in disbelief. He had paid over ten dollars for Katie's gift, and she had broken it in less than thirty seconds. Incredible!

"You hid something in here," said Katie. "I knew it!"

Winston's father, Nathan, leaned over to look. "It has a false bottom," he said, amazed. "The box has a secret compartment."

Winston drew closer. Sure enough, Katie had found a way to remove the floor of the box, revealing a handful of . . . well, what? They appeared to be thin wooden strips with letters on them. What on earth were they?

"What is this, Winston? I don't want to go on another puzzle hunt this year." But when Katie looked up into Winston's face, she saw immediately that he hadn't done this. His expression was one of bewilderment—his eyebrows were arched practically to the top of his head, and that was a look he wore only when faced with a *really* hard puzzle. She looked back into the box at the little wooden strips and then turned the box over and dumped them out.

Four small, thin rectangles fell to the floor. They were made of wood, and each had some kind of inscription in block letters. The partygoers in the living room were utterly quiet as they watched this performance. Even some of the restless kids had crept back in to see why everyone was so fascinated. Winston picked up one of the wooden pieces. It said:

$$\boxed{\textsf{L I N E}}$$

"Line," he said. Why was the *I* in a different color? Heck—why were these words here at all, hidden away in the bottom of this box? He looked at the others.

$$\boxed{\textsf{BALL \quad R}} \qquad \boxed{\textsf{PLACE \quad S}}$$

$$\boxed{\textsf{WAY}}$$

"Winston?" said his mother. "You didn't do this?"

"I swear, Mom."

"Then who did?"

"I don't know," he said. "I have no idea." Winston gazed at the mysterious little strips. BALL. LINE. WAY. PLACE. Simple, everyday words, but what were they doing here? Why those extra letters, the *R* and the *S*? And why the discolored letters in WAY and LINE? Was that done on purpose?

"Ballerina," said Uncle Roger, suddenly. He had been sitting in the overstuffed armchair, looking like a bored emperor. Now he clearly thought he had cracked the whole case wide open and was sitting up excitedly. When he saw that everyone was looking at him with great puzzlement, he said it again, louder: "Ballerina!"

"What about a ballerina?" said Winston's father.

Roger rolled his eyes. "Nathan! Look! You got BALL and then some empty space and then an *R*. What word could that be? Ballerina! That's it!"

Nathan Breen seemed unconvinced. "Well . . . okay. But if that's right, then what does it mean?"

Roger blinked. "Well. Um. I don't know."

Another relative, Aunt Regina, suddenly said, "High!"

Winston thought she had said "hi," even though she had been there for hours and had greeted the whole family with big lipstick kisses upon her arrival. But he didn't want to seem rude, so he cautiously said, "Hello."

Regina shook her head. "No, no. High! You can put the word *high* in front of all these words!"

They looked. Highway—that made sense.

Winston said, "Highball?"

Regina colored a little. "It's a . . . drink for grown-ups."

"Wait a second, wait a second," said Winston's neighbor, Mr. Bernstein. He was a nice man, but also very loud. And also very fat. "Golf!" he said. "It has something to do with golf!"

Uncle Roger couldn't believe his ears. "Golf? How do you figure that?"

Aunt Regina looked irritated. "Hey! What about me? Look! Highway, highball, highline, and . . ." She trailed off. "High place. I thought that was a word. Wait a second . . ." She stared at the floor and tried to recover the answer she had grasped so firmly just a moment ago.

Winston's mother asked, "What's a highline?"

Winston said, "I've never heard of it."

Regina looked up. "Isn't that a word?" She looked sorry she had ever opened her mouth.

Mr. Bernstein, however, was suffering no lack of confidence. He felt he had waited long enough. In a loud voice he said, "I'm telling you, it's golf! Look! You PLACE the BALL on a tee, right? Right?" He looked around for support.

One of Katie's friends, a thin blond girl named Monica, spoke up. "It's a knot."

Winston said, "What is?"

"A highline knot. It's what you use to tie a horse to a post. My parents like to go horseback riding, and they take me, and I'm going to have my own horse someday." She smiled broadly.

Aunt Regina was pleased. "A highline knot! I knew it."

Mr. Bernstein was going to get through his theory if it killed him. "And then you hit the ball in a straight LINE down the fairWAY."

"Fairway is one word!" said Uncle Roger.

"So?"

"So that doesn't work! I'm telling you, it's got something to do with a ballerina!"

Aunt Regina sighed deeply. "Well, I give up. Winston, what's the answer?"

Winston looked surprised. "How should I know?"

"Wait, you mean you really didn't put that puzzle in there?"

"No! Really!" Winston was exasperated. Didn't they see that he was just as perplexed as everybody else?

Winston's cousin, Henry, was eighteen years old and was one of Winston's favorite people. He hadn't said anything up to this point, but now he jumped in, in a calm voice that somehow seized everyone's attention. "Look, let's say for a moment that all four words have something to do with golf. What would that mean?"

"It would mean that golf is the answer to the puzzle," said Mr. Bernstein, as if he thought Henry was playing dumb on purpose.

Henry shook his head. "But what would that *mean*? The answer to the puzzle is golf. Fine. So what? That's not very satisfying."

Mr. Bernstein said, "Maybe Winston bought Katie golf lessons."

Katie said with surprised distaste, "Golf lessons?"

"All I did was buy the box!" said Winston.

Henry waved off this possibility. "No. I've solved a lot of Winston's puzzles. If he gave Katie golf lessons—which I really, really doubt—the answer to the puzzle would be something like, 'Happy Birthday! You have ten free golf lessons.' There wouldn't be any other possibility. All these ideas we're hearing, they're all too . . ." He tried to think of the word.

"Vague," Winston's mother offered.

"Right," said Henry. "Besides, I think it's pretty clear that Katie doesn't golf." Katie nodded vigorously in agreement. "No. Winston says he has nothing to do with this, and I believe him." Winston, grateful, smiled at his cousin. Several others in the room still looked skeptical.

"So what do you suggest?" said Uncle Roger.

"Well," said Henry. "I guess I'm suggesting that we all have some more cake. Winston will solve this. Give him time."

But Winston couldn't solve it.

He sat staring at the wooden pieces as the party went on around him. Occasionally others would sit with him for a few minutes, helping to think up possible solutions. Should the letters all be scrambled together to form some new phrase? (PALS WILL CANE BARLEY was the best they could do, and that seemed unhelpful.) Maybe the wooden pieces should be stacked on top of each other or arranged in some way. (Nope.) Uncle Roger came by, determined to make his ballerina theory fit somehow. He suggested drawing a *line* on a map, from the local ballet studio to . . . well, he didn't know. They got out a map of the town but couldn't figure out where such a line should be drawn or how that might get them closer to an answer. Mr. Bernstein came over several times, and each time Winston had to gently inform him that golf probably didn't have anything to do with it.

After a while, Winston wasn't sure if the puzzle had an answer at all.

Everybody agreed, as the party wrapped up, that Winston had *not* planted the puzzle himself. He was clearly trying too hard to solve it.

"Well, if you didn't create it, who did?" asked Henry. The party was now over. It was evening, twilight, and the house had been restored to its proper order. Henry was staying at Winston's house that night, before driving back to college the next day. The two of them were out on the patio with the wooden pieces on a little table between them.

"I wish I knew," said Winston. His brain hurt—he could actually feel it throbbing, like something out of a science-fiction movie. And he was tired. Sitting in this lounge chair with his feet up, he thought he could easily fall asleep out here.

"Someone put those pieces in there," said Henry. "Maybe someone who knows how much you like puzzles. They thought it was your box. They didn't know you were giving it to Katie."

Winston considered this. "But . . . how did they know it had a false bottom? I didn't even know that."

Henry stared ahead, trying to work around that one. Finally he said, "All right. That's a good point. Put that aside for a minute. Who had access to the box?"

"Well, my whole family, I guess. I brought it home and put it in my room and didn't wrap it until last night."

"Is that all?"

"No—Malcolm and Jake came over and were in my room for a while." Mal and Jake were his two best friends.

"Could it be one of them? Or both of them together?"

"I guess." Winston was doubtful. "I did leave them there when Mom asked me to help her with something."

"Well, then!"

"But if they created a puzzle they wanted me to solve, why not just hand it to me? Why put it someplace where I might not ever find it? And, like I said, how did they know about the secret compartment?"

"Maybe they were going to put it in the box, but then they found the false bottom, so they decided to put it there instead. Maybe they thought you knew about it."

Winston sighed. It was possible, but just barely. He couldn't imagine either of his friends taking the time to engrave letters on thin strips of wood. What would be the point? If either of them had created a puzzle, they would do what Winston did all the time: Jot it down on a piece of loose-leaf paper. "Well, I'll ask them," he said.

They sat there as the twilight turned to full dark. It was starting to get chilly, but Winston was too tired to move. He picked up the pieces again—he couldn't help it—and flipped through them. BALL. LINE. WAY. PLACE. Plus those extra letters. Totally bizarre.

Henry got up and said, "Well, I'm wiped out. I've got to do some reading for school, and then I'm hitting the sack."

"Okay. Good night."

"You know, you usually have a puzzle for me. Didn't have time to create one this time?"

"Hmm?" Winston was back to staring at the wooden pieces.

"Nothing, nothing. Good night." Henry started into the house. "Hey. Where did you get that box, anyway?"

"Penrose's Curio Shop, in town."

"Penrose!" He came back out.

"Yeah." Winston looked up at him blearily. Henry suddenly looked like he was lit from within by a great big lightbulb.

"Isn't that the old guy you told me about? The one who likes puzzles almost as much as you?" Henry was practically jumping into the air. "He's the guy who runs that crazy shop where you can buy anything?"

"Yeah." Winston still wasn't getting it.

"Winston, you nut! You must be totally exhausted if you don't see it. Penrose put that puzzle in there!"

Winston's eyes widened. Of course! He couldn't believe he had missed it. Penrose was the oldest man in the world (or seemed so to Winston), and his brain was stuffed with riddles, word games, and brainteasers. Penrose always had a stumper for Winston, whenever he dropped by the shop. How could he have missed it?

"You're right! That must be it. I'll go there tomorrow," said Winston.

"Will he tell you the answer?"

"If I ask. But, no, I want a hint. I want to solve it myself."

"All right. But when you finally get it, you better tell me. This is driving me nuts. Good night, kid." Henry went inside.

Winston smiled. Penrose! It made perfect sense. Although, if this puzzle was Penrose's creation, it was his nastiest one yet. All this time spent on it and not the slightest bit of progress had been made. But trying to solve something was always fun. That was Winston's opinion, anyway. And he smiled as he thought of the puzzle he had snuck onto Henry's pillow in the guest bedroom earlier that day.

Dear Henry,

Each of the words in this list can be found in the grid, reading across, down, or diagonally, and either forward or backward. Some of the words will cross the shaded middle row, whose letters are all missing—you'll need to fill in these letters. When you've found all the words, the middle row will spell out the title of this puzzle.

AFGHAN	CHIHUAHUA	POODLE
AKITA	COLLIE	SALUKI
BASENJI	CORGI	SAMOYED
BEAGLE	DOBERMAN	SHEEPDOG
BICHON FRISE	MALTESE	SHIH TZU
BORZOI	MASTIFF	TERRIER
BOXER	NEWFOUNDLAND	WHIPPET
BULLDOG	POINTER	

D	N	A	L	D	N	U	O	F	W	E	N	R
T	G	C	H	I	H	U	A	H	U	A	E	A
S	B	N	E	S	E	T	L	A	M	I	G	F
C	B	O	X	E	R	D	A	R	R	U	B	F
O	L	I	R	A	C	K	E	R	Z	P	G	I
R	P	J	B	Z	I	B	E	T	L	O	Y	T
I	I	E	A	D	C	I	P	P	E	D	O	A
K	N	S	G	H	H	Y	E	P	I	L	D	M
U	T	A	L	S	G	E	V	I	L	E	L	O
L	E	B	E	K	H	F	F	H	L	D	L	Y
A	R	D	L	S	O	X	A	W	O	S	U	E
S	E	S	I	R	F	N	O	H	C	I	B	D

(Answer, page 211.)

13

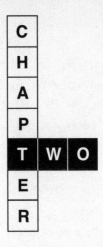

WINSTON LEFT THE wooden pieces on the coffee table in the living room, but when he came down the next morning, they were gone. He blinked at the empty surface and then looked madly about the room. On top of the TV? No. On the bookcase? No. On the floor? No. They were simply gone.

He should have brought them to his room last night! But he had been so sick of staring at them, the same four words again and again for hours.

Did his mother or father throw them out? Mistake them for trash? It seemed beyond imagining. They wouldn't toss an unsolved puzzle into the garbage. That would be like ripping up a baseball fanatic's trading cards. Right?

Right. They knew their son. They wouldn't do that.

Winston ran into the kitchen with the words *Where are they?* primed behind his lips . . . and there they were. Katie was at the kitchen table, eating a bowl of cereal and occasionally rearranging the strips, which were laid out carefully in front of her. Her bright blue schoolbag was at her feet, adorned with shiny stickers.

Katie looked up at Winston as he flew in, and he tried to hastily compose himself. All was well. The puzzle pieces were safe.

Watching her stare at the puzzle, he got himself a bowl and poured some cereal. The newspaper was on the table, and Winston pulled it over as if that's what he'd wanted all along. "Tenth Robbery This Month," said the headline, but Winston wasn't interested. He watched Katie slide the puzzle pieces around, seemingly at random.

"Whatcha doing?" he asked his sister.

She swallowed a spoonful of breakfast and said, "Solving my puzzle." She moved LINE in front of WAY and studied this new arrangement, frowning but bright-eyed.

Winston said, "*Your* puzzle?"

She switched a couple of pieces around. "Sure. You bought it for me."

"I bought the *box* for you."

She shrugged. "And these were inside."

"But—" Winston couldn't think how to respond to that. Katie was such a serious little kid sometimes, serious and smart. And he did buy her the box. And the puzzle pieces were inside. And . . .

He finally said, "But you don't even like puzzles!"

She looked up for the first time. "Yes, I do! Just not as much as you. *No one* likes them as much as you."

He thought, Be reasonable. Calmly, he said, "Katie, I wanted to take those pieces to school today."

"Well, I want to solve it," she said. "It's a mystery, and I want to solve it."

"So write down the words and you can still solve it."

"Why don't *you* write down the words?"

He had known she was going to say that. Winston rubbed his forehead. Slightly less calmly, he said, "I was going to take them to Mr. Penrose today. After school. Maybe he knows something about them."

"So why can't I do that?"

"My school is closer, and Mr. Penrose knows me, and you're not allowed to go into town by yourself yet."

"So why can't you just tell him about it?" she said. "He doesn't need to see the pieces. I'm taking them to school today. I'm going to solve it with Maggie and Debra and Janie."

Those were her three closest friends. None of them, to Winston's knowledge, had the slightest interest in puzzles of any kind. Stuffed animals, yes. Puzzles, no.

"Maybe," Winston said. "Maybe he doesn't need to see the puzzle pieces. But maybe he does. How do I know until I show them to him?"

Katie shrugged. She never threw a screaming fit, but she could be as stubborn as a cement wall. "I wanna show them to my friends. I'm going to bring them to school."

"Your friends saw them! They were all here yesterday."

"Janie wasn't. She couldn't come."

This was going to go on forever. Winston wished he was the kind of kid who could just grab the puzzle pieces and run out of the room. But he understood how that tactic would work out: His mom or dad would punish his greed by awarding her the pieces, permanently.

Their mom came into the kitchen, dressed smartly as usual. As soon as the kids were out the door for the school bus, she would be off to work. She was an office manager at a law firm a few miles away.

Winston lunged at this opportunity. He knew it was childish, but he saw no other way. "Mom, Katie won't give me my puzzle pieces!"

Katie said immediately, "They're my puzzle pieces! Winston bought them for me!"

"I didn't know they were there!"

"They're still mine!"

Winston choked back the words *Are not!* His mother would have frowned on that. A strangled sound of frustration emerged from his throat, making him sound like an angry duck.

"If you both want to solve the puzzle," said their mother, hardly even paying attention as she went about her routine, "then solve it together."

Winston sighed. Every argument he and Katie had was resolved by the same command from his parents: *Share.* Why did Winston continue to go to them, as if they might suddenly say something different?

"Can I have the pieces today, though?" he said.

And then his mother stunned him by saying, "You'll have to ask Katie. You bought those puzzle pieces for her, after all. They belong to her."

Katie sat back in her chair smugly.

"I didn't know they were in there!" Winston said.

"They still belong to Katie, Winston. I'm sorry. Not every puzzle in the world belongs to you."

Winston, grasping about for a reply, said the first thing that came to his mind. "But I think Jake and Mal put those pieces in there for me to find!" Realizing that he did not really believe that, he added, "Or Mr. Penrose! He's always giving me puzzles. He didn't know I was going to give the box to Katie."

Claire Breen stopped and seemed to consider this. Katie's smile dropped off by a degree or two.

"All right," said his mother. "If one of your friends put the puzzle in there, then you can keep it. But if it simply came with the box, then it's Katie's. But either way, I expect the two of you to *share.* Understand?"

"Yes, Mom," they both said dutifully.

Winston was in his usual seat on the school bus when Mal and Jake boarded at the next stop. Jake slid in next to him and Mal took the empty seat in front.

"How was the party?" Jake asked.

"It was fine," said Winston. He was still a little tired. "I had a lot of cake."

"Did Katie get the dead lizard I sent her?" said Mal.

"Yeah, Mal. We had that for dessert, too."

"Good, good. I sent it overnight delivery. Stays fresher that way." Mal was standing on his knees, facing backward in his seat, and bouncing happily. The bus driver would tell him to "cut that out and sit down right" soon enough. This happened almost every day.

"You hide her present this year?" asked Jake. Winston shook his head. "I guess not, since she threatened to kill you if you ever did that again." Jake was the tallest of the three friends and by far the most athletic—he was on the junior high swim team and played third base on the baseball team. He had an unusual talent for being friends with both the boisterous athletes at school, as well as with more studious types like . . . well, like Winston. It was a talent that Winston occasionally found himself envying.

"No, I just gave it to her the regular way."

"How boring," said Mal, digging something out of his lunch bag: a banana. He started to peel it. He was still bouncing lightly in his seat. "What'd ya get her?"

Winston looked at his friend. "That wooden box. The one in my room the other day."

"Oh, right."

"Cut that out and sit down right!" snapped the bus driver. Mal jumped around and sat down properly, facing the bus driver's glare in the rearview mirror. He gave her a smile full of mashed banana.

Winston leaned forward. "Ah, did either of you put anything into that box? Maybe the other day, while I was out of the room?"

His two friends just looked at him. Mal was too mystified by the question to come up with a smart-alecky answer.

"What do you mean?" Jake finally said.

"Not me," said Mal. "It would have been a good idea, but I didn't think of it."

"What was in it?" said Jake.

Winston took out the wooden strips from his coat pocket. After a little more arguing with Katie this morning, he'd won the right to carry them around today to show to Mr. Penrose. Now he held them out to his friends for inspection. "These were in a secret compartment."

"A secret compartment!" Mal said. "Awesome."

"But that box was like . . . this big," said Jake, placing his hands slightly apart.

"It had a false bottom. These were underneath."

They looked at the words. BALL. LINE. WAY. PLACE. "All right," said Jake. "So what does it mean?"

"I have no idea."

"You think it's a message or something?"

Winston shrugged. "I wish I knew. My whole family stared at this for hours yesterday. We didn't get anywhere."

Mal finished the last of his banana as the bus pulled over to the curb. More kids got on board. "What's with those extra letters?" said Mal.

"You tell me. I give up."

Jake was floored. "I cannot believe what I just heard. Winston Breen is giving up on a puzzle?"

Mal threw his arms to the heavens. "Everything is opposite! Day is night! Up is down! Cats are dogs!"

Winston turned bright red. "Shut up. I'm done *temporarily*. I need more information."

Jake took the pieces and flipped through them. "So where'd it come from?"

"My cousin thinks that Penrose put it in there."

"Did you buy it at Penrose's place?"

"Yeah."

Mal said, "Well then, geez. Of course he put it there."

"I have to ask him. I'm gonna go there after school," Winston said.

"No," Jake said. "We gotta go to the library, remember?" The three of them were in history class together, and they all had papers due the following week. "You can't spend your usual day and a half looking at stuffed ostriches or whatever he sells in there."

"All right. I'll just drop in, I promise. A quick stop at Penrose's, just to ask him. Then the library."

"Who are you doing, anyway?" Jake asked.

"Huh?"

"For your report. Your history report."

"Oh," said Winston. "Benjamin Franklin."

"I'm doing Walter Fredericks," said Mal. "Easy as pie."

"He's not historical!" said Jake. The three of them attended Walter Fredericks Junior High.

Mal looked taken aback. "He's dead, isn't he? He was one of the richest guys in town. He was some kind of inventor. Why isn't he historical? Mr. Nelson approved the topic."

"Fine, fine." Jake rolled his eyes to show that he was simply being tolerant of a crazy notion.

"You just wish you thought of it first," said Mal. "Who are you doing?"

"Thomas Paine," said Jake.

"See? That's lame-o. Mine's much better."

Jake swung out at Mal playfully, and Mal ducked his head down, laughing.

Winston was still holding the wooden pieces, and now he went back to flipping idly through them. "I hope Mr. Penrose can explain these," he said. "It's driving me crazy."

"Short trip," said Mal, happily.

"Get a new joke," Winston told him.

Jake said as they all entered the school together, "Hey, I forgot to tell you, I thought of a puzzle over the weekend." Winston was by far the most fanatical of the trio when it came to puzzles, but both Mal and Jake liked a good challenge.

"Oh, yeah?" said Winston.

"Shoot," said Mal.

"All right, here it is." Jake dug out a piece of paper from his pocket and uncrumpled it. Winston looked over his shoulder. It was a list of animals, all of them with three letters:

```
ANT    EWE
CAT    OWL
COW    PIG
DOG    RAM
ELK    RAT
```

Jake said, "Take two of these animals. If you spell them out backward, one after another, you'll get a six-letter word."

They mulled it over as they walked down the hall.

"Targod," said Mal.

Jake stopped in his tracks. "Targod?"

"Sure! DOG and RAT, spelled backward. Targod!"

"Great. Except my answer is a real word."

"Oh, well, in that case, I don't know."

"How about you, Win?"

"I don't have it yet. Give me until history class." He took the list and walked off staring at it.

(Answer, page 212.)

WINSTON FLEW INTO his bedroom, emptied half the contents of his bookbag onto his bed, shouldered the rest, and ran back down the stairs to his bicycle. Did he still have the wooden strips? Yes, they were right there in his inside coat pocket. He avoided Katie, in case she planned to ask for them back.

It was nice—no, it was *great*—to be bicycling again after the long winter. Winston liked snow as much as the next kid, but sometimes it seemed as if spring would never arrive. And now it had. Suddenly, the days would get longer and sunnier, and Winston could bicycle through town with his friends. They'd ride with no hands or attempt extremely lame wheelies or have races that Jake would win effortlessly. Soon they would even stop taking the school bus and would bike to school each morning instead.

Winston met Jake and Mal in Rosetti's Pizzeria, their usual hangout. Sal Rosetti, gruff and dark-eyed and a zillion years old, nodded to him—his usual unsmiling welcome. (Mal said the expression translated to "I'm glad you're here! Don't stay too long!")

The pizzeria was one of a long string of businesses placed all in a row along the border of the large town green—two banks, a hair salon, a fish market, a deli, and a lot more.

Plus Penrose's Curio Shop, Winston's favorite store in the world.

Penrose's shelves were crammed tight with the most incredible assortment of items one could imagine. A small table that was so ornately carved that it must have come from a European palace. A seventeen-pound dictionary that wasn't in English. A peacock feather that was almost five feet long. A lamp made out of coconuts. Where did all this stuff come from? Winston could not imagine.

His first time in the store, he had browsed up and down the three narrow aisles and hadn't even realized that a full hour had passed. And that was before coming across a shelf stocked with . . . puzzles! Puzzles made out of metal and wood, old puzzle books creaky with age. Winston could hardly believe his eyes. Even more amazing, Penrose would let you try them out for as long you wanted. It turned out that Mr. Penrose, like Winston, loved puzzles of all kinds, and the two became unlikely friends. Now when Winston dropped in, Penrose often had a challenge of some kind ready for him. Sometimes Winston solved them. Sometimes he had to ask for a few hints. Occasionally one would elude him entirely, but—and Winston was quite proud of this—not often.

Each of the three boys had a quick slice of pizza before walking their bicycles down a few stores to Penrose's shop. The familiar little bell jingled as they entered. Penrose was in his place behind the counter, and he threw his arms wide in a gesture of mock surprise.

"Winston! You are back so soon!"

"Hi, Mr. Penrose."

"How did your sister like that box you bought her? Eh?"

"Well," said Winston. "She liked it."

"Good! Good." Penrose put on his glasses, which magnified his brown eyes dramatically.

"Mr. Penrose," said Winston. "Did you, uh, did you put one of your puzzles into the box? Before giving it to me?"

Penrose squinted at him. "A puzzle? I gave you a puzzle when you came in here. And you batted it away like a badminton birdie, if I remember correctly."

"But you didn't put anything in the box?"

"Like what?"

"Like wooden strips with words on them."

Penrose was only looking more and more mystified, an expression that Winston was not used to seeing on Penrose's face. "Wooden strips?"

Winston sighed. Penrose hadn't planted the puzzle. He'd have said so if he'd done it. So the most intriguing, mysterious puzzle he had ever come across officially belonged to his sister, and that was that. Oh, well.

He brought out the four simple words from his pocket. Penrose reached out a slightly shaky hand and took them. He held them up to the light and examined them deeply, one at a time.

Jake and Mal were wandering around the store. It was impossible to step into Penrose's and *not* wander. Mal picked up something off a shelf and examined it. "What is this?" he said.

Penrose glanced away from the wooden strips. "That," he said, "is a device for removing the bones from a dead fish."

"Oh, yuck." Mal put it back down distastefully.

Penrose turned back to Winston. "You say these were in the box?"

"Yes. The box had a secret compartment. These were in there."

"Really! Isn't that something." Penrose seemed quite pleased that one of his own items held such an interesting secret.

"Do you know what they are?" Winston said.

Penrose shook his head slowly. "No. I didn't even know they existed until just this moment. Most fascinating. A puzzle of some nature, I should say." He smiled at Winston. "How wonderful that they fell into the right hands, eh?"

"Or nearly," said Winston, mostly to himself.

"If it is a puzzle," said Penrose, "do you have any idea how to solve it?"

It was Winston's turn to shake his head. "Worked on it a long time, too."

"I'll bet you did," Penrose said gravely. He handed the pieces back to Winston.

Jake had wandered back over, and now he said, "Mr. Penrose, where did that box come from?"

"Hmm. That is a good question. It was not very big, correct? A rather dark wood, with a pattern of diamonds. Yes?"

Winston nodded in agreement.

"Yes, I thought so," said Penrose. "That box came from the estate of Livia Little. Nice lady. She died several weeks ago. Do you know who she is?"

The boys just stared.

"Okay, then, no. Perhaps you would know her before she got married and changed her name. Before, she was Livia Fredericks. Is that any better?"

Mal said hesitantly, "Walter Fredericks?"

Penrose nodded. "He was her father. Do you know who he is?"

Mal said, "I'm writing a report on him."

"Tell me, then."

Mal glanced around, surprised at this pop quiz. "Uh. I haven't gotten very far. Our school is named after him. He was one of the richest men in town. He invented things. My father said he invented a new kind of mattress."

"He invented many things," said Mr. Penrose, "And he supported this town in a number of ways. He helped to build this town, in fact. It's quite proper that your school should be named for him. He was a good man."

"You think he put the puzzle pieces in the box?" said Winston.

Mr. Penrose shook his head. "I have no idea. Do you know what you should do? You should ask Violet Lewis."

Jake said, "Mrs. Lewis? The librarian?"

Penrose nodded. "Yes. She, too, is a daughter of Walter Fredericks."

Winston said, "Really? I didn't know that."

Mal looked at him. "Why would you?"

Penrose continued, "She is Livia's sister. Now that Livia has passed on, I think Violet is the only child of Walter Fredericks who is still alive. Ah, that's too bad."

"Do you think she would know about these puzzle pieces?"

"I don't know. I can only suggest you ask her."

"I'll do that," said Winston. "I hope she can tell us something. I was sure that this puzzle came from you."

"No, I'm afraid not. But of course, that doesn't mean I don't have a puzzle to share. If you're interested."

Winston beamed. "I figured you wouldn't have one, since I was here just a couple of days ago."

"Winston Breen, I am always prepared for your arrival."

He jotted something down on a scrap of paper and handed it to Winston, who took it and, with a great amount of effort, did not look at it but simply put it in his pocket. "I'll look at it later if that's okay."

Penrose smiled. "You want to get to the library. I understand."

"We were going there anyway!" said Winston. "We have history papers due."

"Good-bye, then! Let me know what Mrs. Lewis has to say."

The town where Winston lived, Glenville, didn't grow slowly from a few farms, the way many other communities do. It was planned and built a long time ago. The designers (including Walter Fredericks himself) imagined a town green where residents could come and walk around, and they imagined the very row of shops that Winston and his friends had just visited. At one end of the green was the town hall and at the other end was the library, looking like the town hall's younger brother.

The three boys rode up to the library and chained their bicycles at the nearby racks. Entering the large main room, they passed Mrs. Lewis at her usual desk, busy with paperwork. The boys sat down at one of the long blond wood tables so they could spread out.

Two giant shelves were marked BIOGRAPHY, and Jake and Mal disappeared down the aisle. Winston, however, couldn't resist—he had to see what kind of challenge Penrose had for him this time. He uncrumpled the little piece of paper. If I can't solve it right away, I'll save it for later, he thought.

The paper bore Penrose's graceful handwriting and consisted of just a few words.

These six words can all be scrambled to make new words. Which one does not belong?

AMONG   BEARD   CHEAP

LUMP   MILE   PAGER

(Answer, page 212.)

28

* * *

Jake returned to the table with three books about Thomas Paine. Mal was still gone. "He's right," said Jake. "I should have chosen someone more interesting. Jackie Robinson, maybe. Mr. Nelson said 'historical' so I assumed that meant hundreds of years ago. Oh, well." He flipped through the first of the books.

Mal came back, looking stunned. "They don't have anything on Walter Fredericks! No books. Nothing!"

"You're kidding," said Winston.

"He was the richest guy in town!" said Jake. "Nobody wrote anything about him?"

"I couldn't find anything. I can't believe it!"

"Well, why not talk to Mrs. Lewis?" said Jake. "She is the guy's daughter."

"Yeah, I guess so. . . ." Mal glanced back at the biography section as if it had offended him.

Winston said, "I'll go over with you. I'll ask her if she knows anything about the puzzle pieces."

Walking over to the reference desk, Mal said, "That reminds me—I thought of something about those pieces."

"Oh, yeah? What?"

"Two of the strips have extra letters, and two of the strips don't, right?"

"Right."

"What if you took the extra letters and put them into the other words? What does that get you?"

Winston took the strips from his pocket. "What do you mean?" he said.

PLACE S	BALL R

WAY	LINE

Mal said excitedly, "See? The *A* in WAY is a different color. You can replace it with this *R* and get WRY!"

"Yeah," said Winston. "But that doesn't work on the other one. If you take the *S* from this strip and put it in LINE, you get . . . LSNE."

Mal stared at it for a moment. "Well, heck."

"It was a good idea, though. Maybe there's something to it."

They had reached the reference desk. Mrs. Lewis looked up from her stack of books with a firm, businesslike smile.

Mal said, "Mrs. Lewis? I'm doing a report on Walter Fredericks, and I was told that . . . uh, that you were his . . ."

Mal trailed off into silence. Mrs. Lewis didn't seem to notice that Mal existed. Winston saw that her can-I-help-you smile had vanished. She was staring at him with widening eyes.

Winston cautiously said, "Mrs. Lewis? Are you okay?"

Mrs. Lewis pushed herself away from the desk as if Winston had tried to hit her. Was she sick? Was she having some sort of heart attack? He and Mal exchanged a worried glance. What was going on here?

She stood up on legs that were clearly shaky, but made a visible effort to pull herself together. Finally, she said, "Where did you get those?" She pointed a long accusatory finger. Winston looked down and saw that he was still holding the wooden strips.

It took a moment to find his voice. "I . . . I bought them," he said. It seemed the simplest way of cutting through a long story.

Mrs. Lewis all but shouted, "You didn't buy them! Where did you get those!"

Winston glanced around and saw people around the library staring at them. He took an involuntary step away from the desk. This was frightening, and he felt helpless and small. "No, really," he said. "They . . . they were in a box." He thought perhaps the full explanation would be better after all. "Your sister—"

That was as far as he got. "Why don't you people leave me alone?" she said sharply. Now Mrs. Lewis looked just plain angry.

Winston couldn't figure out how to respond to this. He glanced at Mal, but he was no help. He looked as astonished as Winston felt. Finally he said, "Mrs. Lewis—"

But she exploded. "Get out of here! Get out of here!" Then, in an amazing finale, she collapsed back into her chair, weeping loudly.

Mal and Winston ran. They ran back to Jake, who had seen the whole thing and was already rapidly packing up their belongings. "What was that all about?" he asked in a low hiss.

"I don't know!" said Winston. "She just went nuts."

"What did you say?"

"Nothing! We didn't say anything!" Winston threw his stuff into his backpack. He looked back at Mrs. Lewis and didn't like what he saw: She had come out from behind the reference desk and was marching over to them. She had apparently decided she had more to say. The makeup around her eyes was running down her face in dark streaks.

Mal saw her coming, too. "Oh, no!" he whispered hoarsely.

"Let's go, already," said Jake.

They had to run toward Mrs. Lewis to get out. They did this as fast as they could. Her expression was one of blind rage. She yelled at the three boys as they ran through the door, "You just stay out of here! You keep away from me!" Winston cast a glance over his shoulder as the door shut behind them. She was crying again—loud, miserable sobs, her hands to her face.

Winston was prepared to run all the way home, but then he remembered his bicycle, locked up right here. It felt like forever, kneeling by the bike rack and dialing the combination, and then finally pedaling away from the dim but definite sound of Mrs. Lewis.

They rode for several blocks, as fast as they could. As they rounded a corner and started down a side street, Jake said, "Whoa, whoa. Guys, stop. Stop!"

They stopped, panting heavily. Nobody said anything as they tried to process the events of the last five minutes.

"Well," said Jake, finally, "what happened?"

Winston said, "It was the wooden strips from the box. She saw them and—"

"She just snapped," said Mal. "Holy moly. I've never seen anything like that."

Jake said, "You didn't say something?" He was talking to Mal.

Mal looked offended. "Like what? I asked her about Walter Fredericks, and she never even heard me. She saw those puzzle pieces and went berserko. Don't blame me."

"Mal's right," said Winston. "It wasn't him."

They stood there, bewildered. Winston took the puzzle pieces back out of his coat pocket—but not before casting a glance behind him, as if Mrs. Lewis might materialize like an evil genie to scream at them some more. His two friends came closer, and they looked at the little wooden strips, trying to see them through new eyes.

"Well," Mal said after a moment, "I guess she knows what they are."

"I guess *so*," said Winston. "But we don't. And I'm not going back to ask her."

Mal said, "Did you hear what she said? 'Why don't you people leave me alone?'"

Winston nodded. "Yeah. I heard that, all right."

Jake said, "What did she mean by that?"

Nobody had an answer. They stood there, trying to think it through. It made no sense. None at all.

When he got home, Katie was watching television in the living room, stretched out comfortably on the couch. "Well?" she said, the second Winston walked through the door.

"Well what?" said Winston, although he knew what she was referring to.

She sat up. "Is that my puzzle or what?"

Reluctantly, Winston dug the pieces out of his coat pocket. After Mrs. Lewis's disturbing reaction to them, the thin strips of wood felt almost alive, maybe even cursed. Handing them over to his little sister seemed like a terrible idea. It felt like giving her a loaded weapon. But what was he supposed to say? "I can't give you these four strips of wood, Katie. They're too dangerous." He'd be laughed out of the room.

"All right, yes," he said. "They're yours. But listen—"

"I knew it!" she said, smiling as triumphantly as if she had beaten him at arm wrestling. Winston loved his sister, but she was not the most gracious winner in the world.

Winston took a deep breath and tried again. "Katie, listen—"

"Give them to me!" she said, still on the couch but holding out her hand.

Grimly, Winston walked over to her and handed her the pieces. "But you can't show these to anybody," he said. "Do you understand?"

That stubborn look came over her face, the one she wore when she planned to do exactly the opposite of what she had just been told. "Why not? You showed them to your friends."

"I did," said Winston, "but—"

"I'm going to solve it with Janie. And Maggie and Debra."

"Right, right," said Winston. "Fine, you can show it to them but not to anybody else, okay?"

"Why not?"

Sitting next to her on the couch, he told her about the library and about Mrs. Lewis's incredible reaction when she saw the pieces. From Katie's flat, disbelieving expression, it was clear that Winston was not getting across how eerie and bizarre the whole encounter had been.

"You're saying she got upset because of these?" She waved the pieces around.

"I know it sounds weird—"

"Give me a break, Winston. You just don't want me to solve the puzzle."

"Solve it all you want! I'm just asking you not to show those pieces to too many people. Show it to your friends and that's it, okay?"

She shrugged and answered with a curt "Fine," then turned back toward the television. She wasn't agreeing or disagreeing with him. She just wanted him to go away and drop the subject. It was her puzzle, and that was that. Winston stared at her a moment more. He wanted to say something to make extra double sure she would listen to him, but he knew that the more he pressed her on it, the closer they would get to an all-out argument. There was nothing more he could do. He went to the kitchen to get a drink. When he peeked back, Katie was flipping through the pieces and mouthing the words: BALL. LINE. WAY. PLACE.

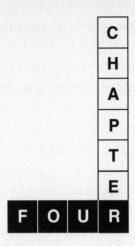

CHAPTER FOUR

MR. PETERSON WAS DRAWING a complex problem on the blackboard, full of numbers and xs and ys. Winston could not concentrate. He had slept badly. The four words had danced in his head all night: BALL. LINE. WAY. PLACE. Four simple words, like something out of a first-grader's schoolbook, but the sight of them had given a perfectly normal woman a five-course nervous breakdown.

Why?

The fact that he had returned the pieces to Katie didn't matter. He continued to manipulate the words in his head, trying every method he could think of to get some kind of meaning out of them. He continued on helplessly even though he was sure that it was pointless—that he was trying to solve a five-hundred-piece jigsaw with only a handful of pieces. But the words would not stop bouncing around his brain. BALL. LINE. WAY. PLACE.

Shortly after the pieces had been discovered, he'd thought it possible—even likely—that the four words were just that: Words, with no additional meaning at all. No puzzle to solve, no big mystery. Just four words inscribed on pieces of wood, hidden by someone long ago, for reasons he would never understand. Before the incident at the library, he was willing to believe this. But Mrs. Lewis's reaction was simply too extraordinary. It was clear there was much more to know.

"Mr. Breen," said his math teacher, "do we have enough information to solve this problem?"

Winston snapped back to attention. Mr. Peterson was looking at him carefully. It was unlikely that he was talking about the words on the wooden strips.

"Uh," he said, scanning the blackboard for the equation under discussion.

"Pay attention, Winston," Mr. Peterson said with some disapproval. "Mr. Drucker, do you have an answer for us?"

"We don't have enough information to find the answer," Ronald Drucker said crisply.

"That is correct," said Mr. Peterson. "There is no way of knowing what x represents. It can stand for any number. It is a variable." He looked up at the clock. "All right, class. For homework tonight I want all the questions at the end of chapter seventeen. All of them!" There were some *awww*s in response to this.

"And for extra credit . . ." He turned and drew some figures on the chalkboard. Winston immediately paid attention. Mr. Peterson's extra-credit problems were more like puzzles than work.

$$1 \; 1 \; 1 \; 1 \; 1 \; 2 \; 1$$

"Can you place mathematical symbols into this string of numbers so that it becomes a correct equation? You can use whatever math symbols you like—plus, minus, multiplication, division, even parentheses. There are a few different ways to do this. We'll hear your answers tomorrow."

(Answer, page 212.)

Jake had a baseball game after school, and Mal and Winston were among the few spectators. They would watch the game, and then all three would head over to Rosetti's for pizza. Winston arrived before Mal and picked a spot in the second row of bleachers. The Glenville Bears were warming up on the field. Winston watched as Jake, standing on third base, caught a blazing throw from the catcher, just in time to tag out an imaginary base-stealer.

Winston opened one of his books on Benjamin Franklin. He had gotten three of them out of the school library—no more trips to the town library for him. The thought of facing Mrs. Lewis again made his stomach do unhappy flip-flops.

A white school bus pulled up and the opposing team filed off, looking somewhat wary, like astronauts taking their first steps onto a possibly hostile alien planet. A few more people wandered over to sit in the stands—parents with video cameras, mainly. A tall gentleman wearing a gray suit climbed up stiffly and sat behind Winston, looking like he felt out of place. Winston guessed he was somebody's father, out of work early to see his son play ball.

Mal arrived, hoisting a backpack full of books. "Let's go, Bears!" he said, plopping down next to Winston.

"Who's this other team?" Winston asked.

"Kids from Maplewood," said Mal. "The Maplewood Warriors, I think."

"They don't look like warriors."

"And our guys don't look like bears," Mal pointed out. "If teams had to name themselves honestly, they'd all be the Pimple-Faced Teenagers."

Winston grinned.

The Bears had retreated to their bench, and the Warriors were limbering up on the field.

Mal said, "I have to go back to the library. Want to come?"

"The *town* library?"

Mal nodded grimly.

"No, thanks. Why not use the school library? That's what I did." Winston raised up his new Benjamin Franklin book as evidence.

Mal shook his head. "I told Mr. Nelson"—he was their history teacher—"that they didn't have any books about Walter Fredericks. I wanted to choose a different topic, but he wouldn't let me. He said there would be plenty of newspaper and magazine articles out there, and that I should go back to the library and look them up."

"So why not the school library?"

"They don't have what I need. Lots of books, very few magazines. So it's back to the lair of the crazy librarian for me."

"Good luck."

"Thanks," said Mal. "I'm hoping that she only remembers being mad at *you*."

Winston didn't hear this last comment. He was gazing out at the field. Five of the Warriors were standing in a row. "Hey, look at that."

Mal glanced around. "What?"

"Those guys down there."

Mal looked at them. "Yeah? So?"

"Look at their uniforms."

Mal instead looked at Winston. "Is this going to be a puzzle?"

"Yup."

"How did I know that? I must be psychic. Okay, what is it?"

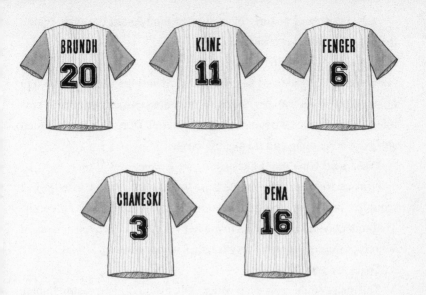

"I just noticed that four of those guys have something in common. Which one of them doesn't belong?"

(Answer, page 212.)

It was the bottom of the second inning when the man behind them suddenly spoke up in a friendly, melodic voice. "You certainly did give that librarian a scare yesterday, didn't you?"

It took a second for the words to sink into their brains, and then Mal and Winston whirled around, astonished. The man was calmly smiling down at them, as if he had simply made a comment about the weather.

Winston said, "What?"

"That librarian," said the man. "You certainly did rile her up."

"We didn't mean to." Winston and Mal glanced at each other. Who was this guy?

"Oh, I'm sure, I'm sure. It's not your fault," said the man. "She's been under a lot of pressure lately."

Mal said, "Are you friends with her?"

"Friends?" He seemed to give the word serious thought. "No, I'm not sure you could call us friends. Acquaintances, perhaps. She seems like a perfectly nice woman, as far as I can tell. Don't you think? When she's not screaming and raving, of course."

"Yes," said Winston, "I guess so."

"But as to your little incident in the library . . . If I were you, I wouldn't pay it any mind. You know, her last sibling died recently. That must be hard. I think it's made her very . . ." He waved a hand, in search of the right word. "Very fragile," he concluded.

"Who are you?" Mal said.

The man's smile grew even wider. "Oh, just another treasure hunter like yourselves."

That really stopped things for a moment. Mal and Winston looked dumbly at each other. Another . . . *treasure hunter?* Winston was attempting to absorb this when the man leaned forward as far as he could. He seemed as old as Winston's father, or maybe older. His long face was inches away from Winston's own. The man wore gold spectacles, and his eyes were quite blue. He was still smiling warmly, like a department store Santa. The man said, "I don't think she's going to be any help. If you want to find the treasure, you're on your own. Or we can work together."

Winston was starting to feel like he had come in late to a movie and had no idea what was going on. Feeling like he had to say something, he said, "You want to work with us?"

Mal added, "To find the treasure?" Winston could tell that word—*treasure!*—was bouncing around Mal's brain as well.

The man sat back again. He seemed to misinterpret Winston's question. "I know, I know. You're Winston Breen. You're supposed to be some kind of puzzle whiz."

Winston's expression of surprise widened yet again. "How do you know all this?" he said.

The man shrugged. "Oh, word gets around. The nice town librarian has some kind of massive fit right in the middle of the library floor, people are going to talk about it. I asked around. Someone happened to drop your name. And here we are."

"So you know his name," said Mal. "What's *your* name?"

"Oh, didn't I introduce myself?" said the man. "My name is David North. It's very nice to meet both of you." He put out a large hand, and awkwardly, not knowing what else to do, both boys shook it. "I have no doubt that we are going to be very close friends," said David North.

Mal raised his eyebrows. He looked at Winston and repeated words he clearly found unbelievable. "Close friends."

"Naturally," said North, ignoring Mal's skepticism. "After all, you boys have the same problem that I have. You don't have all the puzzle pieces."

He leaned forward again. There was now a sharp edge to his friendly smile. Winston thought he looked . . . hungry. "Do you have your pieces on you?" North asked.

Winston shook his head no. He was suddenly very glad that he had given them back to his sister.

"No?" David North looked disappointed. "Hmm." He was staring at Winston closely again. "I have to ask, although I'm sure it's none of my business. How'd you get them? How'd you get Livia's puzzle pieces?"

"I bought them." Again, it seemed like the easiest thing to say.

David North gaped at him. "*Bought* them? You're kidding me."

"No. I bought a small box. They were inside."

North blinked. "A keepsake box? With diamonds on it? Wooden diamonds?"

Winston was surprised. "Yes, that's the one."

"I held that box in my hand! It was empty!"

Winston couldn't help but smirk a little. North seemed to know everything, but he didn't know this. "There was a secret compartment. The pieces were in it."

North rapped a fist lightly on the bleachers. He stared off into the distance, a look of dark frustration clouding his face. He came back after a few moments like a man waking up.

"Well. Good for you," he said, not at all convincingly. He looked for his smile and found it with some difficulty. "But you only have one set of pieces. There's nothing you can do with only one set of pieces. You're not going to get anywhere." He reached into his suit jacket pocket and . . . Winston couldn't believe his eyes!

From his pocket, David North took out four small wooden strips. He waved them quickly through the air. There were words printed on them, but Winston couldn't make them out. "You're not going to find the treasure without these, my friend. So what do you say? You want to be partners?"

"I'll . . . I'll think about it," said Winston. It seemed the safest thing to say.

North nodded as if he had predicted exactly that response. "Sure. You think about it. But I'm not going away. And you're not going to find the treasure without me. When you figure that out, you give me a call." He reached into his inside jacket pocket again and produced a small card and a pen. "I'm going to give you my cell phone number. You can call any time of day." Winston took the card.

North stood up. "I'll be seeing you, boys. Be good." And he stepped purposefully off the bleachers and headed toward the parking lot.

They watched him go. "Holy mackerel," said Mal. "What was *that?*"

"He had four wooden pieces, too. Did you see that?" Winston still couldn't believe it.

"Of course I saw it! I'm sitting right here!"

They sat there thinking about it. In front of them, the baseball game continued, forgotten. Winston saw Jake sitting on the bench, waiting for his turn at bat—he was looking at the two of them with an expression of extreme curiosity.

"Jake saw us talking to that guy," said Winston. He waved, trying to somehow communicate "I'll tell you all about it afterward. You're not going to believe it."

"What are you going to do?" asked Mal. "You going to be partners with him?"

"I don't know. Do you really think these wooden pieces will lead to buried treasure?"

"I thought only pirates buried their treasure," said Mal. "You think there are pirates in Glenville?"

Winston didn't even hear him. "Also, it's not me who'd be teaming up with him. It's Katie. The pieces are hers, not mine."

"Riiight," Mal said. "It's some kind of puzzle that might lead to buried treasure, but you'll just bow out because technically the pieces are Katie's. Now tell me again about the tooth fairy."

"Well, I'd have to tell her about it, anyway. And if we did team up with him, and if there really is treasure, what's to stop him from just taking it away from us? If we even find it?"

They thought about that. Neither of them had an answer.

The Bears won 5 to 3. Jake had two hits, and though he didn't score, he made a fantastic diving catch at third, snatching a bullet of a line

43

drive out of the air as it ripped through the infield. It would have been a double for sure, but Jake leapt sideways like some kind of comic book superhero, and the ball was in his glove before anyone knew what had happened. He got up, covered in dirt from head to toe and grinning wildly, to the loudest applause of the day.

But sitting in a booth at Rosetti's, Jake acted like he'd have gladly missed the game entirely if he could have been sitting with his friends as they met the mysterious Mr. North. "He really had four wooden pieces of his own?" he asked for the third time. "Where did he get them?"

"We didn't ask," said Winston.

"How could you not have asked?" Jake was amazed.

Mal said, "There was a lot going on. This strange guy shows up out of nowhere, he seems to know everything but Winston's birthday, he's talking about buried treasure, for crying out loud. . . ." Mal took a deep breath, and Winston nodded in agreement.

Jake said, "So what are you going to do? You gonna team up with this guy?"

Winston thoughtfully picked at a garlic knot. "I don't know. If there really is treasure hidden somewhere, I'd like to find it. But I'm not sure I trust him."

"Why not?"

Winston said, "Remember what the librarian said? 'Why don't you people leave me alone?' Don't you think this guy's a good candidate to be one of 'you people'?"

Jake frowned. "You think he's doing something to her? Something to frighten her?"

"I don't know. He clearly wants this treasure, whatever it is. Maybe she knows where it's hidden but won't tell him anything. So what does he do?"

Mal said, "Ask her again?"

"Maybe ask her again and again and again," Winston said. "And when she still doesn't tell, then what?"

They thought about that, how easy it would be to harass somebody if you really wanted to. Phone calls in the middle of the night, notes left in the mailbox, perhaps a stone tossed through a window. Small, nasty things that individually would mean little, but taken all together could make someone very afraid. Was David North, well dressed in his neat gray suit, doing these things—or worse—to Mrs. Lewis?

The bell over the door jingled and a man walked in, but instead of heading to the counter to place an order, he walked directly over to Winston's table. All three boys looked up at him. He was wearing a purple-and-green-checked sport coat that badly clashed with the rest of his outfit. (Even Winston, no fashion plate, could tell.) He had a narrow face and eyes that were trying to take in the entire room, as if he thought someone was about to sneak up on him.

"Which of you kids is Winston Breen?"

Winston's mouth was partway open to respond, but Mal was faster. "Who wants to know?"

The man frowned. "Look, kid, it's been a long day. I know one of you is Winston Breen, and you want to find the treasure. Right? Well, I wanna help you out, that's all."

The treasure again. Winston figured as much. Strangers did not often strike up conversations with him, and now it had happened twice in one day.

"I'm Winston," he said.

The man seemed relieved that it wasn't Mal. He stuck out a hand, which Winston, from his seated position, shook clumsily. "Mickey Glowacka. Nice to meet you, kid." He was already moving to join them in the booth, and Jake had to shift over quickly.

"So," said Glowacka. "You boys tried asking that librarian lady about the treasure, huh? And she told you to take a hike."

"Did it get written up in the newspaper or something?" said Mal.

Glowacka continued. "She's crazy, you know. Doesn't want to have anything to do with it. She'd rather leave it buried wherever the heck it is. Can you believe that? She's crazy!" He shook his head as if he pitied a world where such insanity was possible.

Jake said, "So you're looking for the treasure, too."

Glowacka said, "You bet I am."

Winston said, "Do you know what it is? The treasure?"

"What, you don't know?"

"Well, no," Winston admitted. "Do you?"

"Sure!" said Glowacka, as if it were obvious. "Money!"

"How much is there supposed to be?"

Mickey Glowacka snorted as if this were a ridiculous question. "A lot! I don't know. This Fredericks guy was loaded. I'm figuring, a million, two million. At least."

The boys gawked at each other. Winston felt like his brain had just short-circuited. Did this strange man just say that Walter Fredericks had buried one million dollars? At a *minimum*?

Glowacka leaned in and looked at the boys, who were all staring at him, openmouthed. "Plenty for everybody, you know what I mean? None of us is finding it on our own. You know that, right?"

That was the one thing Winston knew. He nodded.

Glowacka said, "You got your pieces of the puzzle?"

He was wearing the same hungry expression that had been on North's face not long ago. Once again, Winston was glad he had given the pieces to his sister.

"I don't have them on me," he said.

Disappointment flickered briefly over Glowacka's face. Then he said, "Smart. You gotta keep them safe." He reached into his ugly sport coat. "Me, I've been keeping mine on my person at all times." He removed four strips of wood and held them out, facedown. Glowacka grinned. "I bet you boys would give anything to know what words are on the other side of these. Am I right?"

Winston didn't say anything. The man was absolutely right.

"Tell you what," said Glowacka to Winston. "Let's say you and I work together to find the treasure. I asked around and it seems like you're a smart kid. We split it fifty-fifty. You in?"

"What about—" Winston stopped himself. Did this guy even know about David North?

Glowacka looked suspicious. "What about what?"

Oh, well. Too late now. "Do you know David North?"

"Oh, no." Glowacka was appalled. "Has that guy been talking to you? What did he say? You didn't show him your puzzle pieces, did you?"

"No."

"I wouldn't trust that guy to pump my gas and give me correct change."

"Why?"

Glowacka shook his head. "Never mind. Just do yourself a favor and stay away from him."

"He has puzzle pieces, too," said Winston.

Glowacka pursed his lips. "Yeah. I know."

"Well, we might need those pieces, too, right?"

"I was hoping we wouldn't," Glowacka said. "I was hoping two sets is enough. We're never going to get all four, anyway."

Jake said, "Wait a second—there are four sets of pieces?"

Glowacka looked at him. "Whaddaya, kidding? Yeah, there are four sets."

"Who has the last set?"

"Don't you know anything? That crazy librarian! And she's not gonna give them up, she's not gonna sell 'em—nothing!"

"Why not?"

"Because she says she doesn't care about the treasure. Can you believe that? I mean, yeah—she has a lot of her old man's money. But who couldn't use more? Right?" Glowacka took a deep breath and made an effort to calm himself down. "Anyway," he said. "That don't matter. What matters is, you and me, we got a real chance to find this treasure, wherever it is. Let's meet here tomorrow. Can you do that?"

"I'm not sure."

Glowacka looked irritated. "What. You got homework? With half a million dollars, you can hire kids to do your homework. You can pay the teacher to never give you homework again. You wanna bring your friends?" he said, gesturing to Mal and Jake. "That's fine. Friends are good. But you pay them out of *your* half."

The man dug around in his jacket pocket again, where he had returned his four wooden pieces. This time his hand emerged with a business card, which he gave to Winston. "That's where I'm staying. You think about it and call me, and maybe when you go to bed tomorrow night, you'll be a half-million dollars richer. What do you think of that?"

Winston glanced at the card. It was for a motel near the highway. "I'll think about it," he said.

"Yeah, yeah," Glowacka said as he got up from the booth. "You think about it, Winston. Nice meeting you kids."

Jake said to Glowacka as he turned to leave, "You really think Walter Fredericks hid a million dollars somewhere?"

Glowacka smiled broadly for the first time since he arrived. "Friend, you don't just bury your spare change. Am I right?"

*   *   *

Somehow, Winston was able to get home and focus on his homework. He didn't think it would be possible to stop thinking about the Mysterious Real-Life Treasure Hunt that was blossoming into life around him, but he managed—probably because he had no choice. If he suddenly stopped doing his homework so he could focus on treasure hunts instead, his parents would come down on him like a great big wall.

He got through a page of algebra problems in twenty minutes. He liked math well enough, and he polished off the equations the way one finishes a bowl of snacks, one nugget at a time. English was harder—it was normally a subject he handled well, but that was before they had started with Shakespeare. He was suffering through *Romeo and Juliet*, a scene or two every night, not understanding a word of it.

No science tonight, thank goodness, although a major test loomed on the horizon—he would have to start reviewing. Science had always been a weak spot. All that vocabulary. *Vacuoles* and *chlorophyll* and *dendrites*. It took a huge amount of effort to attach those words to anything meaningful.

And, of course, history class. There was a chapter to read in the textbook, and the famous report on Benjamin Franklin. It only needed to be five or six pages. A brief biography of the man, his role as one of the founding fathers, and a glimpse of his many inventions—that should do the trick. He tapped out an outline on his computer, occasionally referring to the books he had taken home that day.

Sitting here doing his homework felt so normal after a strange day like this one. It was almost enjoyable to be doing something so calm and boring while everyone else went crazy, running around in search of a million dollars.

A million dollars!

It was impossible to believe, but impossible to forget. The phrase kept leaping into his mind, unsummoned, like an itch that wouldn't stay scratched. He tried to shoo it away and squinted at his history textbook.

A few minutes into the chapter, another familiar thought stole into his brain—a puzzle idea. He rolled it around for a little while and then had to write it down. He could almost hear Jake and Mal making fun of him: Winston could somehow put aside the idea of finding a million dollars, but a new puzzle idea? That had to be dealt with immediately. For most people, it would be the other way around.

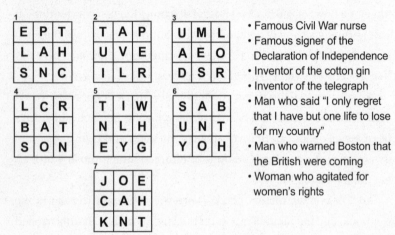

- Famous Civil War nurse
- Famous signer of the Declaration of Independence
- Inventor of the cotton gin
- Inventor of the telegraph
- Man who said "I only regret that I have but one life to lose for my country"
- Man who warned Boston that the British were coming
- Woman who agitated for women's rights

The first and last name of a historical figure are hidden in each of the nine-letter grids. For each puzzle, figure out which letter to start with and then trace out the answer letter by letter, moving one space at a time, up, down, left, right, or diagonally. Letters can be used more than once, and some letters won't be used at all. Clues for each answer can be seen in the list to the left, but are not presented in the same order as the grids.

(*Answer, page 212.*)

Winston heard Katie pounding up the stairs. She had reported no success in solving the mystery with her friends at school, to Winston's complete lack of surprise. He figured he was going to have to tell her—not to mention their parents—about the buried treasure, but that was going to be a very strange conversation, featuring lots of questions he wouldn't be able to answer, and he didn't feel ready to head down that path just yet. Besides, he wanted to keep it as his secret for a while longer.

Katie was suddenly in his doorway. "Don't you hear me yelling?" she said, exasperated.

"What?"

"I'm calling you from downstairs! Someone's at the door for you!"

Winston sat up. "Who?"

"I don't know," as if it was crazy that she might have asked. She ran off before Winston could grill her any further.

Winston nervously went down the stairs. Had David North or Mickey Glowacka come to his house? Holy cow, he hoped not. This whole thing was going to be difficult enough to explain to his parents without one of those guys standing there wearing that hungry intense look.

He entered the living room. Katie had returned to the video game she had been playing. His mother was lying down after a long day, and his father was on the computer in his small home office. Whoever was at the door was still outside—Katie hadn't asked the visitor in.

He opened the front door, convinced it was either North or Glowacka, the gray suit or the checkered coat. It was neither.

Standing there, looking apprehensive and withdrawn, was the librarian, Violet Lewis. In her hand, she held four wooden strips. She looked up as Winston opened the door.

"Can I speak with you for a moment?" she said.

"FIRST OF ALL," she said, "I want to apologize for my out-
burst yesterday. I am deeply, deeply embarrassed by my reaction
when I saw you holding those puzzle pieces. I'm afraid it caught me
off guard. But that is no excuse."

"It's okay," said Winston, a bit uncomfortably. He wasn't used to
receiving such a serious apology from a grown-up.

They were sitting in the living room. Winston had made Katie turn
off her video game. She didn't want to, but when she saw the four
strips in Mrs. Lewis's hand, she got it right away. She was sitting on
the sofa next to her brother, her legs dangling over the side.

From her chair, Mrs. Lewis looked briefly around the room, her
hands folded in her lap. She looked nervous, like a woman on a job
interview, and Winston didn't know quite what to do about that. He
said nothing and waited.

She finally said, "Let me ask you a question first, Winston. The
puzzle pieces you brought into the library yesterday—where did you
get them?"

"They were in a small wooden box that I bought for my sister."

"It was my birthday," Katie added helpfully.

Mrs. Lewis nodded. "Ah. I know that box. It's lovely." She looked at Katie. "What is your name? I don't believe I know it."

"I'm Katie."

"Katie! I hope you make good use of that present, Katie. That box belonged to my sister, so it is only fitting that Winston should buy it for *his* sister." Mrs. Lewis looked back at Winston. "And the pieces were in the box?"

"In a secret compartment. It had a false bottom."

"Really!" She smiled for the first time. "Ah, Livia could be a sneaky one. A secret compartment! I never had any idea. And do you know what those little wooden strips are for?"

He thought for a moment about playing dumb. But he said, "They're supposed to lead to some kind of buried treasure."

Katie jumped in her seat. "Buried treasure?"

Oh, right—he hadn't told her yet. "I just found out today!" he said. "I was going to tell you."

Mrs. Lewis said with a frown, "And how did you find out?"

Before he could answer, Winston's father entered the room with a curious "Hello?"

Mrs. Lewis stood. "Mr. Breen! It's good to see you."

It was obvious that Nathan Breen did not know who this woman was. "Yes? I'm sorry, but . . ." He trailed off in confusion, his arm nonetheless extended to shake her hand.

Extending her own hand, she said, "Violet Lewis. From the town library."

He recognized her now. "Oh, of course. I think this is the first time I've seen you out of the library."

"I do occasionally wander away," she said.

Winston's father's smile still had a puzzled look to it. He cast about for a possible reason that the town librarian would be in his living room. "Are my kids that overdue with their books?" he said jokingly. Then he noticed what she was holding: four wooden strips. He blinked. "Are those . . . ?"

"Puzzle pieces," said Mrs. Lewis. "Made by my father. There were sixteen pieces, and he gave four of them to each of his four children. Now most of the pieces lie in other hands, my brothers and sister having passed on. Winston here apparently owns one set. He found them in my sister's keepsake box."

Katie piped up. "They're mine. Winston bought them for me."

Winston said quickly, "But we're sort of sharing them."

Mrs. Lewis nodded. "Quite right."

"But what are they for?" said Mr. Breen.

"They lead to buried treasure!" said Katie, barely able to stay seated on the couch.

"Let the grown-ups talk for a moment, Katie," said Mr. Breen, patting the air.

"Actually, your daughter is correct," said Mrs. Lewis. "Well, I don't know if the treasure is *buried*. But it's certainly hidden. And these pieces will tell us where."

Winston looked at his father as he attempted to digest this piece of information. Nathan Breen worked for a business magazine, analyzing companies and predicting whether or not they would be successful. Winston occasionally came across his father studying sheets of numbers of dizzying complexity, reading them as casually as one reads the Sunday comics. Winston's father understood business. Buried treasure was another matter entirely. Nathan Breen sat down. "This is a story I think I'd like to hear," he said.

"I think you should," said Mrs. Lewis. "Your son was just about to tell me what he knows about all of this."

All eyes went to Winston. "Well," he said, "the other people who have the puzzle pieces . . . they both came to see me today."

"I was afraid of that," said Mrs. Lewis in a low voice.

His father said, "Who came to see you? When?"

Winston told them about David North and Mickey Glowacka and said that they both seemed to know about Winston's run-in with Mrs. Lewis in the library.

"You had a run-in?" asked his father, increasingly bemused.

Mrs. Lewis colored. "I'm afraid that was my fault. I saw Winston holding the puzzle pieces, and my first thought was . . . well, I'm afraid I lost control of my emotions. I yelled at your son. I caused quite a scene, I'm sorry to say. I suppose word got around about the incident." She shook her head morosely.

Winston continued. "Anyway. These guys hope that the treasure can be found using only two sets of pieces, so they both want to team up with me to find it."

"They're greedy is what they are," said Mrs. Lewis.

"Do you know these two?" asked Mr. Breen.

"I've met them both," she said grimly.

Mr. Breen said cautiously, "I guess you don't like them very much."

She was silent for a moment, and then she said, "Let me tell you the full story."

"My parents had four children. Red was the oldest. Then there was Bruno, and then Livia, and then finally me. Two boys and two girls. In my family, however, the children did not get along very well. We would argue all the time and fight with each other. What did we fight about? I can't even remember. Which means they were stupid, little things."

"Winston and I fight all the time," offered Katie.

"Not *all* the time," said Winston.

"All brothers and sisters fight," said Mrs. Lewis. "But I bet that you don't stay mad at your brother very long, right?"

"I guess," said Katie.

"Well, you're not mad at him now, are you?"

"No . . ."

"No," said Mrs. Lewis. "I can tell that just by the way you're sitting together on the sofa. My brothers and my sister and I were always mad at each other. And it only got worse as we grew up. By the time we were adults, none of us were on speaking terms. I would pass my own brother on the street, and he would pretend I wasn't even there."

"Why were you all so mad at each other?" asked Katie.

Mrs. Lewis could only shake her head. "I don't know. It sounds ridiculous, but I don't. All I can remember are small, silly arguments. I remember one Thanksgiving when we were children—Bruno wanted the wishbone out of the turkey, but Livia got it. Somehow, this turned into a giant screaming match, with accusations flying all around. Right in the middle of Thanksgiving. Over a wishbone. Isn't that the most foolish thing you've ever heard? But that's all I remember of growing up—every day, another fight over something small and ridiculous. All these arguments added up over the years, and the result was four children who wanted nothing to do with each other." She paused, looking for the words that would make all this sound logical. "We . . . we didn't know how to heal the small arguments. We only knew how to make them bigger."

"That's too bad," said Winston's father, trying to be comforting.

Mrs. Lewis nodded sadly, and they all sat quietly for a moment. Winston thought of Katie, sitting next to him on the sofa. Sure, he got mad at her sometimes, but could he really stay angry at her for years and years and years? It seemed impossible. Wasn't it?

The librarian took a deep breath, and it occurred to Winston that telling this story was difficult for her. She said, "My father became a wealthy man, thanks to his inventions. He invented a new kind of mattress that somehow knows to support your back in just the right way. I never really understood the technology behind it, although I sleep on one myself. Anyway, late in his life he started to do a lot of traveling. He went on a safari in Africa, he traveled throughout Europe, he visited ruins in South America. My mother had long since passed away, so he traveled by himself or occasionally took a friend with him.

"One time when he was traveling through Jordan, word got around that this famous inventor was in the country. One of the princes there not only had heard of my father but actually owned one of his mattresses. It seems this prince had a notoriously bad back, and my father's mattress had fixed it like magic! When he heard my father was visiting, he held a banquet in my father's honor. And gave him a jeweled ring."

"A ring?"

"A very beautiful and expensive ring, right off the prince's own finger."

"Wow!" said Katie.

Winston was also impressed but found himself jumping ahead of the story. "That's what your father hid, right? The ring is the hidden treasure."

Mrs. Lewis nodded. "All the children knew that we would inherit a lot of money when my father died. And so we started having silly fights over various possessions. One child would lay claim to, say, an antique lamp that my mother had bought years ago, and suddenly everyone else would want it, too. We were completely selfish and awful, and it's a wonder that my father left us anything at all.

"More than anything, we wanted that ring. The four of us were very greedy, and we all wanted the ring for ourselves. One by one, we would argue with our father about why one of us should be given the ring and no one else. That's probably when my father made up this plan.

"My father liked jokes and puzzles and riddles. He would have liked you very much, Winston. He was a happy, creative man. I've always wondered how such a good man could have raised four such nasty children, and I can't say I understand it. He was always sharing riddles and puzzles with us at the dinner table. One of his favorites was: What is something you can break just by saying your name?"

"Oh, wait, I know that one," Winston said, closing his eyes to think.

They all waited a moment, but when Winston didn't say anything, his father said, "You can work it out later, Winston. Let Mrs. Lewis finish her story."

Winston opened his eyes, a little embarrassed. "Right. Sorry."

(Answer, page 213.)

(Answer, page 213.)

"After my father died, a lawyer called us together in his office. A young man, I remember. Gary Rogers, his name was."

"Oh," said Mr. Breen, "I know Gary. But doesn't he do environmental law? He doesn't handle wills and estates, does he?"

Mrs. Lewis shrugged. "I wouldn't know. He definitely wasn't my father's usual lawyer. But he was asked to oversee the handling of the will. We gathered in his office and signed a lot of papers. And then this young lawyer said, 'Finally, regarding the ring that your father received from the Prince of Jordan.' I'm sure we all sat forward a little. Who was going to get the ring? But the lawyer simply handed each of us an envelope. And in the envelope were these wooden puzzle pieces.

"The lawyer informed us that my father had hidden the ring. The wooden pieces were a puzzle, and we would have to work together to find the ring."

Winston's father said, "Why do you think your father did this?"

She looked surprised. "Isn't it obvious? He wanted to bring us together, force us to talk with one another and solve his puzzle. We were supposed to forget years of arguing and hatred because my father had given us a *puzzle.*" She shook her head. She said that last word with the slightest bit of scorn, and Winston looked at the floor. "A foolish plan," she said quietly. "Never had a prayer of working." Winston supposed she was right. Puzzles had a place in the world, but they couldn't do everything.

"We were already angry at each other for a thousand different reasons. Now we were angry at our father, too. For doing this to us." She stopped and thought back. "Red refused to have anything to do with it at all. No discussion. Nothing. And, well, he left and took his puzzle pieces with him, so what hope did the rest of us have? So nothing came of it. The ring that my father hid is still hidden. Unless, of course, someone has found it and never said anything. It *has* been almost twenty-five years."

Winston hadn't thought of that. Could Walter Fredericks have hidden the ring in a public place? There were a trillion ways for that to go wrong. A couple of kindergartners dig a hole somewhere—because that's what little kids do—and suddenly they find a metal box, which they bang open with a rock. The thought of it was overwhelming. This could all be for nothing!

Mrs. Lewis looked at Winston and seemed to read his mind. "I think it is likely that my father hid the ring very carefully and that it is still there. I can't promise that, of course." She took a deep breath. "In any event, I would like, all these years later, to find it." She looked at

Winston with a slanted kind of smile. "My guess is a treasure hunt is right up your alley, Winston, wouldn't you say?"

This statement was so true that Winston couldn't think how to agree with it strongly enough. His mouth opened and closed. His father finally stepped in and said, "He'd be your guy, all right. You want him to help find the ring?"

"And me!" said Katie.

"The both of you," said Mrs. Lewis.

"But after twenty-five years? Why now?"

Mrs. Lewis frowned and thought about how to continue. She said, "Every so often, I get a call from someone claiming to be a treasure hunter. Somehow, this person has heard about my crazy inventor father and his buried treasure, and they want my help in finding it. Every time, I politely decline. The fact is, Mr. Breen, I don't care if the ring is ever recovered. As far as I am concerned, it can stay buried forever. All it reminds me of is my own greed and the fact that I had two brothers and a sister that somehow I never got to know."

Nathan Breen said, "So what happened to make you change your mind? Is it these two men?"

Mrs. Lewis nodded. "Both of them have approached me in the past, although not at the same time. I assumed at first that they would be like the others—once I gave them a firm no, they would simply go away and leave me alone. But these two men are a little more . . . determined."

Winston said, "Where did they get their puzzle pieces?"

"The first fellow, David North, bought many of my brother Red's belongings after he died, obviously hoping to find the pieces hidden somewhere. I guess it worked. The other fellow, Glowacka, told me that he'd bought them from Bruno. Bruno rather squandered his inheritance and needed money toward the end. I'm sure he suckered

Glowacka into buying the puzzle pieces without telling him that they were useless without all the others."

Winston said, "He thinks the treasure is a million dollars. At least."

Mrs. Lewis looked startled. "A million dollars!" She laughed. "My father may have been a little eccentric, but he was not a complete raving lunatic. A million dollars, in cash? My goodness. Mr. Glowacka is quite off base."

Nathan Breen said, "What happened when they came to see you?"

"Pretty much the same thing happened each time," said Mrs. Lewis. "Because they had puzzle pieces of their own, they both felt entitled to my assistance, and they were both very angry when I refused to give it to them. They left, and I assumed that I would never see them again."

"But you have," said Winston, leaning forward.

Mrs. Lewis paused, frowning. "Not as such," she said. "A couple of weeks ago, my sister died."

Winston said, "Your sister Livia."

She nodded. "A week or so after her death, someone broke into her house."

Winston's father was astonished. "What?"

"I don't know it for a fact," she continued, "but I think it must have been either David North or this Glowacka fellow."

"Whoever it was, he must have been looking for your sister's puzzle pieces," said Winston's dad.

Mrs. Lewis said, "Of course."

Winston thought back to his conversations with the two men. He gasped suddenly as he remembered. "It must have been David North," he said excitedly.

Everyone looked surprised at this. "How could you know that?" asked his father.

"He told me that he'd held the keepsake box in his hands. He must have broken into your sister's house and found the box, but he didn't know about the secret compartment."

Mrs. Lewis shook her head. "Maybe. Maybe. But many of Livia's possessions were sold at an estate sale shortly after her death. David North could just as easily have looked at the box then."

"Oh." Winston was deflated.

Winston's father said, "And maybe the robbery had nothing to do with this treasure. Right? Why couldn't it have been just a random burglary? Haven't there been a few of those lately?"

"Because shortly after the break-in, I began getting phone calls. A man with a deep voice, berating me for not letting people look for the treasure. He demanded my puzzle pieces and said if I didn't mail them to a certain address, I would be asking for trouble. Well, you better believe I didn't mail them anywhere."

Winston said, "Did you recognize the voice?"

Mrs. Lewis shook her head. "But I only spoke to Mr. North and Mr. Glowacka once or twice each. And the man on the phone was trying to disguise his voice anyway."

"What happened next?"

Mrs. Lewis looked at the floor for a moment, as if steeling herself. "A couple of nights ago, someone broke into my house. I heard him down there. It was very scary."

"You were home at the time?" asked Mr. Breen.

"I was."

Katie said in a low, frightened voice, "Did you call the police?" Winston had forgotten she was sitting next to him, so absorbed was he in Mrs. Lewis's story.

"You bet I did. And then I called my neighbor, Ray Marietta. He used to be a policeman himself, and he came right over. By that time, the man had fled. But he left a piece of paper on my kitchen table, with a message on it."

"What was the message?" Katie was holding her breath.

"It said WHERE IS THE TREASURE? in big block letters." Mrs. Lewis looked around at them. "I filled out a report, although nothing from my house was stolen. Ray thinks the burglar, whoever he was, was only trying to scare me. I have to admit that it worked."

Winston said slowly, "So when I showed up at the library with my puzzle pieces . . ."

Mrs. Lewis nodded. "I thought it was another attempt to intimidate me. Some kind of grand conspiracy. After you ran out of the library and I calmed down, I thought about it and realized that I had probably just made a fool out of myself over nothing. I discussed it with Ray— my neighbor—and he agreed that whoever was doing this would be unlikely to involve some random teenager. Actually, at first, Ray wondered if perhaps you weren't the one behind all this, Winston—making threatening phone calls and breaking into my kitchen."

All three Breens sat up straighter at that and began talking at once. Winston said with great alarm, "Me?" and Katie said, "Winston wouldn't do that!" and Mr. Breen, loudest of all, said, "Is he out of his *mind*?"

Mrs. Lewis patted this clamor down with two hands. "He doesn't think that anymore. I've known your son for years, Mr. Breen. I know it's not him." Winston's father calmed down slightly, but still looked ready to go on the offensive if needed.

Mrs. Lewis continued, "Eventually, I figured out that somehow your son had gotten hold of Livia's puzzle pieces. And here we are." She sat back, looking tired.

Nathan Breen said, "So you want to find the ring before this guy does. This North character or the other one, Glowicky, Glow . . . uh, whatever his name is."

Winston said immediately, "That won't work."

Mrs. Lewis nodded. "I know."

Winston's father looked around, confused. "What? Why not?"

"Because we can't find the ring without all the pieces," said Winston. "Including the ones owned by whoever is doing this—Mr. North or Mr. Glowacka."

"So you're going to split the treasure with somebody who broke into your house?" Winston's father was incredulous. "And how can you split a ring, anyway?"

"I'm going to sell the ring, should we be so lucky as to find it," said Mrs. Lewis. "In fact, I am going to sell it to the daughter of the man who presented it to my father in the first place. I contacted the royal family of Jordan, and they will be more than happy to have the ring back in their collection."

Katie said, "So I would get some treasure? Because I have the puzzle pieces?" Her eyes were now so wide that Winston thought they might soon pop out and fly across the room.

Mrs. Lewis smiled. "Yes, dear, you would. Assuming we find it."

"But in order to find the ring," said Winston's father, "you'll also have to split the money with the person who has been threatening you."

"No," she said. "Ray plans to catch the burglar before that happens."

Winston blinked. "Really? How?"

"I'll tell you in a minute. First things first. Can you help find the ring this weekend? Say, Saturday?"

"Can we, Dad?"

Winston's father looked deeply bothered. He said, "You're telling me that one of the people involved in this treasure hunt is potentially very dangerous."

Mrs. Lewis said, "I honestly don't think so. Whoever was doing this wanted me to help him find the treasure. Now he's getting what he wants."

Mr. Breen leaned forward. "But a person like that, maybe he'll try to take the ring entirely for himself. He's still a dangerous person, don't you think?"

"I have a great deal of faith in my friend Ray, Mr. Breen. The former policeman I was telling you about."

"He'll be there? On Saturday?"

"Oh, yes," said Mrs. Lewis. "He's very important to the plan. And he'll have an assistant with him as well, another policeman." Seeing that Mr. Breen's thoughtful frown had not vanished, the librarian said, "I wish I had brought a picture of my neighbor with me. He is a big fellow, and, as I say, a former policeman himself. And he assures me that his friend is an excellent officer. There is absolutely no way either of these two treasure hunters would try something with these men around."

"Why the second police officer?"

"Ray has the fingerprints of the man who tried to break into my house. He took them off the glass on my back door. Over the course of the day, he's going to make sure to get the fingerprints of both David North and Mickey Glowacka. His friend has promised to analyze the prints as quickly as possible. If either of them is the thief, we'll know it long before we find the ring."

Winston said, "Please, Dad? It's a hunt for buried treasure! We have to go!"

Katie said, "Yeah!" Her eyes were still shining.

Mr. Breen nodded slowly. "All right," he said. "Two policemen definitely helps put my mind at ease. But I want you and your sister to stay in the presence of those policemen the entire time. The entire time! Do you understand?"

"I'll make sure of it," said Mrs. Lewis. "You can be there yourself, if you'd like."

Mr. Breen shook his head. "I wish I could, but I can't. Not this weekend. I'll be traveling starting Friday evening. And my wife has to work on Saturday, on some big project at her office. But if these two policemen are everything you say they are, then it's okay with me."

Winston said, "Do you want me to contact Mr. North and Mr. Glowacka?"

The librarian cocked her head. "How would you do that?"

"They both gave me business cards."

"Did they?" she said with some curiosity. "Well, of course they would." Mrs. Lewis stared at a point on the ceiling for a moment. "Can I use your phone for a moment?"

"Of course," said Mr. Breen. "It's right there in the kitchen."

Mrs. Lewis crossed the room. She seemed much happier now.

Katie said, "We're going on a treasure hunt! I'm going to get treasure!"

"Which I am sure you'll share with your brother," said Mr. Breen, steadily.

Katie looked appalled. "Dad! Mrs. Lewis said only the owners of the puzzle pieces get to share the treasure!"

Nathan Breen gave his daughter his darkest look, a look that when aimed his way made Winston want to climb under the nearest piece of furniture. Katie instantly understood that she had stepped over an invisible, but very important, line.

"The only reason you are going on this treasure hunt is because your brother is going with you," said Mr. Breen. "His first priority is to take care of you." He turned that look momentarily on Winston. "Is that clear?"

"Yes, Dad," Winston said soberly.

"And I think we can all agree that in addition to his role as a big brother, Winston is a good person to have around when solving puzzles that might lead to buried treasure. Wouldn't you think so, Katie?"

"Yes," said Katie in an even softer voice.

"And do you think that might be worth something?"

"Yes." Katie was staring at the floor as if she wanted to melt into it.

"Good. These are your puzzle pieces, so you'll decide what his help is worth. You give him a nickel, or you give him all of it. But you *will* share. I trust you to do the right thing."

Winston arched his eyebrows but said nothing. He had thought his father was about to demand that Katie evenly split her share with him. Instead, their father was letting Katie make that decision on her own. Which was crazy. She'd give him a dime. But this was no time to speak up and demand a fifty-fifty split, not unless he wanted that dark look aimed back at him.

Mrs. Lewis walked back into the room, and if she caught a whiff of the momentary family tension, she indicated nothing.

"I spoke to Ray. He suggests that Winston call both Mr. North and Mr. Glowacka. Have them meet him on the steps of town hall, tomorrow at four. Ray will be there, and he'll explain everything to our two friends. But don't let on that anybody else will be there, Winston. The more we keep these two on their toes, the better off we'll be."

"Okay." Winston was smiling now. It was really going to happen. The wooden pieces were not meaningless—far from it. They were going to lead to buried treasure, and Winston was going to help find it. Amazing.

Mrs. Lewis was smiling, too. "All right. Thank you for listening to me this evening. I'm sorry again about how I reacted to you the other day, Winston, but I'm very glad that you and your sister will be helping me. I'll see you soon."

*   *   *

There was one person that Winston had to tell immediately, and that was his cousin Henry. Winston wrote him a long e-mail explaining the whole remarkable story, with TREASURE HUNT written several times in boldface capital letters. Five minutes later, a return e-mail arrived—Henry must have been sitting right at his computer.

Win,

Wow, that sounds exciting! And who better to look for buried treasure than you? Fantastic! I can't wait to hear about it.

Funny thing that you e-mailed me because I was just about to e-mail <u>you</u>. I've got a puzzle for you to solve. I attached it as a file—give it a shot!

See you soon!

Henry

Winston called up the attached file and found himself looking at three interlocking circles:

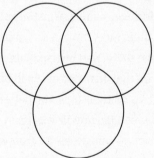

Winston:

Can you draw this figure with a single continuous line that never crosses itself? —H

(Answer, page 213.)

WINSTON, JAKE, AND MAL biked over to the town hall right after school and planted themselves on the cement steps.

"How are we going to know what this guy looks like?" said Jake.

Winston said, "Mrs. Lewis kept saying what a big guy he is."

"Big tall or big fat?" asked Mal.

"I don't know. Just plain big."

They looked around. It was late afternoon, and most people were still at work, but there were quite a few people walking around the green, and the town hall itself was a fairly busy place. But nobody stood out as being particularly tall or fat.

Jake said, "Well, does he know what you look like?"

"He's a cop," said Mal. "He'll figure it out."

"Ex-cop," said Winston. Far across the green, he could see the awning to Penrose's shop. Winston thought he should stop in after this and tell his friend the latest news. Penrose would undoubtedly be delighted to learn about where that little gift box had led him. Winston wondered if maybe he should have invited Penrose to come solve the treasure hunt as well. But he'd already invited Jake and Mal, and probably he shouldn't invite too many more people. Although there was no doubt Penrose would be a good guy to have on your side during a treasure hunt. . . .

Jake suddenly said in a low, amazed voice, "I think that might be him."

Winston looked at Jake and then out toward the green. A definitely *big* man was heading toward the town hall, with large purposeful steps. Winston's eyes involuntarily flicked to the statue in the middle of the green, to see if it hadn't come to life.

"If that's not him," said Mal, "does that mean there's someone bigger out there?"

But no, it had to be him. The man was close enough now that he saw the three kids, and Winston saw him change course to head directly toward them. Marietta wore a crewneck shirt that revealed large, muscled arms. Mostly bald up top, he nonetheless sported a bushy blond-gray mustache. Winston had no doubt that he would have been an excellent gym teacher, had he chosen to go that route. Retired or not, he could probably be an excellent gym teacher right now, after scrunching up their present gym teacher, Mr. Giano, into a tiny little ball.

Marietta stopped in front of them. He was even taller than Winston had first thought.

The large man looked at the three of them. There was no hello. He said, "I was expecting one kid. Not three."

Winston said, "Um. They're my friends. I told them they could come."

There was a tense pause as Marietta seemed to digest this concept. After a moment, Jake said, "We don't want any of the treasure! We just want to help find it."

Winston said, "They're smart. They'll be really helpful. Really."

Mal said, "Yeah, I know . . . er . . ." He couldn't seem to think of something he knew. ". . . all kinds of things," he finished lamely.

Marietta finally shook his head. "No, I'm sorry. This isn't an open invitation party. We're keeping the group small and under control. That means no friends and no guests. End of story."

The boys looked at each other, stricken.

Winston said again, "I told them they could come."

"That's not something that's up to you, son. I'm the guy in charge of this operation. I'm sorry, they're out. You can tell them all about it afterward. Frankly, I'd rather not have any kids on this thing, but Violet insisted that you and your sister be allowed to come along."

"Then I guess she's the one in charge," said Mal.

Winston felt his heart freeze in his chest, and he heard Jake suck in his breath. Marietta turned his head slowly to face Mal, and his stare turned several degrees colder. It would not have surprised Winston if laser beams zapped out the large man's eyes, blasting Mal to smithereens.

Thankfully, this did not happen. In tones of grim finality, pointing to Jake and Mal, he said, "You and you. Good-bye. Your friend will call you later."

Understanding that there was no arguing with this, Jake and Mal stood up without a word and walked over to their bicycles, parked nearby. Winston saw Jake slug Mal in the arm. They glanced back only once, then bicycled slowly away.

Marietta watched them go for a moment before turning his attention back to Winston. "All right," said the former cop. "These are the rules. Are you ready?"

"Yes," Winston said. He felt about as small as a gerbil.

"When they get here, these two guys, I don't want you to open your mouth. I'll do all the talking. All right?"

Winston nodded. Maybe the no-talking rule was already in effect. Better not to take chances.

"I especially don't want any kind of talk about Walter Fredericks's ring or how we're going to go about looking for it. Those wooden pieces—you didn't bring them here, right?"

"No, I didn't think—"

"Good," said Marietta abruptly. "The only reason we're here is to establish the ground rules. Is that clear?"

Another small nod.

"All right," said Marietta. "They're going to be here any minute. Before that happens, I want you to do something for me," he said.

"Wh-what?" Winston couldn't imagine.

"I want you to look me in the eye and tell me you haven't been making threatening phone calls to my friend Violet. Tell me you didn't break into her house."

Winston swallowed, suddenly feeling as guilty as if he *had* done those things. Nonetheless, he pulled himself together, looked Marietta directly in his chilly blue eyes, and said, "I didn't make any threatening calls. I wouldn't have the slightest idea how to break into someone's house."

Marietta stared at him unblinkingly for a moment more and decided he was satisfied. "All right, then," he said, nodding.

With that, Marietta leaned up against a concrete pillar and crossed his arms, content to await the arrival of North and Glowacka. Winston felt a small obligation to continue conversing with this giant stern man, but Marietta was apparently done talking. After a short wait, Winston took a puzzle magazine out of his backpack and flipped through it, looking for something he hadn't yet solved.

Place the twenty languages into the crisscross grid. When you're done, you'll be able to rearrange the shaded letters into the name of yet another language.

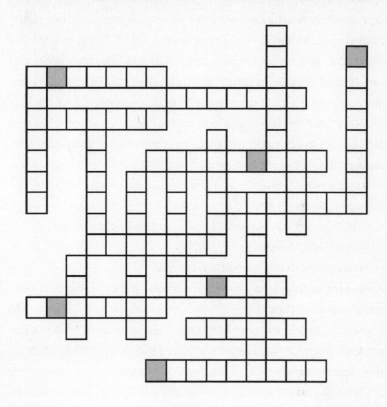

4 Letters
THAI
URDU

6 Letters
GERMAN
HEBREW
POLISH

7 Letters
ENGLISH
ITALIAN
PERSIAN
RUSSIAN
SPANISH
SWAHILI
TAGALOG
TURKISH
YIDDISH

8 Letters
JAPANESE
MANDARIN
ROMANIAN

9 Letters
CANTONESE
ESPERANTO
NORWEGIAN

(Answer, page 213.)

*   *   *

Winston was filling in the last few letters when the sound of distant shouting reached his ears. He looked up, mentally betting on what he was about to see. Sure enough, David North and Mickey Glowacka, still some distance away, had run into each other and had started arguing instantly. North held a briefcase in one hand and had a light jacket draped over his arm. He was doing his best to look dignified. Glowacka was making no such effort—his thin face was an angry red color. Winston couldn't hear what they were saying, precisely—all that carried across the green was a muted, hectoring sound. But it was clear that neither was happy to see the other.

"That them?" said Marietta, still leaning against the pillar.

"Yeah," said Winston.

"Don't seem to like each other much."

North and Glowacka seemed to simultaneously realize they were being watched. They broke off from their quarrel and turned to see Winston seated on the town hall steps, looking at them. With one last unhappy glance at each other, each man composed himself. Side by side, they walked the rest of the length of the green.

"Winston," said David North as he approached. "I don't know what you're planning, but I hope it has nothing to do with this man here." He jabbed out a thumb at Glowacka. "He is a liar and has a deeply unsavory character."

Glowacka turned red again. "Me? *I'm* a liar? I wouldn't trust you to tell me the weather! You say sunny, I'm bringing an umbrella!"

North's jaw set, and for a moment he looked ready to throttle Glowacka. But then Ray Marietta noisily cleared his throat, which seized the attention of both men. Neither of them had registered his presence, but they certainly did now. North was fairly tall, but Marietta had a full six inches on him. And to see Marietta's face, Glowacka had to angle his neck so drastically that he looked like a man considering the height of the mountain he was about to climb.

Marietta said, "Which one of you is North?"

North looked suddenly on the spot. "I am," he said.

Marietta nodded and said, "Which makes you . . . Glowacka, is it?"

"Yeah," said Glowacka, looking this huge stranger up and down. "That's me. Who are you? The kid's bodyguard?"

"My name is Ray Marietta. I'm a friend of Violet Lewis. I'm representing her in this meeting. Now, sit down, both of you." He pointed to the staircase. Winston looked around and saw other pedestrians glancing at this odd scene as they walked by.

Glowacka said with some surprise, "Violet Lewis? That crazy librarian?"

Winston grimaced. Marietta's eyes widened. He stepped in closer to Glowacka, who immediately understood he had made an error.

"I don't think she's crazy," said Marietta in a soft voice. "But even if she is, at least she will still be alive at the end of the day. Would you like to be?"

Glowacka, barely perceptibly, nodded.

"Then sit down." Marietta pointed at the staircase again. Glowacka sat.

North, perhaps from being taller, wasn't as intimidated. "What is this meeting about?" he asked, politely.

Marietta said, "Mrs. Lewis will agree to help find the treasure her father hid, as long as the three of you agree to certain rules that I shall now lay out. Interested?"

North had to smile. "I'm interested. I'll sit down." And he did, one step up from Winston.

With the three of them seated on the cement stairs, Marietta marched back and forth like a general.

"Okay, gentlemen," he said. "These are the rules. The treasure hunt will begin at ten o'clock sharp Saturday morning. We will gather in one of the meeting rooms on the lower level of the town library. Prior to that meeting, there will be no contact with each other. None. Do not contact Mrs. Lewis. Do not contact this boy Winston or his sister or anybody in his family. And the two of you would do well to avoid each other, too. Is that understood?"

There were studious nods all around.

Marietta nodded as well, content that his message was being heard. "The hunt will continue until the ring is found. If it becomes necessary to meet again on Sunday morning—"

Glowacka said in a surprised tone, "Ring? What ring?"

Marietta didn't like being interrupted. "The ring you're all so hot to find. What else?"

Glowacka stood up. Winston didn't even think he was aware of it—Glowacka just rose slowly as if lifted by a giant invisible hand. He had an anguished look on his face. "A ring? We're running around like a bunch of loonies over a ring? One ring? What happened to the million dollars?"

North, from behind Glowacka, said, "You thought Fredericks hid a million dollars?"

Glowacka turned on him. "What did you think it was?"

"I don't know. I just thought it would be valuable. Treasure usually is. I didn't think it would be a million dollars, though. In cash?"

Now Glowacka looked embarrassed. "That's what I was told."

"By whom?" asked North. "Bruno Fredericks? And you believed him?"

"Never mind that!" Glowacka flapped his arms in frustration. "Who hides a ring? Who sets up this whole cockamamie production with puzzle pieces and treasure hunts and who knows what else over a ring?"

"It's a very nice ring," offered Winston.

"Yeah? How would you know?"

"Mrs. Lewis told me."

Glowacka's look of dismay deepened further. "Mrs. Lewis told you? When?"

"Yesterday. She came to my house and—"

"She came to your house? And told you about the treasure? I ask her a thousand times for a crumb of information and I get nothing! And she just comes to your house and tells you everything?" Glowacka seemed ready to pull out all of his thinning black hair.

Marietta said in an even voice, "If you don't want to be a part of this, Mr. Glowacka, then you're perfectly free to hand over your puzzle pieces and go away."

That stopped Glowacka—seemed to freeze him in place entirely. Then, slowly, he thawed out and sat back down, although he looked like he had a great deal more to say on the subject.

Marietta nodded, satisfied. "Now, then. The hunt will continue until the ring is found. If it becomes necessary to meet again Sunday morning, we will do so." He stopped pacing and said slowly, giving great weight to each word, "Everybody is expected to be on his best behavior and to do what is necessary to find the ring. No bellyaching, grousing, moaning, or complaining will be tolerated." This last was said directly to Glowacka, who crossed his arms with some aggravation. "If and when the ring is found, it will be sold and the proceeds divided up among the four holders of the puzzle pieces."

"How much are we talking here?" Glowacka said. "How much is the ring worth?"

Marietta said, "I don't know, and I don't care. You'll get what you get."

Glowacka made a snorting sound of disgust. Behind him, North raised his hand tentatively like a child in a schoolroom. "Wait a moment. I don't want to get snapped at," he said, seeing that Marietta was close to doing just that, "but something doesn't quite work. Who are we selling the ring to? Are they coming along, and are they going to write out a check right then and there?"

"I doubt it," said Marietta.

"Who keeps the ring in the meantime?"

"Mrs. Lewis will keep the ring." Marietta's tone made it clear he thought this was a stupid question.

North said, "And who's to say that we'll ever get our share?"

Marietta was getting annoyed again. "You can trust Mrs. Lewis."

North arched his eyebrows. "As a matter of fact, I cannot," he said. "Put yourself in my shoes, sir. I've invested a lot of time and quite a bit of money in this endeavor, and if we find the ring, I cannot just hand it over to someone—even Walter Fredericks's daughter—and merely hope I get my share of the profits somewhere down the road."

Marietta looked thrown by this. Winston could see he hadn't been expecting anybody to raise a valid point. "She's selling it to a princess from some rich nation," he said. "This princess is actually gonna fly in, but not until after we get the ring. There is going to be a delay between finding the ring and paying you people off. It's unavoidable."

"Then I don't think that I'll be participating in this after all." North stood up. "Good luck finding the ring without my pieces."

Glowacka gawked at him. "Sit down, you idiot," he said.

"No, I don't think so. I'm not going through all this just to come up empty."

Winston's heart sank into his stomach. Was this whole thing about to fall apart?

Marietta gazed at North coolly. "All right," he said. "What do you suggest?"

"The ring needs to be put somewhere safe," said North. "Someplace that none of the four parties can access. A safe-deposit box at the bank would be ideal—it could be set up so that it cannot be opened unless all four parties are present."

"We're doing this on a Saturday," said Glowacka. "Banks are closed on Saturday."

"Actually, ours is open until noon," said Winston.

North, who was still standing, looked down at Winston. "I think we would be very lucky indeed if we found the ring in less than two hours."

"So why don't we start earlier?" Glowacka said. "Start at nine. Start at eight. For crying out loud, let's start now."

"We're not starting now," said Marietta.

"There's still no guarantee we'll find the ring before the bank closes," said North.

Glowacka said, "Well, why don't we do this on Friday? Or tomorrow? Why wait until Saturday?"

"I have school," said Winston softly. Glowacka rolled his eyes and shook his head, as if this was an impossibly lame excuse.

"I am not available until Saturday," Marietta said, a tad sharply. "And Mrs. Lewis isn't going to take a step near you gentlemen unless I'm around. As little as you trust her, she doesn't trust you twice as much."

North looked unoffended. He simply shrugged and said, "Well, then, I don't know."

Marietta sighed. "All right. I got an idea. You want the ring safe. How about this: They've got a vault over at the police station. We put the ring in there, seal it up like evidence. Only a cop can get it out of there. None of you four can touch it. It'll stay there until this princess gets into town. Then we'll all go and get it."

Glowacka said, "You're a cop?" This fact seemed to make him even unhappier, if that was possible.

"I used to be. And I still have friends. They'll help me out."

North thought it over and finally nodded. "All right. That will do."

"Good," said Glowacka. "So sit down."

North sat, calmly refolding his jacket onto his lap.

From there, it was easy. Everybody agreed to the ground rules, and everybody agreed to be at the library at ten o'clock. The meeting ended with a curt nod from Marietta. "Good. See you Saturday. Stay away from each other until then." The large man turned around and started walking back across the green.

"Do tell Mrs. Lewis how pleased I am that she's decided to help find the ring," North called after him. Marietta made no indication that he'd heard.

Glowacka said to Winston, "That's one interesting friend you have there." He seemed to be holding back a number of other adjectives he would have preferred to use.

"I just met him right before you showed up," said Winston.

North stood up. "Well, gentlemen. Since we've been told to stay away from each other until Saturday, I think I'll be off for an early dinner. Winston, I suggest you get on your bicycle and go home. I don't want to leave you here with—" He gestured to Glowacka, who turned red all over again.

Glowacka said, "With me? Like you're trustworthy? Like this kid should be hanging around a con artist like you?"

North said darkly, "Don't call me a con artist."

"Why not?" Glowacka wanted to know. "You're not good at it or anything. You're not successful at it. But you're just as crooked even without the talent."

North took a step closer to Glowacka. "That's pretty rich coming from a greasy little thief like you."

Winston was dying to ask what on earth these two had against each other, but he did not want to get between them while they were arguing.

But the argument ended right then and there. North seemed to realize they were causing a scene. He took a step back and adjusted his tie. He tried on a tight, ill-fitting smile. "Gentlemen. I'll see you both Saturday." He turned and walked away, the way Marietta had gone.

Winston said, "I should go, too."

Glowacka looked tired. Between arguing with North, being threatened by Marietta, and finding out the treasure wasn't a million dollars but a ring, he'd had a long day. He raised a hand of acknowledgment at Winston but didn't look at him. "Fine, fine. Get home safe, kid. See you Saturday."

Winston got on his bicycle and started home. When he glanced back, Glowacka was sitting on the steps again, looking up at the sky. He seemed to be thinking very, very hard.

"Well?" Katie said right as he walked through the door. That was getting to be a very annoying habit.

Winston took off his jacket. "Well, it's on. Saturday at ten just like Mrs. Lewis said."

She sat up on the couch. "We're going to find the treasure?"

"We're going to try."

"Both those other guys are going to help?"

"Of course. I didn't think they would say no."

Katie jumped up and reached for the phone. "I'm going to invite Maggie and Janie!"

"Uh—"

"Don't you tell me I can't! I know you invited your two doofus friends."

Winston almost let her, just for the sight of giant Marietta dealing with three slightly bratty ten-year-old girls. It'd be like watching a Great Dane fending off a bunch of poodles. But he said, "This policeman, Mrs. Lewis's friend, he doesn't want any extra people coming along. He kicked out Jake and Mal." After a moment, knowing he shouldn't, he added, "He wasn't too crazy about you being there, either."

Instant outrage. "What? They're my puzzle pieces!"

"That's why he's allowing it."

"Well, he better!" Katie stuck out her chin as if she meant to find Marietta and punch him in the nose. With the help of a fairly tall ladder, perhaps.

Winston left Katie stewing in her mild indignation and went upstairs to his room. Once again, he had to put aside all thoughts of the treasure hunt in order to focus on his homework, and tonight it was nearly an impossible task. He lost a solid ten minutes just staring into space, his math book open and useless in his lap.

Finally he decided to turn to Mr. Peterson's extra-credit problem. Okay, it wasn't technically homework, but it was close enough. Anyway, it was closer to homework than what he had been doing, which was nothing.

SUN
+ MOON
EARTH

Can you replace each of the letters above with a digit from 0 to 9 so that the equation is correct? (The two Ns must be represented by the same digit, as must the two Os.) There are eleven possible answers to this puzzle— you only need to find one.

(Answer, page 213-214.)

OH, IT WAS A long week. Wednesday, Thursday, and Friday passed with impossible, deadly, maddening slowness. Most of Winston's brain was taken up with the idea that he would soon be hunting for hidden treasure. He was barked at by his teachers for not paying attention. His parents had to say things to him two or three or four times before the words penetrated his ears. Watching television, he realized he was halfway through some show or other and had not the slightest idea what was going on. He might as well have been watching a fish tank.

Saturday seemed as distant and unreachable as China.

He spent a long time after school at Penrose's, finally bringing his friend up to date on where those mysterious wooden pieces had led. He told the story practically in a single breath.

Penrose shook his head in fascinated disbelief. "Simply fantastic, Winston," he said.

Eagerly, as if Penrose might really know the answer, Winston said, "Do you think the ring will still be there? Do you think it's just been sitting around for twenty-five years?" It had been eating at him, the idea that they might travel down this long road for nothing.

Penrose did nothing to put his mind at ease. He pursed his lips and shrugged. "Who can say?" he said. "Walter Fredericks was a crafty man, but even he might not have thought that it would take this long to find what he had hidden. I'm afraid there's only one way to answer your question."

Winston nodded tiredly. "Find out where he hid it and go there."

Penrose adjusted his glasses. "And, honestly, Winston. Let us pretend that we know the ring has already been found. Yes?"

Winston frowned. "Okay."

"The ring has been found!" Penrose said. "Long ago, or perhaps only yesterday. The treasure is gone." Penrose leaned over the counter. "Wouldn't you want to solve Walter Fredericks's puzzle anyway?"

Winston thought about that. "Yyyeah, I suppose so," he said dubiously.

Penrose waved this waffling answer away. "I know so. Winston Breen, I know you well by now. Walter Fredericks could have hidden an old fountain pen," said Penrose, picking up an old fountain pen. "But if the puzzle intrigued you—and I've yet to find one that didn't—you'd be there solving it."

Winston had to smile. Penrose was right. If somehow Mrs. Lewis called him tonight and announced that she had found the ring in the back of her closet, and there was no point to solving the puzzle, Winston would immediately ask to see all the puzzle pieces so he could try solving it anyway. He hadn't thought of it that way before. "All right," he said. "But I sure hope the ring is still there. It'll be really disappointing if it isn't."

Penrose nodded. "Of course. Treasure hunts make much better stories when there's treasure at the end. In the meantime, if you are looking to warm up that brain of yours, perhaps I might be able to assist with that."

Winston grinned. "Hit me with your best shot."

Penrose leaned forward slightly with a mischievous expression and said, "I have a friend named Marisa.

She likes CARAMEL but not CHOCOLATE.

She likes MACARONI but not SPAGHETTI.

She prefers NEVADA to RHODE ISLAND.

She'll drink COCA-COLA but not GINGER ALE.

She might become a POLICEWOMAN, but she'll never be a WAITRESS.

Which of these musical instruments is Marisa most likely to play— the TUBA, the PIANO, or the SAXOPHONE?"

(Answer, page 214.)

Jake and Mal's enthusiasm for the treasure hunt had dimmed only slightly since being ejected from it. They were waiting for Saturday as eagerly as Winston, and in the meantime, the three of them discussed what the secret of the wooden puzzle pieces would turn out to be, wondered about where the ring would finally be found, and gave serious thought to North and Glowacka. One of them had broken into Mrs. Lewis's house—which one?

"It's that Glowacka guy, for sure," said Jake. It was after school, and they were hanging out in Winston's room.

Mal looked amazed. "For sure? Why for sure?"

Jake shrugged. "Process of elimination. I don't think it's Mr. North."

"Well. I guess that settles that," said Mal.

"I can sort of see both of them doing it," Winston said quietly.

"Me too," said Mal. "I think they're working together."

Jake, who was spread out on the floor of Winston's bedroom, made a face. "Working together? Those two guys hate each other!"

"It might be an act!"

"An act. That's one heck of an act." Winston had told them of the accusations they threw at each other after Marietta had left.

"I didn't mean they were working together," said Winston. "Just that both of them seem capable of it. They both really want the treasure, and they probably both want to divide it with as few people as possible."

Jake said, "Or better yet, keep it entirely for himself."

"You bet," said Winston. "I wonder why they hate each other so much."

Mal said, "Unless they're acting."

Jake looked around for something to throw at him. "They're not acting!"

"*You* don't know," said Mal.

Jake said something that sounded like "fuff" and waved his hands disgustedly.

Winston said, "You think that cop is going to get the guy? Whoever broke into Mrs. Lewis's house?"

"I don't know that I'd want to bet against him," Mal said.

"I wish you guys could be there on Saturday," said Winston, not for the first time. If anything could dampen the excitement of going on a treasure hunt, it was having to do it with the town librarian, his increasingly bratty sister, two mysterious guys who were constantly arguing, and an extremely unfriendly policeman watching over them all. Jake and Mal would be much better teammates. Even if they didn't find the ring, they'd have fun trying.

Then Mal said to Jake, "Tell him."

Winston glanced at them. "Tell me what?"

Jake gave Mal a look that clearly said "You have a big mouth."

"We're going to be there," Jake said to Winston.

Winston was confused. "Where? At the treasure hunt?"

"At the library. We're allowed to be at the library, right? We'll be upstairs working on our history papers."

"Yeah," said Mal. "So, you know, if you guys are having trouble downstairs and need someone else to think about something—"

"We're right upstairs!" said Jake.

Winston was pleased. "That's a really good idea. I'll come up and tell you how it's going."

"I'm gonna spend the day reading magazine articles about Walter Fredericks," said Mal. "Maybe I'll discover something about him that solves the whole thing!"

"Right," said Jake. "A newspaper article. 'Walter Fredericks Hides Treasure Under Rock. See Page Fifteen for Map.'"

Winston said, "What fun would that be?"

And then, finally, Saturday seeped into the world. Winston was up at dawn and spent the next few hours wandering uselessly around the house. Katie was up soon after. They spent some time looking at the original wooden pieces, even though there was nothing further to learn from them. Winston rubbed their delicate wooden texture with his thumb and again tried to process the idea that these simple words would lead to treasure—honest-to-goodness treasure—hidden somewhere in town.

Unless it *wasn't* in town. Who knew what Walter Fredericks might have been up to? Or unless it was buried in town, but dug up years and years ago—the possibility still itched in the back of Winston's brain.

Or unless they couldn't solve the puzzle.

Their mom got up and was not the least bit surprised to see her children already fed and dressed. Their father had left the evening before for a weekend-long business trip. Before leaving he had taken Winston aside and told him again, in a stern voice that Winston definitely heard the first time, that his first priority was *not* solving puzzles but looking out for Katie. Winston promised his father that he would do so.

It was still way, way too early when Winston and Katie decided to walk to the library. Their mother had offered to drive them on the way to her office, but that would have meant waiting even more, and both kids were anxious to get out of the house. Finally, with repeated promises that they would call with updates throughout the day, they were allowed to leave. Winston and his sister walked for a time in silence, each in an invisible, vibrating pocket of excitement.

Katie finally said, looking at the ground as they walked, "Am I going to be able to help today?"

Winston looked at her. "Of course. Why not?"

She shrugged. "I'm just a kid."

"But you like puzzles."

"I like them, but I'm not great at them," she said. "I don't solve them all day long."

Normally, this would have been a jab at Winston. Now Katie seemed truly concerned that she hadn't spent her whole life preparing for this day.

Winston felt a need to cheer her up. "Katie, you're very smart. I'm sure everybody will be able to help today, even you."

"Give me a puzzle," she said.

"Huh?"

"Give me a puzzle to solve. Let me see if I can solve it."

Winston thought. If he gave her one that was too easy just to boost her confidence, she would see right through it. But he didn't want to give her a really hard one, either. He finally said, "All right. What do these things have in common: A SANDWICH SHOP, A COMPUTER, and A CASINO?"

"A computer and a casino?" Katie said sharply, as if Winston must be kidding.

"Yes," said Winston. "And a sandwich shop. What do they all have in common?"

They walked in silence for a bit, Winston mentally crossing his fingers that she would solve it. They were just stepping into the town green when Katie looked up suddenly, with a slight gasp. She smiled. "I got it!" she said.

(Answer, page 214.)

Upon entering the Glenville library, most people either go straight ahead to the main reading room or take a quick left into the children's library. But you can also go down a flight of stairs just inside the main entrance, which leads to a number of small, plain meeting rooms, where a variety of town events are held. Winston had never before used these stairs. But now, at last, after waiting through a week that took nearly a year to pass, he was about to. He swung open a gate that blocked the stairs from wandering toddlers and descended, Katie close behind him.

He had known they were going to be the first ones here, and he was right—the hallway was dim and had an empty echoey feeling. A second staircase led even farther down, into total darkness. Impossible to guess what was down there, and Winston had no desire to find out. This whole place felt rather creepy, quite different from the comfortable library above them.

"Maybe we should wait upstairs," Katie whispered.

Winston had been thinking the same thing but didn't want Katie to think he was afraid.

"No," he said. "People will be here soon." He peeked once more down the second staircase—the darkness down there looked solid—then walked briskly away and opened a door at random. Winston found a light switch, and numerous bright fluorescents flickered to life. There were a couple of long tables and a few dozen metal folding chairs set up in neat rows. "Come on, we'll wait in here," he said.

As they walked into the room, they heard the gate clang shut from above them—someone else was coming down. Whoever it was was doodling a little nonsense song as he came down: *Dum de dum de DAH de dee de DOO. . . .*

That would seem to rule out Marietta—Winston couldn't imagine him singing.

It was a policeman in full uniform. He was a young black man, much younger than Marietta, and he had a wide, friendly face. He was cradling something in one arm and held a plastic bag in his other hand. A brief glimmer of surprise showed on his face when he saw Winston and his sister, but that quickly melted into a smile.

"Hey. You must be the kids," he said. "Something Breen. Sorry, I forget the name."

"Winston."

"I'm Katie."

"Right! I'm Officer Louis Stokes. I'm a friend of Ray Marietta. He asked me to ride along on this little shindig today. This where we're setting up?" He was looking past them into the room.

"We just got here ourselves," said Winston.

"Well, seems as good a place as any, what do you say?" He walked in and put his packages on one of the tables. Winston could now see that one of them was a coffeemaker.

"You kids like coffee?" said Stokes. He was looking around the room thoughtfully, like he was trying to solve a problem.

"Yuck," said Katie. "I tried some of my dad's coffee once, and it's awful."

"Well, maybe you'll like it more when you're older," said the policeman. "Ah, here we are." He had found what he was looking for: an electrical socket. Stokes dragged one of the tables over to the wall and plugged in the coffeemaker. "Katie, howja like to do me a favor? Take this coffeepot down to the ladies' room and fill it up to here with some water." He smiled at Katie, who took the pot from him carefully and left the room.

Stokes opened up the plastic bag and removed a number of tall plastic cups, like Winston's mother had for drinking coffee in the car. "So, Winston," he said. "You think we're going to find this ring everybody's so hot about?"

"I don't know. I hope so."

Stokes removed a foil packet and shook it, and then tore it open and dumped its contents into the filter. "There we go. Fresh coffee in no time."

"You like coffee, I guess," said Winston, just to say something.

"Never touch the stuff. Kills my stomach."

"Oh," said Winston, now officially mystified.

Mrs. Lewis came into the room holding the coffeepot filled with water. Katie trailed in right after her.

"Officer Stokes!" she said warmly. "It's nice to see you."

"Violet! Let me take that." Stokes took the coffeepot in one hand and gave Mrs. Lewis a quick hug with his other arm. Katie came and sat next to Winston.

Mrs. Lewis turned her attention to Winston with a smile. "So, are you excited?" she said.

"You bet," said Winston.

"Me too!" said Katie.

Mrs. Lewis nodded. "I am, too. After all these years, it's hard to believe we're really doing this."

"Good morning, everybody!" They all turned to look, and there was David North, standing in the doorway, looking exceptionally pleased. "It's going to be a lovely day for our little quest." He saw the librarian and nodded politely, unsure of his standing. "Mrs. Lewis."

"Mr. North." She was standoffish, but nodded back.

North said with great seriousness, "This is the first chance I've had to thank you for allowing us to seek out the final piece of your father's estate. I know it wasn't an easy decision."

Winston could see that Mrs. Lewis didn't want to be impolite, but she also didn't want to be particularly gracious toward this man. She finally said, "We'll start in a few minutes. Why don't you have a seat."

North came into the room and folded his light jacket over the back of a chair. "Of course, of course. Oh, fresh coffee! Wonderful idea!" He looked pleased enough to start tap dancing.

Glowacka came in a few minutes later, with a hard expression on his face, as if he was expecting an immediate confrontation. But North saw him and said, "Mickey! Exciting day, wouldn't you say?"

Glowacka blinked. "Yeah. Yeah. Very exciting. Why wouldn't it be?" He looked around the room, saw the librarian, and became the slightest bit flustered. "Mrs. Lewis. Um, hi there. Good to see you again. This is your library, huh? I mean, I know it's not *your* library. . . . And Winston. Hey, kid." He finally found himself a chair and sat down.

"Why, it looks like we can start, doesn't it?" said North, looking around the room, his grin widening. "I assume we all brought our wooden pieces."

Stokes had been standing in the corner, leaning against the wall.

He spoke up. "We won't be starting until Ray Marietta arrives. Have some coffee and relax."

That knocked North's grin clean off his face. But he took the policeman's advice, taking one of the travel mugs and pouring himself some coffee. "Will you be joining us all day, Officer?" he said.

Stokes shrugged. "You never know."

An uncomfortable silence descended on the room. Nobody knew what to say, and the sense of anticipation was awful in its intensity. Finally, five eternal minutes later, Marietta came in. He looked around and said, "We're all here. Good." He nodded to the policeman. "Lou, thanks for joining us."

"Hey, Ray, no problem. This is going to be fun." Stokes's grin was loaded with good-natured mischief.

Marietta looked around the room as if for security problems. "All right," he said. "I guess we can get started, unless anybody wants to discuss anything first." Nobody wanted to discuss anything. "Okay, then. Let's go."

On these words, a physical buzz shot through the room. The hunt was about to begin.

"You brought your puzzle pieces with you?" said Marietta.

There was agreement from all four parties. Katie was already holding hers. Mrs. Lewis raised up her purse to indicate where hers were. Glowacka dug his out of the purple-and-green-checked sport coat he seemed to wear everywhere. North removed his pieces from his pants pocket.

"Then why don't we gather around this table here," said Marietta, pointing to one of the long tables. Glowacka, North, Mrs. Lewis, and—looking very little indeed—Katie each took a position around the table. Together, they looked like they were about to perform some strange, ancient ritual.

North looked down at Katie, aware of her for the first time. "And who are you, miss?"

"Katie," said Katie, in a low voice.

Winston said, "She's my little sister. The puzzle pieces are actually hers."

"They are?" North seemed surprised.

"Well, we're sharing them."

Glowacka said to Katie, "How old are you, kid?"

"I just turned ten."

"Ten," repeated Glowacka. "A ten-year-old treasure hunter." Glowacka shook his head in disbelief.

"Do you want to do this, people?" said Marietta, with a touch of annoyance. "Let's get started. Now everybody put your pieces down on the table, and—"

There was a voice from the doorway. "Excuse me?"

Heads whirled. There was a young woman with long blond hair, a small camera draped around her neck. She seemed aware that she had just interrupted something important. She said shyly, "Mrs. Lewis . . . ? We met the other day?"

Mrs. Lewis seemed pleased to see her. Everyone else just looked baffled. "Brenda! It's nice to see you again."

Marietta said, "Who is this?"

"I'm Brenda Bethel. I'm a reporter for the *Glenville News*?" She said it as if she wasn't even sure herself. "I spoke to Mrs. Lewis about covering your treasure hunt today?"

Marietta turned to Mrs. Lewis accusingly. He could not possibly have looked less pleased.

Mrs. Lewis blushed. "I'm sorry, Ray. I meant to mention this to you the other day, but in all the excitement—"

"I won't get in the way, I promise," Brenda piped up. "But this is a wonderful story, and I would love the chance to cover it. A treasure hidden by one of the founders of our town!"

"I told her she could, Ray," said Mrs. Lewis. "I didn't really think you'd mind."

He minded. Winston could see that. But he couldn't seem to think of a way to *say* he minded.

North said, "I don't see where it does any harm. Do you, Mickey?"

Glowacka shook his head. "Hey, she wants to take a picture as we finally find this thing, that's fine with me."

"Fine," said Marietta, in a low voice.

Brenda smiled and bounded into the room. She took out an assignment pad and a pencil and looked alert.

Marietta turned to the group at large. "All right. Where were we?"

"We're about to start," said Glowacka.

"Right. Right," said Marietta. "Okay. Everybody put your puzzle pieces faceup on the table . . . *now*."

LINE	SHOW V	BY T	WAY
TIME O	PARK O	TABLE R	KICK E
MEAL T	ST AND	BALL R	A PIECE
PLACE S	L SIDE	TENNIS	DRIVE S

CHAPTER EIGHT

"LOOK," SAID GLOWACKA for the hundredth time. He was holding a map of the town and staring at it intently. "I'm telling you, you gotta shuffle the words around in some crazy way. You gotta make a sentence out of them. You put the words in the right order, it'll tell you where to go. What else can this be except directions to some location? And that's where the treasure is hidden! We have to arrange them into some kind of . . . sentence."

"It can't be done, Mickey," said North. "There's no sentence in there." He was pacing and frowning at the floor, his hands clasped behind his back in a gentlemanly fashion.

"Well, what else? You come up with something, then."

"I am trying to do just that," North said calmly.

Winston was sitting on the table, his legs folded under him, the pieces laid out before him in a neat rectangle. Katie was standing next to him, and she would occasionally switch the position of two or more pieces. Winston didn't stop her. He wasn't really looking at the pieces anymore. At first, he thought Glowacka had a good idea, arranging the words into one or more sentences. But that had been nearly two hours ago, and Winston now thought there was no way to do that, although Glowacka continued to grip the idea with a kind of desperation.

He kept seeing two-word phrases in there—combining KICK and STAND to make KICKSTAND, for instance. Great, but what did that accomplish? Nothing, as far as he could tell. And so he sat and stared.

Ray Marietta and his friend, Officer Stokes, had prepared themselves for a long day. When it was clear the group wasn't going to solve the puzzle quickly, Stokes brought out a deck of cards, and the two of them were now playing gin rummy. Brenda was trying, mostly unsuccessfully, to interview Mickey Glowacka. She was seated near him with her assignment pad at the ready, but he was too interested in the map he had retrieved from the library upstairs.

"How did you find out about Walter Fredericks's treasure?" she asked.

"Huh? I was friends with one of his sons," Glowacka said, utterly distracted. "Bruno. Bruno Fredericks."

"He gave you his part of the puzzle?"

"He *sold* it to me, that . . ." Glowacka's sentence trailed off into an angry mutter. Winston thought Mrs. Lewis was right: Her brother must have sold Glowacka on the idea that the treasure was a million dollars. Winston wondered how much Mickey Glowacka had paid for his puzzle pieces and if he would make that back with his share of the ring.

Mrs. Lewis came over to Winston, looking glum and a little embarrassed. "I'm sorry," she said. "I feel like I should be better at this, since it's my father's puzzle. But I just don't know what to make of any of this."

Winston said, "Do any of the words mean anything special to you?"

North stopped pacing. He came over to the table, surprised and pleased. "Yes. That's a good question!" He looked down at the wooden strips. "To us, they're just a bunch of words, but this was a father talking directly to his children. It might be a message only they could interpret. That never occurred to me."

Mrs. Lewis frowned at the words. "Nothing here really leaps out at me. . . ."

Glowacka joined them. "What about your old man? Did your father play tennis?" He picked up the TENNIS piece and waved it to make his point clear.

"Yes, sometimes."

"Where?"

"He belonged to a club. I don't remember which one."

Katie, who had said very little since the treasure hunt began, suddenly spoke up: "Maybe the words don't mean anything at all."

North looked at her politely. "Sweetie, they're all we've got. If they don't mean anything, what are we supposed to do?"

"But maybe it's these extra letters that are important."

Glowacka looked up. "You know, she may be right. We haven't paid nearly enough attention to those letters."

North reached for some paper and a pen. "All right. I'm game. Can we make any words out of them? Let's see. . . ." He started writing.

"I wonder why some of those letters are in front of the word and others are in back," said Mrs. Lewis.

"To drive us completely crazy," Glowacka said promptly.

Winston shook his head as if to clear it of dust. He jumped off the table, and the joint of his right knee made a small popping sound like an air rifle. He'd been sitting in one position for much too long. He thought he might take a break and go upstairs, to see if Jake and Mal were there, as they had promised.

But just at that moment, North said excitedly, "The word SOLVE is in here!" Glowacka came around and gawked over the larger man's shoulder. Brenda took a picture of the two of them. Her camera's flash was remarkably bright.

Mrs. Lewis said, "What letters do you have left?"

"Just a minute, just a minute," North said. He was scribbling fever-ishly. Winston, on the other side of the table, couldn't decipher North's upside-down handwriting, but he hoped the man really had cracked the puzzle.

North stopped writing. He held the piece of paper in both hands. He said, "START OR SOLVE." North looked around the room with bright hope in his eyes. But everybody simply stared at him, waiting for more.

When it was clear that there was no more, Glowacka said, "So what the heck is that supposed to mean?"

North turned morose. "I don't know."

"It's nothing! It's another dead end!"

"All right, Mickey. At least I'm trying something new here."

"Aaaaah." Glowacka shooed this away with a frustrated wave of his hand. "We're getting nowhere."

"Gin," said Officer Stokes.

"Ah, you got me again," said Marietta.

"I'm glad someone's having fun here," said Glowacka, sitting back down with a thump.

With that momentary excitement over, Winston went upstairs to see if Jake and Mal had shown up. They had. In fact, the second they saw Winston they waved him frantically over, as if he had been heading somewhere else.

"It's about time you came up here," said Jake.

"Show him," said Mal.

"I will, I will."

"Show me what?" Winston was tired and sluggish after two hours of getting nowhere on that puzzle, but he began to notice that his friends were nearly bursting with exhilaration.

Jake said, "Mal was researching Walter Fredericks, looking him up in the magazine database."

Mal said, "Show him!"

"I will," said Jake. "I'm just explaining things first. It's this big computer database, and you just type in a word or phrase, and it gives you back all these magazine articles you can look up."

Winston said, "You found out something about Walter Fredericks?"

Mal said, "No, better! Jake, *show him!*" Mal looked like a machine that was set on too high a speed. He was about to vibrate into a thousand pieces.

Jake selected a piece of paper from the pile in front of him on the table and held it to his chest. His eyes were glowing. "We got the idea to look for treasure hunters. I don't know why. Just to see, right? So we typed in the phrase 'treasure hunters.' This is one of the articles we found." He gave the paper to Winston.

It was a black-and-white printout of a magazine article. The top half of the first page was completely taken up with a single photograph—perhaps thirty or forty men and women, grouped together for a portrait. Under that, a banner headline: "Gold Diggers." The caption for the photograph read "Attendees of the National Treasure Hunters' Association's annual convention, held this year in the Wyerbrook Hotel."

"But what is this?" Winston didn't get it.

Jake looked at him with surprise and then thrust his finger at the picture. "Look."

Winston looked. Jake was pointing at . . . David North! At least, it might have been David North. The photograph hadn't printed very well.

"It's much clearer on the screen," said Jake. "It's him. Mal's sure of it."

"Absolutely," said Mal. "And look here."

Mal pointed. Winston knew what he was going to see, and he was right: Mickey Glowacka, glowering at the camera. Smudgy, but undoubtedly him.

"They were at a treasure hunters' convention together," Winston said with wonder. "When was this?"

"July, two years ago."

"Does the article say anything about them?"

Jake shook his head. "Nothing. They weren't interviewed. And we looked up both their names in the magazine database—"

"And on the Internet, while we were at it," said Mal.

"Right," said Jake. "And for Mickey Glowacka, there was nothing. Flat-out nothing."

Mal said, "I think maybe it's not his real name."

Jake shrugged to show he doubted this. "Not everybody in the world has been interviewed in a magazine. Or has a Web page."

Mal said, "Anyway, we looked up David North, too."

"What did you find?"

Jake shook his head again. "The opposite problem. Too many of them."

"There's like a zillion David Norths out there," said Mal. "They should form a club."

"We looked up a few of them, hoping we'd get lucky," said Jake. "You want to read about David North, the jockey? He's won a lot of horse races."

"I guess our David North is a little tall to be a jockey," said Winston.

Jake shook the printout of the treasure hunter article again. "So what do you think this means?"

Mal said immediately, "Well, duh. It's like I said. They've been working together the whole time. They've known each other for years."

"We *knew* they knew each other," said Jake. "It doesn't mean they're working together."

"Maybe," said Winston, "maybe this is where they met. Maybe something happened there to make them dislike each other."

"I wish we knew what," said Jake.

Mal said, "How's it going down there, anyway?"

"Terrible. We're not getting anywhere. I want to snap those wooden pieces into a bunch of matchsticks."

"Well, if you need help, you've got two mighty brains sitting up here," said Mal. "Or, anyway, one and a quarter."

Jake slugged Mal's arm. "I knew you were going to say something like that, you jerk."

"I should get back downstairs," said Winston. "I'll try to come up again later."

"Should we keep researching those two guys?" said Jake, anxious to help somehow.

"If you think you'll get anywhere. Or look into Walter Fredericks. Mal said he would find something that would lead us to the treasure. Boy, could we ever use that."

Mal, in his usual cheerful mood, saluted. "Aye, aye, Cap'n. We're on the case."

Winston went back downstairs. He expected to hear Glowacka and North arguing, but instead there was only moody silence. Mrs. Lewis had pulled a chair over to the table and was moving the wooden pieces around. Nobody else seemed to be paying attention to the pieces at all. Katie was sitting with her feet up on another chair, looking bored and depressed. North was sitting almost exactly in the position of a sculpture Winston's dad kept in his office—a statue called *The Thinker*. Brenda was pacing in the back of the room, talking on a cell phone. And Marietta was playing cards with . . . Mickey Glowacka. Officer Stokes was gone.

Mrs. Lewis looked up as Winston came in and waved him over. "I was thinking about what you said before," she said, "About all the two-word phrases you can make out of these words. Like KICKSTAND."

"Yeah?"

"I'm wondering if there's a way to make a chain of two-word phrases. Like here we have PLACE and KICK, which makes PLACE KICK. And then you have KICKSTAND. And then maybe STAND can be the beginning of another phrase. Maybe there's a way to use all these pieces at once."

Winston thought this was a pretty good idea. He felt himself getting excited again, even though a hundred similarly good ideas had all led nowhere. "Let's try it out." He pulled up a chair, and they began shuffling the pieces.

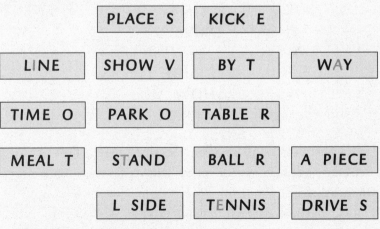

(Continue reading to see the answer.)

"This has to be significant," said David North, looking at the completed chain of words. Winston agreed with him. This couldn't simply be a coincidence.

They were all gathered around the table, staring at the reorganized wooden pieces. The reporter, Brenda, was taking notes furiously. Even Marietta, who until now had expressed no interest in the details of the treasure hunt, came over to look at the result.

```
MEAL  T
TIME  O
TABLE  R
TENNIS
BALL  R
PARK  O
PLACE  S
KICK  E
STAND
BY  T
LINE
DRIVE  S
WAY
L  SIDE
SHOW  V
A  PIECE
```

"It's very nice," said Glowacka, "but what does it get us?"

"There must be a message in the leftover letters," said Winston. "There has to be."

Katie said them out loud: "T-O-R-R-O-S-E—"

"Wait a second, wait a second," said North. "What about the *E* in

TENNIS? It's a different color from the rest of the letters. If you include that in your list, Katie, the first six letters spell out the word TORERO!"

Katie squinted at him. "What's a torero?"

"It's a Spanish word for bullfighter."

Glowacka said immediately, "Is there a famous bullfighter in this town? Maybe a statue of a bullfighter?"

Marietta shook his head. "No."

Glowacka was annoyed. "You know every statue in town?"

The big cop shrugged. "There aren't that many of them, friend."

"Maybe it's not a public statue," said Glowacka. "Maybe one of Walter Fredericks's friends owned it." He looked at Mrs. Lewis, hope gleaming in his eyes.

"Maybe we should look at the rest of the letters," suggested Mrs. Lewis, gently. They had all learned by now that Glowacka did not come easily away from an idea once he had sunk his teeth into it.

At that moment, Brenda shrieked—a startlingly loud sound, as if something had bitten her. Everybody flinched. Katie, standing next to Brenda, jumped halfway to the ceiling. Brenda noticed none of this. She wasn't frightened, Winston saw—she was nearly overwhelmed with excitement. Brenda pointed at the chain of words and said, "Rosetti! Rosetti!"

Glowacka said, "What? What's that?"

"Rosetti! His name is right there! Look!"

Marietta was curious. "Rosetti? The pizza guy?"

Winston saw it. Starting with the word BALL and reading the extra letters or the colored letters, ROSETTI was spelled out clear as day.

North said in a hoarse voice, "That has to be right."

Glowacka said, "Who is this guy?"

"Salvatore Rosetti," said Mrs. Lewis. "He owns a pizza parlor right near here."

"That's where me and my friends were the day you found us," Winston said to Glowacka.

"Oh, that place."

Now it was Mrs. Lewis's turn to gasp. She bent forward and slid the bottom five words up to the top of the chain. "Look at this," she said. "It's not a chain. It's a circle. The word at the bottom connects back with the word up top."

"Piecemeal," said North.

"Look what happens when you start the chain with DRIVE."

```
DRIVE S
   WAY
  L SIDE
SHOW V
 A PIECE
MEAL T
TIME O
TABLE R
TENNIS
BALL R
PARK O
PLACE S
KICK E
STAND
 BY T
LINE
```

She was right. Now the extra or colored letters spelled out Salvatore Rosetti's full name. Somehow, the man who had served countless slices of pizza to Winston and his friends was now the key to finding Walter Fredericks's treasure.

Glowacka said, "Was this guy friends with your dad?"

Mrs. Lewis shrugged, mystified. "I knew they knew each other. I don't know if they were friends."

"I guess we should go see the gentleman," said North.

"I guess we *should*," said Glowacka.

Marietta took charge. "All right. Let's assume we're not coming back here. Everybody take your stuff, and we'll go over as a group. The pizzeria is right across the street. Nobody needs to drive anywhere."

There was a mild hubbub as everybody gathered up their belongings—even in just two hours, they had done a fine job of spreading out and taking over the room.

"Officer Stokes left his coffee machine here," said Mrs. Lewis.

"Leave it for now," said Marietta. "He'll come back for it. I'll get him on walkie-talkie a little later."

Katie said, "You have a walkie-talkie?" Marietta pointed to his hip, where a small black box was clipped, making soft crackling noises. Katie seemed deeply impressed at this.

They all made their way up the stairs, an awkward group. Just before the exit, Winston remembered Jake and Mal. "I'll be right back!" he said, and ran off before Marietta could react. Winston raced into the reading room. Jake and Mal looked up as he ran over. "We're going to Rosetti's. That was the answer to the puzzle," he said.

"What? It was? How?"

"I can't explain it now. I'm just telling you where we're going. I gotta go." And Winston turned back and ran to the rest of the group, leaving his two friends blinking at each other in bewilderment.

"What was that about?" said Marietta as Winston came back.

"Nothing. I . . . just wanted to see something. But it was nothing."

Marietta grunted, and the full group headed across the green to the pizza parlor. They passed Penrose's shop on the way, of course, and Winston felt an urge to run and tell the old man the latest news. But he thought breaking off from the group again would be frowned upon by Marietta.

Sal Rosetti wasn't behind the counter at the pizza parlor. His son, Frank, was there, stretching out the dough for a fresh pie. A second worker, a bored-looking teenage girl with a whole artist's palette of makeup on her face, sat working the cash register.

Frank continued kneading out dough as the group approached the counter, but he said, "Hey, all. What can I get for you?"

North took charge. "You're not Salvatore Rosetti, are you?"

Winston said in a low voice, "This is his son."

"That's right," said Frank. "Sal's my dad. Is there a problem?"

"We need to see him on a matter of utmost importance," North said.

"Yeah?" Frank seemed mildly curious and nothing more. "What is it?"

Mrs. Lewis stepped up. "Frank. Hello."

"Oh, hey, Mrs. Lewis. How are you?"

"I'm fine, thank you. Frank, this is going to sound very strange. Many, many years ago, my father—you remember my father?"

"Well, sure."

"I believe that, years ago, he may have given your father a ring."

Frank tried to absorb this odd information. "A ring?"

"A very nice jeweled ring. And he may have told him to keep it until one of his children asked for it. I'd be interested to know if your father still has that ring."

Frank shook his head. "I don't have the slightest idea. He's home today, if you want to go ask him. I don't know anything about a ring."

"Well, you would have been just a little boy when he received it. Thank you, Frank. I guess we'll go ask your dad."

Brenda took Frank's picture.

They drove over in two cars. Marietta drove Glowacka and North in a black SUV so large it looked like it could go straight through a tree without getting dented. Brenda escorted Winston, Katie, and Mrs. Lewis in her far more modest sedan. The backseat was filled with all kinds of random items—maps, an old briefcase, a jug of antifreeze—and Katie sat with her legs folded under her, because there was no place else to put them.

"Sorry about the mess," said Brenda as she started the engine.

"It's okay," said Winston as he felt around for the jagged item that was jabbing him in the rear end. He found it: A small ice scraper. He tossed it on the floor.

Mrs. Lewis, in the passenger seat, said, "I'm not sure of his exact address, although I'll remember his house when I see it. He lives near the playground by Edison Elementary."

"Oh, I know where that is," said Brenda, and she took off.

They drove in silence for a few minutes. Then Brenda glanced into her rearview mirror and said, "Katie, I understand you found your puzzle pieces by accident."

Katie seemed down about something. "Yeah," she said. "They were in a box that Winston bought me as a birthday present."

"Yeah? That's really interesting! You gonna share your part of the treasure with your big brother?"

"I guess."

Winston leaned over to his sister and said in a low voice, "What's the matter?"

Shrug.

"Katie, what is it?"

"I didn't get to solve anything. I knew I wouldn't."

Winston was taken aback. "It was a very hard puzzle, Katie. And besides that, what are you talking about? You're the one who pointed out how important the extra letters would be."

"That's not solving anything. That was just something I said."

"Well, it was important, anyway. Everybody made suggestions, because nobody knew which suggestions were going to be right. That's how it works when a lot of people are trying to solve something really difficult. It's called brainstorming."

"Hey, Katie?" said Brenda. "When I saw Rosetti's name in that bunch of letters, I just got totally lucky. I'm sure you're much better at puzzles than me in general."

"I'll never be as good as Winston."

Brenda frowned. "So what? I've got a brother who's a state champion soccer player. I'll never be as good a soccer player as he is, but I can still enjoy playing the game." Katie looked at Brenda in the mirror, intrigued by this notion. Brenda smiled and continued, "One day you're going to discover something you love almost as much as Winston loves puzzles. And he'll never be as good as you at that. Whatever it is."

Winston felt his stomach do a flutter as he watched Brenda easily talk his little sister out of her funk. He and Mal and Jake had once made a list of the prettiest girls they knew. He was only twelve, so this was not a tremendously long list. Brenda Bethel had just skyrocketed to the top of it. On top of this, she was just plain nice. Of course, she was also ten years older than him, at a minimum. He doubted she would be accompanying him to the Spring Dance at the junior high, assuming he ever got up the nerve to ask her, which would never happen in a million, trillion years. But the stomach flutter was not unpleasant in the meantime.

"Make a left here," said Mrs. Lewis.

They turned onto Autumnside Lane. Salvatore Rosetti lived about halfway down the block, in a white house with a slightly crumbling paint job and a large wooden porch. Marietta had arrived first, and he and North and Glowacka were standing there waiting.

"I hope this guy is home," said Glowacka when they had all reassembled.

Marietta said, "Let's go see."

They marched toward the house as a group, and Winston, finding himself at the front, rang the doorbell.

There was a minute of silence, and then the door opened up to reveal Salvatore Rosetti. He answered the door in an old white T-shirt and loose-fitting gray pants with a hole in the knee. Winston felt a small wave of unreality wash over him—he had only ever seen this man in his own pizza parlor, in a red-and-white-striped jacket.

"You must be the group looking for some kind of ring," Rosetti said.

Mrs. Lewis again stepped to the front of the group. "Yes. I guess Frank called you."

"Well, I don't know anything about any such ring."

"My father would have given it to you around twenty-five years ago. He might have asked you to hang on to it until one of his children came looking for it."

Rosetti was shaking his head. "No, no. No ring. The only thing your father gave me was a bunch of envelopes."

From the back of the assembly, North said, "Envelopes?"

Rosetti continued, "But as you say, that was a long time ago, and I don't know where they are. If I had them, I would give them to you. I am sorry."

Glowacka muttered, but not quietly enough, "He probably had the ring and sold it ages ago."

A whole weather pattern of thunderstorms passed over Rosetti's old face. "I would not do any such thing." His voice was choked with sudden anger. "You accuse me of stealing from Walter Fredericks? Is that what you've come here to do?"

North waved his hands as if to magically avert disaster. "No! No, sir. We just thought—"

"I'm through with this," said Rosetti. "Go find your ring somewhere else." He glared at the lot of them and then slammed the door shut.

NORTH TURNED ON Glowacka. "You are a horse's ass!"

"He doesn't have the ring, anyway! You heard him."

"He still could have been of help to us. You accused him of stealing the ring!" North shook his head, incensed. "I still can't believe it."

Katie said, "So is that it, then? Did we lose?"

"I don't know," said Mrs. Lewis.

"He mentioned envelopes," said Winston. "What would your father give Mr. Rosetti in a bunch of envelopes?"

North fumed, "Well, we're not likely to find out now, are we?"

Mrs. Lewis said, "Maybe it's another puzzle." She considered this for a moment and then added, "In fact, I'm sure of it. The first puzzle originally came in four envelopes, one for each of us."

"You see that?" said North, talking directly to Glowacka. "He never had the ring in the first place. He's got the next leg of the treasure hunt in there, and now he's slammed the door on us because of *you*."

"I think," said Glowacka, slowly and precisely, "that I get the point."

Marietta suddenly announced, "All right. Everybody head down to the playground and wait for me there."

"What are you going to do?" asked Mrs. Lewis.

"Talk to the man. But maybe it's better if I do it alone." He cast a glance at Glowacka.

Who caught the glance and its meaning. "I'm not going to say anything else!" he said. "How stupid do you think I am?"

North said, "That has yet to be determined."

Glowacka looked like he had a sharp reply to this, but Marietta interrupted him. "Everybody down to the playground. Let me talk to the man and see what I can do. Go!"

So they went, hesitantly marching as a group down to the end of the block. Halfway there, Winston looked back to see that Marietta had managed to summon the pizza maker to the porch again. Rosetti looked angry and was jabbing a finger at Marietta as he spoke, while Marietta patted the air with both hands in an attempt to calm the pizza maker down. After a moment, Marietta gestured questioningly into the house. Rosetti seemed to consider this for a second and then led him inside, closing the door behind him.

The playground at the end of the block was one of the nicer ones in town. The centerpiece was a huge metal-and-plastic apparatus with all kinds of fun things for little kids to do. A group of toddlers was cavorting around it with great glee, while their parents chatted amiably at one of the three nearby picnic tables. The parents stopped talking abruptly as this group of strangers descended upon the playground, claiming the other two picnic tables for themselves. Deciding that this new group posed no threat, they continued their own conversation.

"Do you think he'll get the envelopes?" asked Katie.

"I don't know," said Winston.

North sighed. "I should have brought some food with me."

Mrs. Lewis nodded. "Yes, that would have been a good idea. But it's not like I go on treasure hunts every week. I didn't think about it."

There was a moody silence, punctuated only by the shrieks of the little kids. After a little while, Glowacka said with some regret, "I got a big mouth." He stared down at the ground. "I'll go back and apologize. What was I thinking, saying he stole the ring? What a thing to say! I'm just tired."

North said, "Let that policeman do what he's doing, Mickey. Maybe he'll get the envelopes we need. If not, then you can go apologize."

Glowacka nodded. "Yeah, okay." He continued staring morosely at the ground.

Brenda came over to Winston, who glanced up at her, surprised. Yes, she was sitting down next to him. Winston tried not to redden. "So, Winston," she said. "Is it Winston? Or Win?" She had her assignment pad and pencil out again—she was in reporter mode.

"Winston."

"I understand from Mrs. Lewis that you might be the biggest puzzle fan in the group."

Winston agreed. "I've always liked puzzles."

"What's the first puzzle you remember solving?" she asked with a smile.

That was a surprising question, and he had to think about it. His parents would buy him word search magazines when he was a child. He'd been doing those since he was six, circling the words in the grid with a sloppy, uneven scrawl. But even before that, he had dim memories of making his own impromptu puzzles—choosing a bunch of plastic toy letters at random and seeing how many words he could make from them. Even his attempts to build the tallest possible tower out of blocks now struck him, in a way, as a kind of puzzle.

"Wow," said Brenda. "So you really have been solving puzzles your entire life. That's amazing."

"I guess." People sometimes told him that his love of puzzles was amazing, but to Winston, it was just who he was. His friend Jake had loved sports since he was very small, and now he was on the baseball team at school—what was so amazing about that? If he had played baseball, football, and soccer all through his childhood and then suddenly dropped it all to join the sewing club, *that* would be amazing.

"So what's your favorite puzzle ever?" Brenda asked.

Winston blinked. "Wow, I don't know. There's a lot of puzzles out there."

"All right. What's one of your favorite puzzles?"

He thought about it. Then he said, "This is an old puzzle, and it drove me crazy for the longest time. I think the solution is really neat." He took a pencil and wrote down a string of letters:

O T T F F S S __

"What's the next letter in this series?" he asked.

Brenda stared. "Can I think about it?"

"Sure. I'll tell you the answer later, if you want."

(Answer, page 214.)

Brenda asked a few more questions, and Winston enjoyed answering them, but after she was done, nobody in the group had much to say. Time passed, and they all sat there, eyes glued to Rosetti's house a hundred yards away. At some point, Marietta was going to come back out that door, and what would happen then? They were all dying to know, but there was nothing they could do to make that moment happen any faster.

It seemed like a good time to check in with his mom, as he had promised to do. Winston asked to borrow Brenda's cell phone, and she gave it to him.

"How's the treasure hunt going?" his mother asked when she answered. She was still at her office.

"Well, we're a little bit stuck at the moment," Winston said.

"Is Katie with you?"

"Of course she is!" Winston said, surprised. "I'm not going to lose her."

"Is she having fun?"

He looked around at the group. "I don't think any of us are having much fun, actually."

"Oh," his mother said. Over at Rosetti's house, the door opened, and Marietta stepped out. A surge of energy went through the whole group at the picnic tables. Marietta shook hands with Rosetti. They seemed to be on much friendlier terms now. Rosetti shut the front door, and Marietta descended the porch and headed toward the playground. Throughout this, Winston's mother's voice was ringing in his ear, but he didn't hear a word of it.

"What?" he said.

"I said, if neither of you is having any fun, why don't you go home? I thought treasure hunts were supposed to be fun."

Winston saw that Marietta, now halfway to them, had one arm behind his back. He brought this arm out now. He was holding a number of envelopes. He had done it. Plus, to Winston's amazement, Marietta was grinning like a pleased kid. A six-foot-five-inch, three-hundred-pound kid.

"I think the fun might be starting again," he said to his mom, and hung up—and then realized that he had just hung up on his mother.

Oh, well. She would understand when he explained later. Probably.

"How did you do it?" asked Mrs. Lewis, amazed and pleased, when Marietta arrived at the picnic tables.

"Simple," he said. "Just a little bit of sweet talk. Plus I gave him a hundred bucks."

"Really?" said Winston. "You bribed him?"

Marietta frowned. "*Paid* him. Policemen don't bribe people."

"Okay," Winston said quickly.

"I also told him I would break Glowacka's spine," Marietta announced.

Glowacka, who had been smiling as much as anybody at the sight of those envelopes, grimaced. "I already made my apologies to everyone," he said. "You missed it."

"I'll take your word for it," Marietta told him.

"He still had them after all this time?" Mrs. Lewis couldn't believe it. She stared at the envelopes in Marietta's hand like they were an original copy of the Declaration of Independence.

"They were at the bottom of a drawer," said Marietta. "He was amazed himself that he was able to find them. But one look around his home and you knew those envelopes had to be somewhere. The man saves everything."

North said, "Well, how about we open them already?"

"Good idea," said Winston.

Marietta distributed the envelopes to Mrs. Lewis, North, Glowacka, and Katie. Winston hung anxiously over Katie's shoulder. The envelopes were yellow and splotchy with age. Katie ripped open her envelope and shook out the contents. Winston was not entirely surprised to see that they were more wooden strips. Two of them this time, each engraved with a series of letters:

Katie looked up at her big brother and said, "Here we go again."

Glowacka groaned as he took out his own wooden strips. "We're going to be at this until the middle of spring."

Brenda glanced at him. "It *is* spring," she said, gesturing to the green world around them.

"*Next* spring," Glowacka said.

North said, "Do we all have the same thing again? Two wooden strips, each with four letters?"

There was general agreement from the group.

Winston said with some surprise, "You know what? I think I know what this is."

"You do?" said Brenda.

Winston glanced at North, Glowacka, and Mrs. Lewis, all of whom were studying the letters on their puzzle pieces. "I think it's going to be an anaquote," he said.

Glowacka said, "A what?"

"What is that?" said North. "I've never heard of it."

"Here, let me show you how it works," said Winston. "Does someone have some paper I can borrow?" Brenda gave him a page out of her assignment pad and her pencil. He bent over, wrote some letters, and ripped the paper into four strips. He scrambled them up and laid them on the picnic table.

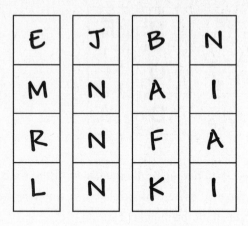

"Look," he said. "Here's an example of what I'm talking about. By switching the order of these strips, you can spell out the name of a famous person, reading across all four rows."

(Answer, page 214.)

"All right," said Glowacka after the group had solved Winston's puzzle. "I get the idea. Now why don't we solve the real puzzle?"

At that moment, Marietta's walkie-talkie crackled. "Ray, you there?"

Marietta snatched the walkie-talkie off of his belt and took a few steps away from the group. "Go ahead, Stokes."

"What's your location? I'm ready to catch up to you." The staticky reception made Officer Stokes sound like he was on the moon.

"We're at the playground on Autumnside."

"Check. I'll be there in ten."

"You got news?" Marietta asked.

"I do, but you're not going to like it. I'll see you in a few." The crackling abruptly stopped. Marietta frowned.

Winston wondered what that was about. What news could the policeman have for Marietta? Why would it be bad news?

Then he remembered with a jolt: Stokes was going to somehow collect the fingerprints of North and Glowacka. He must have done exactly that and taken them back to the police station to analyze them. The idea was, one set of prints or the other would match the fingerprints taken from Mrs. Lewis's windows the night someone broke into her house.

So what could the bad news be? Only one thing that Winston could think of: Both prints were on the windows. Mal was right. North and Glowacka were working together. He glanced at them—the two men—and saw that they were standing together, staring back at him, frowning.

Had they also figured out what Stokes's bad news was bound to be? Were they going to try something?

North leaned forward slightly and said to Winston, "Are you ready?"

"What?"

Glowacka said, "Are we going to solve this puzzle or what? Snap out of it!"

Winston realized they were staring at him for a far simpler reason. He was holding Katie's new wooden pieces, and everyone was waiting for him. "Right," he said, trying to sound like everything was perfectly normal. "I'm ready. Sorry."

Everybody laid their pieces on the table.

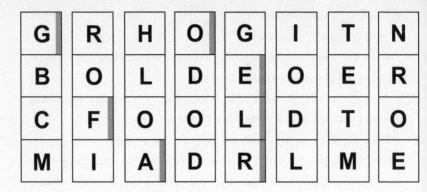

G	R	H	O	G	I	T	N
B	O	L	D	E	O	E	R
C	F	O	O	L	D	T	O
M	I	A	D	R	L	M	E

"Are you sure about this, kid?" asked Glowacka. "About this anaquote thing?"

Winston shook his head. "Nope. Not at all. It could be something totally different."

"And what about these stripes on some of the letters?" said North. "What do you suppose they're for?"

"I've been thinking about that," said Winston. "My guess is, they mark the end of words."

"Oh, that makes sense."

Mrs. Lewis said, "In any event, it's a good place to start, don't you think? Let's see if Winston is right."

"I'll bet he is," said Brenda, smiling broadly at Winston, who tried not to look overly pleased.

(Continue reading to see the answer.)

The group was about halfway to solving the puzzle when two cars pulled up at the same time. The first was a blue-and-white Glenville police car, out of which emerged Officer Stokes, looking grim. The second was a small hatchback with a Rosetti's Pizza sign clipped to the roof. A young man came out carrying three pizza boxes.

The two men walked over to the picnic tables simultaneously, regarding each other as they did so.

The pizza man spoke first. "Are you the guys looking for some kind of treasure?"

They all looked at him with surprise. "Yes . . . ?" said North.

"Oh, good," said the pizza man, relieved. "I was sure this was some kind of dumb joke. Anyway, these pizzas are for you. Mr. Rosetti sent me over with them. They're on the house."

Mrs. Lewis said, "Well, wasn't that nice of him!"

"Yeah," said the pizza guy. "You know, he lives right up the block here."

"We know," Glowacka said dryly.

The pizza guy put the boxes down and waved away the tip from Marietta. "Mr. Rosetti already tipped me and everything. It's totally on the house." He glanced around at the group as if a joke might yet be sprung on him. Deciding he would leave before that could happen, he gave a short wave and said, "Happy treasure hunting, I guess." He walked back to his car and drove away.

Mrs. Lewis said to Marietta, "I guess you did make a friend today."

Marietta said cheerfully, "I've got what it takes sometimes. I'm not always the heavy." They smiled good-naturedly at each other.

"Aha!" said North. He and Glowacka were still bent over the puzzle. "These two pieces are in the wrong order. Look!"

Everybody gathered around again and stared at the rearranged pieces:

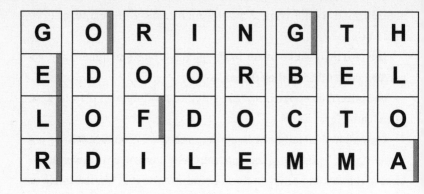

G	O	R	I	N	G	T	H
E	D	O	O	R	B	E	L
L	O	F	D	O	C	T	O
R	D	I	L	E	M	M	A

"You were right, Winston," said North. "Good boy! An anaquote! I'd have been here the rest of my life."

Brenda said, "I knew he was right," and tousled Winston's hair. Winston beamed.

Glowacka said, "Yeah, yeah, that's great and all. But what kind of message is this? Go ring the doorbell of Doctor Dilemma?" He looked around at the group. "Who the heck is Doctor Dilemma?"

That stopped everybody. Glowacka turned to Mrs. Lewis. "Well? If someone's going to know, it should be you, right? He's your dad."

Mrs. Lewis only shook her head, mystified. "I have no idea who that could be."

Katie said, "It sounds like a comic book bad guy."

"It does at that," said North. "Can that possibly be right?"

"How are you going to ring the doorbell of a comic book character?" Glowacka just about shouted.

Winston glanced over to Marietta, who had stepped away from the group with Officer Stokes. The two of them were having a low, intense conversation. Marietta looked like he had lost all the good humor he had discovered over the last hour or so. What was going on?

"If it's not a comic book character," said North, "then what is it? A store?"

Brenda said, "Maybe it's actually somebody's name. There are people with strange names out there."

North nodded. "I suppose that's possible. We need a phone book, then. We'll have to go back to the library."

Marietta came back to the group, followed by Stokes. "We're not going anywhere just yet," he said. He looked as deeply serious and humorless as on the first day Winston had met him. Winston thought, This man is about to arrest somebody.

North looked at him, mildly puzzled. "We're not? Why not?"

"We're going to have the very nice pizza that Mr. Rosetti sent over," said Marietta. "And while we're eating, Winston is going to tell us why he broke into Mrs. Lewis's house."

C
H
A
P
T E N
E
R

IT TOOK A MOMENT for Marietta's words to sink in, and
when they did, Winston felt everything below his neck suddenly freeze
into a solid block of ice. He gaped at the large ex-cop, who was staring
at him with a mix of disappointment and anger.

Brenda said, "Winston did what?"

Katie found her voice next. "He wouldn't do that!" she said shrilly.
She looked almost as furious as Marietta.

"I . . ." said Winston, although he didn't know where that sentence
might go. He had to deny it, of course. "I didn't do it. I really didn't."

North said, "What exactly are you accusing him of? I don't
understand."

Marietta, still gazing intently at Winston, said, "Someone broke
into Mrs. Lewis's sister's house shortly after she died. Soon after that,
someone broke into Mrs. Lewis's house. And between those events
were a number of veiled, creative threats, demanding that Mrs. Lewis
assist in this very treasure hunt."

"And you think it was this kid?" Glowacka seemed incredulous.

"Well, it's not you or Mr. North," said Marietta. "Your fingerprints didn't match."

Glowacka's eyes widened. "Our fingerprints?" he said. "Didn' match?"

North looked equally surprised. "Our fingerprints didn't match what?"

"Those coffee mugs you drank from this morning," said Marietta, without taking his eyes off Winston. "Perfect surface for collecting fingerprints. When Officer Stokes left, he took the mugs with him. He lifted off prints from each mug and compared them to prints we found on the outside of Mrs. Lewis's windowpane and door. They didn't match. They didn't come close to matching. So if it wasn't Mr. North, and it wasn't Mr. Glowacka, who was it?"

They all considered that. And they all turned and regarded Winston.

Mrs. Lewis said, "I can't believe Winston would really . . ." But she trailed off, as if figuring out how she might believe it after all. She looked at Marietta, and then over to Winston, her expression questioning, looking for answers.

Winston still couldn't believe this was happening. He wished he could simply melt into the earth and vanish forever. But no, he was stuck here. "I didn't do that!" he said, a bit desperately. "I didn't break into anybody's house! I wouldn't have the slightest idea how to even go about it!"

"You're a smart kid," said Marietta. "You'd figure it out."

"But why would he?" said North. "I don't understand."

"Isn't it obvious? He loves puzzles. He wanted to go on this treasure hunt. Maybe he read about Walter Fredericks's hidden ring and he wanted to find it. But he couldn't without Mrs. Lewis's cooperation. So he called her up, disguised his voice, even broke into her house. Then he actually took the puzzle pieces he had to the library when she's working there, to really shake her up. That was a bold move, Winston."

Winston suddenly realized he was getting angry. "I didn't do anything like that!" he said, trying not to sound defensive and shrill, but his voice was shaking. "I mean, we just found our puzzle pieces last weekend. Mrs. Lewis was getting those calls even before that. Right?"

Mrs. Lewis said softly, "Um, Ray, he's right. Those calls started coming after Livia died. I don't think Winston had his puzzle pieces yet."

Marietta crossed his arms. "When do you say you found them?"

"Sunday," said Winston. "At my sister's birthday party. My entire family was there."

"And Violet's house was broken into Sunday night."

"But she got those phone calls *before* Sunday!"

Marietta mulled it over. He glanced over at Officer Stokes, who shrugged. "What I keep coming back to," Marietta said, "is that the only people who stand to benefit from finding that ring are all right here. Those are the only people with any reason to break into Violet's house and leave threatening notes. Glowacka's fingerprints didn't match. North's fingerprints didn't match. What would you like me to think?"

"You didn't take *my* fingerprints, did you?" Winston asked.

Marietta looked somewhere between embarrassed and irritated. "No," he said. "You were not originally one of my suspects."

Glowacka said, "You didn't take his fingerprints? Then what are you talking about? You don't got anything on this kid but your own crazy ideas."

"Like I said," Marietta said with a calmness that no one believed, "it's someone involved in this treasure hunt. Someone who's going to get a piece of it. If it's not you and it's not North, then who is it? The girl here?" He pointed at Katie, who, Winston saw, was fighting back hot tears.

Marietta didn't notice. "No," he said. "Maybe someone else made the phone calls, maybe there's something else going on. But as far as I'm concerned, when it comes to who broke into your house, Violet, there's only one logical suspect left."

Winston was shaking—literally shaking. He wondered how noticeable it was, but he couldn't stop. He didn't want to be afraid, but he was. As coldly as he could manage, he said, "Why don't you take my fingerprints, then?"

Marietta said, "I will. But you're a minor. I have to talk to your parents first."

"I can call my mother right now."

Marietta looked a bit surprised and uncomfortable at this. But he stuck to his guns. "All right. You go right ahead. Lou, can you do this now?"

"I've got the stuff in my car," said Stokes.

Marietta nodded. "Go get it."

Stokes broke away from the group and walked back to his car. Winston asked to borrow Brenda's phone again, and she handed it to him solemnly. As he dialed, he looked at his sister. Tears were streaming down her face.

"It's all right," he said, knowing it was a ridiculous thing to say. There was nothing all right about this and his sister knew it, but he had to say something.

Katie whispered to him, "But what if they match?"

Winston winced. What an idea. "Katie. They're not going to match. They'll take my fingerprints and look at them and that will be the end of it. It's going to be okay." He finished dialing the phone.

"I lost you before," his mother said when she heard Winston's voice.

"Uh, I hung up accidentally. Sorry about that."

"Are you having more fun now than you were before?"

Winston made a sound halfway between laughter and choking. "Not really. But for a different reason. I have to tell you something."

"What?"

He spelled it out, and actually, she took it pretty well. There was the initial "WHAT?!", but then she listened to Winston as he told her what was going to happen.

"Do you need me to come over there?"

"No, Mom. I don't think so. I just want them to take my fingerprints so they can see I didn't do this."

She thought it over for a moment. "Okay. Let me talk to this policeman."

Winston waved the phone at Marietta. "My mom wants to talk to you."

Marietta didn't look thrilled to hear this. He took the phone from Winston, took a deep breath, and said, "This is Ray Marietta." Then he said, "Yes" and "No" and "I understand that" for a minute or so in a conciliatory tone, and finally said, "Well, this way, we'll all know for sure, and he does seem to want to get this cleared up. Okay, Mrs. Breen. You can be sure we'll call you when we get the results. Thank you." He hung up the phone and handed it back to Brenda. And he said to Officer Stokes, "Do it."

Stokes nodded. He said to Winston, "Sit over here," gesturing at one of the picnic tables. Winston went over and sat. As he did so, he glanced down the block and saw something that, amazingly, made him sigh with gratitude: Mal and Jake, bicycling like mad toward them.

Stokes had an ink pad and a stiff card marked into ten sections, one for each finger. He took Winston's hand and gently guided his fingers, one by one, first mashing them lightly into the ink and then rolling each one back and forth in a space on the card. Mal and Jake pulled up partway through this process.

"What on earth?" said Mal when he saw what was happening.

Marietta noticed them. "What are you kids doing here? I told you to stay out of this, didn't I?"

Jake said, "Why is he being fingerprinted?"

"He'll tell you all about it later. Now get out of here."

Katie said, "They think he broke into Mrs. Lewis's house."

Jake and Mal looked at Marietta with bald amazement. Mal said bluntly, "You think that? You're five hundred pounds of crazy."

Winston had to suppress a grin. He covered it with a cough, then covered the cough with his hand and got ink on his face. That seemed pretty funny, too. Once, a few years back, he had burned himself badly on the kitchen stove, and he recalled giggling helplessly in the emergency room. He was in terrible pain, but he couldn't stop laughing. His father told him he was in shock. He wondered if he was in shock now, too.

Marietta wasn't laughing. He had turned a bright pink. "I'm going to ask you one more time to leave, and then Officer Stokes is going to escort you boys home in the back of that police car. Believe me when I tell you this. There's nothing for you here."

Jake said loudly, "It's not Winston, it's one of these two guys." He pointed at North and Glowacka.

Neither of them looked particularly concerned at this accusation. Glowacka shrugged. "Hey, don't look at me, kid. My fingerprints didn't match."

"Then why did Mr. North call you a thief?" Jake wanted to know.

North and Glowacka glanced at each other, suddenly a bit more concerned than they were a moment ago. Glowacka's long face seemed to get longer, and North paled a bit. Marietta, almost despite himself, looked increasingly interested in what Jake was saying. He turned curiously to look at the two men, who were standing together as if for protection.

Jake said, "Winston told us all about it. After you guys met Mr. Marietta for the first time, you got into an argument, and Mr. North called you a thief."

Marietta said, "Is that true?"

North said, looking around, "Well, well, maybe I spoke out of turn a bit—"

"So it is true. You think he's a thief?"

Mal spoke up. "It probably has something to do with what happened at the treasure hunters' convention they were both at."

That one *really* surprised North and Glowacka. They now wore identical expressions of pained astonishment. "How do you know about that?" North asked.

Mal shrugged. "I know lotsa stuff."

"What are these kids talking about, North?" Marietta said impatiently.

North and Glowacka exchanged an anxious look. North finally said, "I met Mickey a few years ago. At a treasure hunters' convention, like this boy said. Considering that we were both looking for the same man's treasure, it's no surprise that we found each other pretty quickly."

"And Glowacka stole something from you?" Marietta said.

"No!" said Glowacka. "I only—"

North said, "It's all right, Mickey. Let's tell them the whole thing." He looked around at the group. "Shortly after we met, I tried to . . . *fool* Mr. Glowacka into giving me his puzzle pieces. I told him that I knew for a fact that there was no treasure and that I was only at the convention as a historian of sorts. I offered to buy his pieces from him for a couple hundred dollars."

Glowacka said, "And that was much, much, *much* less than I paid for them. Bruno Fredericks told me outright that the treasure was at least a million dollars. I know he was your brother, Mrs. Lewis, but he was a bad character. He'd talk a bird into giving up its feathers, just for the fun of it. And that wasn't the only whopper he told me. I don't even want to get into it. So then I run into this guy," he said, pointing a thumb at North, "who tells me the pieces are worthless. Do I believe that? No. I decide this guy is just another con man out to make a fool of old Mickey Glowacka." He paused and looked around at the group. "So later in the weekend, I tried breaking into his hotel room. I was going to steal his puzzle pieces."

Marietta said, "Aha!"

Glowacka shook his head. "Aha nothing. I had no idea what I was doing. You know how people in TV shows can open any door with a credit card? You know what? In real life, it ain't so easy. I stood there jamming a credit card into the door, sweating like a bull, trying to get that door to open."

"And that's where he was when I found him," said North.

"So you can see how we didn't become instant friends on the spot," said Glowacka. "We had a big, loud argument and nearly started fighting like schoolkids."

"I've never been in a fight," said Mal.

"Me neither," said Jake.

Glowacka gave them a sour look. "It's a figure of speech! So that's why North called me a thief, and that's why I called him a con man. But it doesn't mean either one of us broke into Mrs. Lewis's house."

Marietta nodded, as if satisfied. He turned to Jake and Mal. "All right? And besides that, like I said, neither of them had fingerprints at the crime scene."

Jake said, "So one of them has a partner. Someone who did the actual break-in so they wouldn't have to."

"They don't."

"How do you know?"

Marietta gazed at North and Glowacka again. "Because I had my friend Officer Stokes keep an eye on them for the past few days. Neither of them has a partner."

Glowacka's looked aghast, while North said in a faint, horrified voice, "You had us followed?"

"I did. And since it helped to put the two of you in the clear, I guess I won't hear any complaining about it." Marietta turned back to Jake. "I don't know the full story yet, but I think your friend has something to do with this. If that turns out not to be true, I'll apologize. You got what you need, Lou?"

Stokes, still sitting with Winston, said, "Just finishing up."

"Good," said Marietta. "And you two," he said to Jake and Mal, both of whom looked angry and helpless. "Now that you've heard what you need, I don't want to see you anymore. Get on your bicycles and go. Go *now*."

Jake and Mal, giving one last glance at Winston, got on their bicycles.

Glowacka, sitting on one of the tables, said generally, "Unless one of them knows who Doctor Dilemma is."

Marietta stared at Glowacka. "They don't."

Glowacka shrugged. "They seem to know everything else."

Mal, still on his bicycle, said brightly, "I *do* know who Doctor Dilemma is."

Marietta looked as if he was ready to throw Mal like a human javelin. "You don't even know what we're talking about. Lou—take these kids home. Put their bicycles in the trunk." Officer Stokes had finished fingerprinting Winston. He advanced on Jake and Mal.

Mal, seeing him coming, said in a loud voice, "I know who Doctor Dilemma is! Why do you want to know?"

North stepped forward and said with some interest, "You don't really know who he is, do you? How could you?"

"I'm doing a history report on Walter Fredericks," said Mal. He got off his bicycle and unslung his backpack. He set it on the ground, kneeled, and began to unzip it. "I saw the phrase in an interview with him. It was his nickname for somebody. Wait a second." He pulled out a messy sheaf of papers and began flipping through them.

Marietta muttered, "This is ridiculous." He waved for Stokes to wait.

Jake took the opportunity to come quietly over to Winston. "You all right?" he said.

Winston shook his head. "I was pretty upset a few minutes ago. That guy really thinks I did it."

Jake spread his arms as if to say, That's that. "Hey, it's nothing. They check the prints, they don't match, and he looks like an idiot."

Winston nodded. "I hope so."

Mal was still trying to find what he was looking for. His notes were hopelessly disorganized. A breeze took one of his papers and sent it scuttling across the grass. Stokes, acting reflexively, stomped on it, leaving a big dirty footprint.

"Aha!" said Mal. "Here it is." He held out a paper to Marietta, who snatched it with a look of pure skepticism. North came over and looked over the ex-cop's shoulder. They scanned the paper, and then, simultaneously, North's face melted into an expression of delight while Marietta looked mad enough to bash all that playground equipment into rivets.

"He's right!" said North, taking the paper away from Marietta. "It's right here. 'Fredericks gave playful nicknames to many of his closest assistants. Dr. Grady Dilmer was known as Doctor Dilemma.'" North beamed down at Mal like a proud father.

"Grady Dilmer!" said Mrs. Lewis. "I remember him."

"Toldja," said Mal.

Marietta said in a calm voice, "Fine. Thank you. That was good work. But you still can't stick around here, and that's final. So get on your bicycles and—"

"Whoa, whoa, whoa!" said Glowacka, hopping down from his perch on the picnic table. "What's the problem? If this kid's got a backpack full of information on Walter Fredericks, I want him to stick around!"

North said, "I have to agree with Mickey, Mr. Marietta. Who knows what other obscure fact we might need before this is all over? The boy has already proven himself more than useful."

Marietta glanced at Mal. It was obvious that Mal's presence was grating the ex-cop to no end. But he also knew that North and Glowacka were right. "Fine," he said, with visible effort. He pointed at Mal. "But keep your smart mouth shut unless you've got something useful to say."

Winston waited for one last jibe—Mal could sometimes go too far, and then one step beyond that. But Mal, looking pleased with himself, simply nodded. Winston breathed a sigh of relief.

Marietta gestured to Officer Stokes. "I guess you can go run those prints. Stay in touch by walkie-talkie. I want to know as soon as you've got anything."

"Of course," said Stokes, and he got into his police car.

There was silence as they watched the policeman drive off. Winston looked at his fingers, which were still smudged with ink. Officer Stokes had given him some baby wipes, but they had merely smeared the ink around.

North said, "So now what?"

"Now," Marietta announced grimly, "I am having a slice of pizza."

They all did. Winston, despite having been accused of a crime and fingerprinted, found that he was absolutely starving. He took a slice and went to sit at one of the empty tables. The little kids and their parents had abandoned it a while back.

Jake and Mal joined him with slices of their own just as Winston said, "Oh, yuck."

"What's wrong?"

"This ink on my fingers is rubbing off on the pizza. It tastes like a bicycle tire."

Mal said with some delight, "Man, wait until I tell everyone at school you were fingerprinted!"

"Don't you dare," said Winston.

"Why? It's not like anyone will believe me."

"Seriously," said Jake. "On the list of kids at school I thought would be fingerprinted one day, you were, like, at the very bottom. Boy, did you prove us wrong!"

Katie came over with a slice of pizza and sat down next to her brother. She didn't look angry or sad anymore—just very, very tired.

"You okay, Katie?" Winston asked.

"I guess. What if your fingerprints match those other fingerprints?" She looked anxious at the possibility. "Will you go to jail?"

"Katie, I don't even know where Mrs. Lewis lives. I was never at her house. It'll be okay."

Katie seemed to accept this and nibbled broodingly at her pizza.

Winston said to Jake, "How'd you find us, anyway? The guy at Rosetti's tell you?"

Jake nodded. "Went in and asked where all those treasure hunters had gone. He told us to come here."

"Good, I'm glad. And that was amazing with that Doctor Dilemma thing, Mal!"

Mal, though seated, somehow performed the elaborate bow of a bad actor. "It was nothing for a genius like myself," he intoned gravely.

"Just don't wise off to Marietta anymore," Winston said in a low voice.

"Please?" He made his eyes big and wide, like a begging puppy dog.

"No."

"Okay." He resumed his normal expression just as quickly and tucked into his pizza.

The adults were at the other two tables—Marietta and Mrs. Lewis sitting side by side at one, and North, Glowacka, and Brenda at the other. Brenda was facing the kids, and she sometimes glanced over as if curious about something. Winston was still hungry after finishing his slice and was thankful that the pizza boxes were not on Marietta's table.

North was saying as Winston approached, "We'll have to head back to the library to find out where this Dilmer fellow lives."

"Heck, let me call my editor," said Brenda. "He can look it up in the phone book."

"Good, good, that'll save us some time."

Glowacka was looking at Winston. "Hey, kid, how you doing?"

"Fine, I guess."

Glowacka lowered his voice and leaned over. "Just between you and me, I don't see you even breaking into your sister's piggy bank."

"Thanks."

"Of course," said North to Glowacka, "that would mean one of us did it."

Glowacka raised his eyebrows. "Well, I didn't do it. Are you volunteering?"

North dabbed his lips with a paper napkin. "No."

"So that's that—it wasn't any of us. Maybe whoever broke into her house didn't know anything about any treasure. It was just a co-incidence. People break into houses. They shouldn't, but they do." Glowacka shrugged, as if none of it was worth worrying about.

There was a whole pizza left untouched, covered in sausages and mushrooms. As Winston considered which slice to take, Brenda said to him slyly, "So, Winston, is there a puzzle in that pizza there?"

North glanced at the pizza. "A puzzle? In the pizza? You think Rosetti left us some kind of clue?"

"No, no," she said. "I was interviewing Winston before, and he told me he often found puzzles in unusual places. I thought maybe he saw a puzzle in the pizza."

Although Winston hadn't been thinking about it, now he reflexively examined the pizza for its puzzle potential. He didn't expect to find much—this was the most puzzle-filled day he'd had in a long time, maybe ever, and his brain felt old and tired. But he hadn't been lying when he told Brenda that he saw puzzles in strange places—by now, his brain was trained to see them almost without effort. And within a minute, he indeed had a glimmer of an idea for one. After another minute, he laughed to himself. "Yeah," he said to Brenda. "There's a puzzle there."

Brenda squinted at him. "You're kidding. What is it?"

Winston said, "Suppose there are four people who want to split this pie. Can you give each of them two slices so that they also receive the same number of sausages and the same number of mushrooms?"

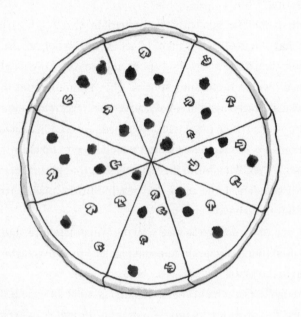

(Answer, page 214.)

They finished eating, and everyone helped clean up. "Rosetti could have sent some soda, too, while he was at it," said Glowacka.

"Oh, hush, Mickey," said North, gathering up a wad of grease-stained paper napkins.

Brenda called her editor on her cell phone and paced back and forth as he looked up the address of Grady Dilmer. After some time, she snapped her phone shut and turned to the group. "We might have a little problem," she said.

"Uh-oh," said Glowacka. "Now what?"

"There's only one Dilmer in town, but it's not Grady Dilmer. According to the phone book, it's a first initial Z."

North said, "Maybe he's not listed."

"I don't suppose," Glowacka said to Mrs. Lewis, "that you simply know where he lives?"

She shook her head. "I'm afraid not. But we can go back to the library and do some research online."

"That's exactly what my editor is doing right now," said Brenda. "He suggests we go to this Z. Dilmer's house to see if it's the right place, and if he finds out anything more, he'll call me."

"Where?" asked Marietta.

She looked at her notepad. "Hill Street. West of here—118 Hill Street."

"All right. Is that what we want to do?" Marietta looked around at the group.

North shrugged. "It's as good a plan as any, I'd say."

"Okay. Then it's the same deal as last time. North and Glowacka with me," Marietta said. "Brenda, you take these two," meaning Winston and Katie. "Violet, why don't you come with me this time?"

"All right," said Mrs. Lewis, getting up.

Jake and Mal tentatively raised their hands, like shy students in the back of the classroom. Jake said, "What about us?"

Marietta glanced at them. "Oh, right. What about your bicycles?"

Jake said, "We'll chain them up to a tree."

"Fine. You have room in your car, Brenda?"

"If you're taking Mrs. Lewis, I can take one of them."

"Good. You take *him*," Marietta said, pointing at Mal. "You, come with me," he said to Jake. He turned around and walked toward his giant car. Soon, they were off to Hill Street and whatever awaited them there.

A few slices of pizza had given Winston a new burst of energy. He wanted to enjoy the rest of this treasure hunt, and he was glad that Jake and Mal had found a way to join in. But just as he couldn't fully focus on anything else in the days leading up to the hunt, now the treasure hunt itself was getting interrupted by the idea that somewhere in town, a policeman was analyzing his fingerprints.

He thought of Katie's question: Was there any possibility in the world that the fingerprints could match those lifted from Mrs. Lewis's house?

He tried to picture it: Officer Stokes pulling up, getting out of his car with handcuffs already in his hands. "It was a match, Winston. It was a perfect match." The application of the handcuffs—*click!* The metal would be cold, and the manacles would be cinched tight, his arms at a crazy angle behind his back. Marietta would take Katie (who would be crying uncontrollably) home, and while he was there, he would inform Winston's mother of what was happening.

It was impossible, but it was also all too easy to imagine, and it gave him the shivers.

At just that moment, Mal twisted around in the front seat and said, "I thought of a way that your fingerprints might match."

That got quite a reaction from everybody else in the car. Katie's jaw dropped, Brenda took her eyes off the road to gape at Mal, and Winston himself went completely wide-eyed. "What are you talking about?" he asked, appalled.

"Listen. What if Marietta is the thief?" Mal said this in a low voice, as if the car might be bugged and someone listening in.

Relief swept through Winston. That was a ridiculous idea. Mal was either joking—which was always a possibility—or was just wildly off base—which was *also* always a possibility. "He used to be a policeman!" he said. "You think now he's a thief?"

Mal shrugged. "I don't know. Why not?"

Katie said, "He's Mrs. Lewis's friend, you dope."

"He could be pretending. Or maybe he *was* her friend, but now he wants the ring for himself. Maybe he needs money or something. So he rigs it so that somebody else gets blamed for breaking into Mrs. Lewis's house, when he did it all along."

Winston leaned back and shut his eyes. He didn't need this. For one flash of a second he wished Marietta had been successful at getting Jake and Mal to just go home.

Brenda said, "But Mr. Marietta's not analyzing the fingerprints. Officer Stokes is doing that."

Mal shrugged again. "His accomplice," he said simply. Katie made a sound of disgust.

Winston said tiredly, "I guess we'll just have to see what he says."

Mal nodded. "But there's one other thing."

Of course there was. "What's that?" Winston asked.

"Let's say he comes back and he says your fingerprints didn't match. Right?"

Winston said, "Okay."

"So that means you didn't do it, and North didn't do it, and Glowacka didn't do it. So who did?"

The question hovered there. Winston didn't have an answer. Maybe the whole thing was a coincidence, like his father—and later on, Glowacka—had suggested. A random burglary. Nothing to do with any hidden ring.

But, no—what about the phone calls and the threats to Mrs. Lewis?

The note on her kitchen table? "Where is the treasure?" it said. That wasn't a coincidence. That was someone playing a very nasty game. But that immediately circled back around to the first question: If the thief was someone who knew about the treasure, who was it? It had to be either North or Glowacka, didn't it? They were both mad to find the treasure. They attended a treasure hunters' convention, for crying out loud. But then why didn't either of their fingerprints match? How could a person break into somebody's home and leave someone else's fingerprints?

It was maddening. Around and around, Winston's brain whirled, getting nowhere. There had to be something he was missing, something he was mentally dancing around without seeing.

"This is it," said Brenda, pulling over. Winston looked around, blinking. He was hardly aware they'd been moving.

This wasn't such a great area of town. And 118 Hill Street wasn't a house but, rather, a series of small apartments, connected by a large parking lot. Brenda pulled into a space, and Marietta pulled into the one next to her.

"Which one of these things is he in?" asked Glowacka as he got out of the car.

"I don't know," said Brenda. "I guess the apartment number wasn't listed in the phone book."

They looked around and considered their options.

"Why didn't we call first? That would have been bright," said Glowacka.

"I'm sorry," said Brenda. "I didn't think of that. I didn't even get the phone number."

"We can just start knocking on doors," said Mal.

"I don't think we should start bothering people at random," said North. "Not yet, anyway. Is there a directory somewhere?"

Winston pointed. "How about the mailboxes there?" he said.

A wall of mailboxes stood by itself off to the side in the parking lot, each one sealed with a little metal door. The group shuffled over and looked at the names on each door, written on strips of masking tape.

"Yep, there we go," said Glowacka. "Apartment 15. Dilmer."

"I think that's this way," said Brenda.

They all started walking over. "Remember, this might not even be the right guy," said Marietta.

"And then we're totally stuck," said Mal.

"We'll figure out something," said North. "I'm sure of it."

They approached the door of Apartment 15, and North rang the doorbell—a faint *bing* could be heard inside. The whole group stood there uncomfortably, waiting for whatever was going to happen next.

The door opened, and a man peered out at them, baffled by the crowd at his door. The man was probably in his mid-thirties. He had a tan scruff of beard and held a sandwich in one hand. The expression on his face told Winston he was expecting to see a single person outside his door—a salesman, or someone collecting for charity. He wasn't expecting to see . . . well, what was this? A bunch of disorganized and out-of-season Christmas carolers?

"Um, yes?" the man said.

North said with some disappointment, "I don't suppose you're Grady Dilmer."

The man looked around at the group once more, clearly wondering just what was going on here. "Grady Dilmer was my dad," he said. "But he's not here. He died over five years ago."

CHAPTER ELEVEN

GLOWACKA SAID, "Grady Dilmer is dead?"

"A while back, like I said," said the man. "I'm his son, Zach. What's this all about?"

There was a moment of confusion while everyone in the group looked to everybody else to take charge. Finally, Mrs. Lewis stepped forward and said, "Hello, Mr. Dilmer. A long time ago, your father worked closely with my father, Walter Fredericks."

Zach Dilmer looked interested. "You're Walter Fredericks's daughter?"

She nodded. "I am."

"Huh," Dilmer said. He offered a puzzled smile, still waiting for all this to make sense. "Nice to meet you."

"And you, too," said Mrs. Lewis, with a polite smile. She cleared her throat and got to business. "Mr. Dilmer, a very long time ago, my father may have given something to your father, with instructions that he should hold on to it until I came to claim it."

Winston had expected Dilmer to offer a blank stare, but instead his jaw dropped open. Dilmer had gone instantly from a state of mild curiosity to one of total astonishment. "Holy crow," he said. "This is about the envelopes! Isn't it? You're going to ask me for the envelopes! Right?"

Everyone was surprised by this abrupt shortcut straight to the heart of the matter. Mrs. Lewis stared at Dilmer for several seconds before responding, "Why, yes."

North said, "You know about the envelopes?"

"Yeah, yeah, sure I do. Hang on a second," he said, and he turned and ran like a little boy into his apartment, leaving his front door open, giving a view of a messy living room stuffed with furniture.

With Dilmer gone, the group exchanged startled glances.

"I guess he has the envelopes," said Glowacka. "That's the good news."

Marietta said, "What's the bad news?"

Glowacka said darkly, "It's going to be another puzzle. I was hoping he'd just have the ring and we'd be done."

Dilmer was gone for several minutes. At one point, a distant crash was heard within the house. Mal said to Winston and Jake, "Maybe we should go in there and help him look."

But just then Dilmer came running back to the front door. In his hand were a number of plain white envelopes. Working to catch his breath, he said, "I found them. Amazing I remembered where they were after all this time. So you're here to claim these, huh?"

"If that's okay," Mrs. Lewis said.

"Sure, sure. Of course," Dilmer said. "I mean, they're yours. But what are they? Can I ask?"

"Oh, it's a long story," said Mrs. Lewis. "Basically, it's a part of my father's inheritance. He hid it somewhere, and these envelopes hold a clue to its location."

"Wow." Dilmer seemed deeply impressed. "That's pretty excellent. I'm glad I hung on to them."

"We are, too," North replied. "What did you think the envelopes were?"

Dilmer shook his head. "I had no idea! But a few years before my father died, we were going through all his papers, throwing out a lot of junk. We came across these sealed envelopes, and I started to open them, but he stopped me and told me that I should just keep them safe. That he was keeping them for an old friend. I guess that was your father," he said to Mrs. Lewis, who smiled emotionally and nodded. "Anyway, he said someone might come around one day and ask for them. I hung on to them, and I guess I wondered about them for a while, but then I forgot all about it. I didn't think anyone would ever claim them, though."

"Neither did I," said Mrs. Lewis.

"Well, here. I guess these belong to you." He extended the hand with the envelopes, which were fanned out like a deck of cards. Winston saw that there were three of them.

He said, "Just three this time."

Dilmer frowned. "Yeah. Is that okay?"

Winston shrugged. "I guess so. There've been two other sets of envelopes before now, and each set had four envelopes."

Dilmer said, "I'm sorry. This is all I've got. Just the three." He extended them again to Mrs. Lewis, who took them.

"I'm sure it's fine," she said. "Thank you for keeping them safe all this time."

"Can I ask . . ." said Dilmer, looking like he didn't want to say the wrong thing. "Can you open them here? I'd love to know what's actually inside these things."

"Well, sure," said Mrs. Lewis. "It's going to be a puzzle of some kind. That much I can tell you right now."

"A puzzle," Dilmer repeated, fascinated. "So you're going to solve it?"

"That's the idea," said Glowacka.

"Well, why don't you solve it here?" Dilmer said, gesturing into his apartment. "Please. I'd love to see how this all turns out."

Again, the treasure hunters exchanged questioning glances. North said, "I don't see why not. We'll have to work on this somewhere."

"Beats standing out in the parking lot," said Glowacka.

Marietta said, as if to make it official, "Yeah, that's fine."

Awkwardly, the whole large group filed into Dilmer's home. The living room was just barely large enough to accommodate them all, and it reminded Winston of the one time he had visited his cousin Henry's dormitory at college. The place was a mess, with an assortment of glasses and bottles on a low coffee table, a small tower of pizza boxes, and various books, papers, and magazines scattered about.

Dilmer was clearly embarrassed by the mess and hastily tried straightening up, but it was impossible. "Just throw things off the chairs," he said. "Sit anywhere you like." He swept a stack of *TV Guide*s from an armchair and gestured to Marietta, who sat with some discomfort.

When everyone was as settled as they were going to get, Mrs. Lewis, who was still holding the three envelopes, said, "I suppose we should see what we have here." She handed one envelope to North and one to Katie. Glowacka, the odd man out, set his jaw to show that he was the slightest bit insulted but wasn't going to make a big deal about it.

There was the sound of ripping paper. Winston again looked over his sister's shoulder as she shook out the inevitable wooden strip. This time it had been etched with a long string of numbers:

$$\boxed{385198918512114 5}$$

"Hoo boy," Winston said.

North looked up from his own piece. "Do you have numbers?" he asked.

Winston said, "Yeah. Do you?"

North leaned forward from his spot on the raggedy brown sofa and laid his strip on the coffee table, which Dilmer had busily cleared off. North's strip read:

$$2351920121144192018520$$

"How about you, Mrs. Lewis?" asked North.

Mrs. Lewis was sitting in an old but fancy-looking chair. She looked like she was going to host a tea party. She handed her wooden strip to Jake, who was sitting on the floor in front of her. "Mine's a little bit different," she said. Jake glanced at it, raised his eyebrows, and put it on the table.

$$18\text{-}25\text{-}11$$

There was a stunned silence. Numbers? What were they supposed to do with a bunch of numbers? Winston didn't have the slightest idea where to start, and looking around the room, it was clear no one else did either.

"This is supposed to be a puzzle?" asked Dilmer with some disbelief.

"Apparently so," said Glowacka.

"Well, how do you solve it?"

Glowacka rubbed his eyes. "If you've got a suggestion," he said, "I'm sure we'd all love to hear it."

Jake said, "What do the numbers add up to?"

Mal said immediately, "926."

Glowacka frowned at Mal. "You added them up that fast?"

Mal said, "No. I'm just kidding."

Glowacka glared.

North said, "Let's see. This first string of numbers is 11, 16 . . ." He trailed off, mumbling numbers to himself. "This first piece adds up to 71."

Winston said, "The second one adds up to 68."

"This doesn't sound helpful at all," said Glowacka.

Brenda, who by now considered herself a full-fledged member of the team, said, "What's going on with this third strip? Is that supposed to be a math equation: 18 minus 25 minus 11? That's a negative number."

North agreed. "Negative 18," he said.

"It looks like a locker combination," said Mal.

"It does at that," said North, showing a faint spark of excitement. "Perhaps we're in the home stretch. The ring might be hidden in a locker somewhere!"

Jake looked at Winston and said, "At school? It would make sense to hide it at the Walter Fredericks Junior High School!"

"But it wasn't named for my father until after he died," Mrs. Lewis said. "While he was living, it was just the Sobol Lane School."

"Oh," said Jake, deflated.

Glowacka said with some urgency, "But a locker somewhere, that makes sense. And the other two strips are the clues to finding that locker."

Marietta chimed in from his deep armrest. "Or a safe. A lot of safes have the same kind of dial, with a three-number combination."

They all chewed on that for a moment. Glowacka said to Mrs. Lewis, "Did your father have a safe? In his house?"

"Yes."

"Maybe we should go there and look in it."

Mrs. Lewis shook her head. "I knew the combination to my father's safe. All of his children did. He wouldn't need to tell us the combination."

Katie was seated on the floor, right by the table. Now she said something that sounded like "ar-why-kay."

Winston said, "What?"

"*R* . . . *Y* . . . *K*," she said. "*R* is the eighteenth letter of the alphabet, and *Y* is the twenty-fifth letter, and *K* is the eleventh letter."

"All right," Winston said slowly. "But that doesn't really spell anything. How does that help us?"

"I don't know. I just want to help solve something!" Katie said, her voice shaking a little. It had been a long day for all of them, but a particularly long day for a ten-year-old. She looked tired and emotionally at the end of her rope.

Winston didn't see that RYK led anywhere, but didn't know how to say that in a way that wouldn't frustrate Katie even further. "Well," he said, "let's keep that in mind in case it's important." It didn't work—Katie frowned angrily, feeling dismissed.

North had picked up the strip with the longest string of numbers and was feeling it as if trying to absorb the answer right out of the wood. "What could these numbers mean?" he asked again.

"There's a lot of numbers in the world," said their host, Dilmer. "Phone numbers, license plate numbers, bank numbers—"

"A bank account," said Glowacka. "Those are always long numbers. The ring could be in a safe-deposit box somewhere."

"Pretty ironic," said Marietta, "since that's where you want to put the ring if we find it."

Mrs. Lewis said, "If it is a bank account number, is there a way of figuring out the bank?"

That question earned nothing but silence. Meanwhile, Dilmer's inventory of the numbers of the world went on. "Social security numbers, credit card numbers, computer passwords . . ."

"The ring was hidden twenty-five years ago, Mr. Dilmer," said North, sounding irritated. "I don't think it will be a computer password."

Winston was starting to think that solving in Dilmer's apartment was a bad idea. The living room was too small—there was no place to move around. He often liked to pace when he was thinking, but sitting here trapped between Glowacka's knobby legs and the coffee table was like being in a straitjacket. Plus, Winston would occasionally glance at Marietta and see the former policeman looking right back at him. Marietta seemed to be itching to get the message that the fingerprints matched so he could place Winston under arrest.

All in all, not the ideal conditions for solving a difficult puzzle.

Winston tried to focus. Numbers, numbers. What could they mean?

Dilmer said, "Can I get people drinks? I've got some soda, water, juice. . . ."

Several people wanted something, so Dilmer got up to play waiter. Brenda went to help him—the two of them went down the narrow hall to the kitchen. Glowacka said in a low voice, "How's he going to get us drinks? All his glasses are in here."

"Maybe he has a lot of them," said Mal.

They batted around more theories. Jake noticed that the 18 on the smallest strip was also smack in the middle of one of the other strings of numbers. They all tried to figure out if that meant anything and got nowhere. They mentally divided up the numbered strings into pairs, into triplets, into groups of four. None of it amounted to anything. Winston saw that Katie was counting on her fingers with a very serious expression on her face. She must have had a theory that she wasn't willing to share, lest she be wrong.

The drinks were served—it seemed that Dilmer did indeed have a large supply of glasses, because he and Brenda carried out two trayfuls of them, to join the many mismatched empties already scattered around the living room.

"Any luck?" Brenda asked when she returned. The gloomy silence was more than enough answer.

They had their drinks. They thought about numbers. For a long time, no one said anything at all.

"I still want them to be letters," said Katie, softly.

"Sure," said Mal. "What's the three-billionth letter of the alphabet?"

"Well, what if . . . ?" she said, and then faded out. Winston looked over at her and was surprised by what he saw. Her mouth hung slightly open and her eyes were shiny, staring at an invisible point on the wall. This was someone in the middle of having a Big Idea. Winston thought if you x-rayed her head at just that moment, you would see a number of gears spinning very fast.

And then everybody flinched when Katie shrieked—a sudden, fantastic car-alarm noise—and jumped to her feet, spilling her soda on the table and the floor. Glowacka hurriedly snatched the pieces off the table before they got soaked. "Watch it!" he cried.

But Katie was practically in another dimension. "What if you put in the spaces first? What if the numbers are letters, but you have to put in the spaces?"

There was a moment of stunned silence. Winston knew right away that Katie had to be right. Her idea just *felt* right.

Glowacka said hoarsely, "Can it really be that easy?" He looked at the strips he was holding.

North barked at him. "Put them back on the table, man! Let's all see them."

Glowacka did so.

$$3851989185121145$$

$$2351920121144192018552 0$$

$$18\text{-}25\text{-}11$$

"See?" said Katie. "The 3 is *C*. The 8 is *H*. The 5 is *E*. . . ."

"Wait a second, wait a second," said North. "*C-H-E-A-I?* That can't spell anything."

Winston shook his head. It seemed so obvious now that the solution had been presented to him. "No, she's right," he said, nearly out of breath from excitement. "It's 3, 8, 5, but then 19, for the letter *S*. Once you put the spaces in correctly, you can turn all the numbers to letters, and it will spell out a message. Katie, you're right!" He couldn't remember the last time he had hugged his sister, but he did so now, almost before he was aware of it. And under any other circumstance, she might have said "Oh, yuck!" and shoved him away. But now she simply beamed with pride.

(Continue reading to see the answer.)

"I wish I could go with you," said Dilmer, "and see how this all turns out. I gotta get to work soon."

Brenda said, "You can read all about it in the *Glenville News*. I'm writing a story."

"Well, I'll have to look for that, won't I?" Dilmer said with a broad smile.

They had all moved to the parking lot outside Dilmer's apartment. It was time to go to the next location—the corner of Westland Street and Cheshire Lane, the two places encoded by the long strings of numbers. Nobody knew just what they were going to find there, but everyone hoped that somehow, it would involve a safe with the combination 18-25-11. How that might be so, nobody could quite imagine.

But the only thing to do was to go there and see. The group piled into the two cars. Katie was still filled to bursting with pride and happiness. She had solved the puzzle! She looked like she could spread her arms and glide over to Cheshire Lane, floating on the slightest breeze.

Zach Dilmer waved and shouted "Good luck!" as they drove away.

Brenda waved back, and they were off.

Mal turned around to face Winston and said excitedly, "This should be it, don't you think? Those last numbers have got to be a way of opening a locker or a safe or something."

"I hope so," said Winston, "but somehow I don't think there's been a huge metal safe sitting on a street corner for the last twenty-five years. Someone would have noticed it."

"Well, whoever lives on that corner, then," Mal said.

"I hope so," Winston said again. He was still distracted by the matter of the fingerprints—when would Officer Stokes call with the results? Shouldn't he have done so already? Winston had no idea how long it took to analyze a set of fingerprints. What if, by wild coincidence, the fingerprints were close enough that Stokes just wasn't sure one way or another? What were the odds of that happening?

Winston brooded on that. Brenda, meanwhile, caught Katie's eyes in the rearview mirror. "Hey, you," she said. "That was really good back there."

"Thanks!" said Katie.

"I gotta tell you," Brenda said generally, "this is the most fun I've had in a while. I didn't think I liked puzzles, but going on a real-life treasure hunt is a blast."

"I'm having fun now, too," said Katie.

"My editor's going to kill me," Brenda continued. "I haven't taken many notes in the last couple of hours. Oh, well, I'll remember everything. It's going to be a great story."

They drove for a while more, and parked near the intersection of Cheshire and Westland, pulling in right behind Marietta's SUV.

This part of Glenville was more upscale—the houses striving to be mansions without quite getting there. The cars in the driveways were shiny and new. The neighborhood was almost eerily quiet, as if kids never dared to make noise in these streets.

"All right," said Glowacka when they had gathered. "Now what?"

Nobody knew. They were directly under the Cheshire and Westland street sign, as if something magical might occur when they stood in the right spot. But nothing happened.

North walked into the middle of the street and looked around. "This has to be the place, right?"

"It certainly seems so," said Mrs. Lewis. "The puzzle gave us the names of two streets, and those streets intersect. Where else should we go?"

Glowacka said, "She's right. But we must be missing something."

North walked back to them. "Well, it must have something to do with that final strip of numbers."

"The locker combination," said Jake.

"Maybe it's not a combination," said North. "Maybe those numbers mean something else entirely."

Glowacka was curious. "Yeah? What?"

North took a deep, frustrated breath. "I don't know. I had hoped it would be obvious once we got here."

The house closest to them was surrounded by a thick eight-foot-tall hedge, and Mal was trying to see through it. "Maybe it has something to do with one of these houses," he said.

Mrs. Lewis said, "I was thinking the same thing. Standing here isn't accomplishing anything."

Brenda said, "But which house?" There were four of them, one on each corner.

"And why didn't your father simply give us a name?" growled Glowacka. "Why put us in the middle of the street like this?"

"I don't know," said Mrs. Lewis, defensively. "Maybe he had a good reason that we'll soon discover."

North said, "I suggest that we break up into four groups, and each group go to a house and see if they know anything. Maybe they have more envelopes. Or maybe they have a safe to which they don't know the combination, doubtful as that may seem."

"Maybe they'll have the ring right there on a coffee table," said Glowacka. "And all we have to say is 'trick or treat.'"

They paired up. North and Glowacka went to one house, Marietta and Mrs. Lewis to another. Brenda took Katie to the third, and the three boys went to the fourth. They passed a mailbox with the name Garr painted on it in gold cursive letters. The brick stoop had a welcome mat that, in fact, said WELCOME!—complete with exclamation point.

"Friendly, anyway," said Jake, and he rang the bell.

Winston said to his friends, "How are we going to say what we want? We're on a pretty strange mission."

Mal suggested, "We're here to inspect your safe?"

At that moment, the front door opened. A woman around Winston's mother's age peered out through the screen door that still separated them. Presumably, this was Mrs. Garr. She was wiping her hands with a dish towel.

"Yes?" she said.

Still not sure what he was about to say, Winston started saying it anyway: "Um, good morning!"

Mal said under his breath, "It's afternoon."

Winston shot Mal a look and started over. "Good afternoon. This is going to sound very, very strange, but we are researching the life of Walter Fredericks, one of the founders of this town?"

"I know who he is," said Mrs. Garr, in a voice that said she was waiting for the sales pitch to begin, at which point she was going to close the door.

"Oh, good," said Winston. "Well, one of the things we discovered is that Walter Fredericks, long ago, hid a ring somewhere in town. He left it there to be found by . . . whoever finds it. The three of us are looking for his ring, and we've done a lot of work on this, and the path has taken us to somewhere in this neighborhood. This street corner, in fact."

Winston waited for the Mrs. Garr to express interest in this fascinating story, but she was just staring at him. He decided to move it along. "We're not quite sure what we're supposed to do next, so we thought we'd ask people who live closest to the corner if they knew anything."

"I don't know anything about any of this," said Mrs. Garr. She was quickly losing patience with this conversation.

Winston hurriedly asked, "Do the numbers 18, 25, 11 mean anything to you?"

Now Mrs. Garr, still staring at Winston, added something to her expression that indicated she thought Winston was out of his mind. "No. Those numbers don't mean anything to me."

Mal then said, "Do you have a safe?"

This question froze Mrs. Garr like a blast from a ray gun. She unfroze just as quickly, gave each boy one last glance, and said, "I'm not going to talk to you boys anymore." She shut the door, and Winston heard her lock it.

Jake rubbed his forehead. 'Do you have a safe?' Why not just say, 'Can you just step out for a few minutes while we rob you?'"

Winston said, "She didn't know anything. She's not a part of this at all."

Jake said, "I don't think so, either, but what's the point of spooking her?"

"Sorry, sorry. I didn't think it was such a spooky question," said Mal.

"Let's go back to the others," said Winston.

They walked back to the intersection. "I bet next time we come here, that same welcome mat won't be out," said Mal.

Nobody had had any luck. The other homeowners didn't know anything more than Mrs. Garr did. No one was home at the house Brenda and Katie went to, so there remained a small crumb of hope that these missing people might come home and answer all their questions. But no one thought that would happen. As Glowacka had noted, if they were supposed to ask a particular person about the next step in the treasure hunt, why not supply the name of that person, as Fredericks had done with Sal Rosetti and Grady Dilmer?

No. The street corner itself was important. Somehow. But none of them could imagine how.

They stood there and they paced impatiently like animals in a cage, and a few minutes later, Marietta's walkie-talkie began to crackle. "Ray? Come in, Ray."

Winston's stomach did twenty-five backflips in a row. It was Officer Stokes.

Marietta unclipped the walkie-talkie from his belt. Looking directly at Winston, he spoke into it. "Go ahead."

Snackle, crackle. "I got your results," said the staticky voice.

"Yeah?"

"The kid didn't do it. He doesn't match."

Mal said, "Ha!" in a loud voice. Marietta scowled and stared at the ground, as if he'd been secretly expecting this result all along. And Winston experienced the greatest sense of relief he had ever known. He'd heard the phrase "a huge weight off my shoulders" and even used it himself, but this time it really did feel like he'd been carrying a five-hundred-pound barbell and only now was allowed to let go of it. Winston didn't mean to poke fun at Marietta's profound disappointment, but he couldn't help grinning from ear to ear. He also felt like he had to sit down right this second. He did so, on the curb. Jake came over and sat next to him, also grinning broadly. He clapped Winston on the shoulder in celebration.

Marietta was still talking to Stokes. "Are you sure?"

"I grabbed a rookie who's been learning the ropes and had him redo everything. He couldn't make it match either. The kid didn't do it, Ray. None of them did."

Marietta shook his head with wonder. "Somebody did," he said.

"I don't doubt you, buddy," said the walkie-talkie, "but it's none of the three we checked."

"All right," said Marietta. "Thanks for your good work, Stokes."

"No problem. Give a holler if you need me."

Marietta, stone-faced, replaced the walkie-talkie on his belt. Everyone was looking at him, wondering what he was going to say.

What he said was, "I missed something. I don't know what. But I'm going to figure it out. Someone broke into your home, Violet, and it's the same person who's been after your father's ring. It doesn't make any sense otherwise." He glanced down at Winston, sitting on the curb. "Sorry, kid. I jumped to conclusions. I shouldn't have." He looked around at the group in general. "Although I'll tell you now, if the robber is anybody in this group and I figure out who it is, you better pray another cop gets his hands on you before I do." With that, he crossed his arms and leaned back against his SUV, brooding, staring at the ground.

An hour later, the sun began to set. The treasure hunters had batted around dozens of ideas, none of them amounting to anything. The people in the remaining house had come home, and they too knew nothing about Walter Fredericks's treasure. Katie had gone to sit in Marietta's SUV, and it looked like she might have fallen asleep. Winston had noticed people in the surrounding houses moving their curtains aside to watch the strange assortment of people on the street corner.

North finally said what Winston knew someone would say eventually. "I think we lost the game, my friends. I think it's time to give up."

Glowacka made a sound that was close to a howl. "No! Are you crazy? We're so close!"

North shook his head sadly, very sadly. "We knew the treasure hunt might be broken, Mickey. I'm amazed we made it this far, to tell you the truth. The more I think about it, the more I believe that there was something here on this street corner twenty-five years ago that would have explained these three numbers. But it's not here now, and I don't think we'll ever know what it was."

Mrs. Lewis said, "We can do research. We can go to the library and see if we can find any information."

"What would you look for?" Winston asked.

"We have historical records. We can look through them."

"I guess the best thing we could find," said North, "would be a picture of this very street corner taken a quarter century ago. Think you have that around somewhere?"

"I'm not sure," Mrs. Lewis said in a low voice.

"I'll be happy to help do research," said North. "But not tonight. We've been at this all day, and frankly, I'm tired. What do you say?"

The group looked around. Weariness was on every face. Nobody needed to answer David North, because it was absolutely clear: They were stuck. It was over. They had lost.

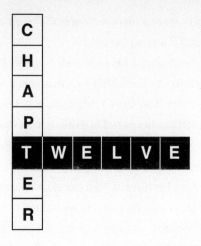

WINSTON SAT ON the couch in his living room, exhausted and depressed. After all they had accomplished, the ring still eluded them. Katie sat in the easy chair with her legs folded under her, looking about as weary as possible without being asleep.

"I thought we would find it," she said simply, staring at a point on the floor, her voice flat with disappointment.

Their mother was fixing them some kind of quick dinner. Winston was not the least bit hungry but couldn't muster the energy to protest. He supposed she was right, and he should eat. That pizza seemed like a long time ago.

At first, Glowacka had continued to protest loudly at the idea of breaking up the treasure hunt, and Winston was on his side. But even while Glowacka tried to argue that they should continue, Winston could see that somehow it had all slipped away from them. The last wooden piece—with the three numbers that might or might not be a safe's combination—just would not give up its secrets. North was probably right: The puzzle was broken, was probably unsolvable, and the ring would therefore never be found. They could try to bully their way through with research of some kind—going through Walter Fredericks's papers in search of additional clues—but doing so would probably take years.

Brenda decided about then that she had enough material for her story. "I just wish it had a happier ending," she said. Her announcement seemed to mark the official end of the treasure hunt. Brenda drove Mrs. Lewis, North, and Glowacka back to the library so they could retrieve their cars. Marietta drove all the kids in his SUV—first dropping off Jake and Mal at the playground for their bicycles and then driving Winston and Katie home. Marietta's dark mood had persisted, and he glowered the whole time, lost in foul thoughts of his own.

As they pulled up in front of Winston's house, Marietta, still staring straight out the windshield, said, "I just want to say I'm sorry again. I shouldn't have accused you of harassing Violet. I thought it was one of those other guys—North or Glowacka. When neither of their fingerprints matched, it took me by surprise."

"It's okay," said Winston. "Who do you think did it?"

Marietta shook his head. "I don't know. Maybe North or Glowacka hired someone when we weren't watching. But neither of them lives around here—they just came in to find the treasure. How would they find someone to break into a house for them? I can't make it work. There must be somebody else. But I don't know who."

Winston didn't have any ideas either, and he was tired beyond belief, so he and Katie got out of the SUV. He could feel Marietta watching them as they made their way into the house—not in an angry way, but simply to make sure they got home safe, as he had promised to do.

"The soup's ready," their mother now said, entering the living room. She looked at her kids, noted their exhaustion, and immediately said, "But I can just put it in the refrigerator if you don't want it. You can have it for lunch tomorrow."

"No, I guess I'm hungry," said Winston, getting to his feet. Katie followed. Winston, as usual, grabbed a puzzle magazine to glance through while he ate. Katie gawked at him.

"You're going to solve *puzzles*?" she said. "Aren't you sick of them by now?"

Winston hadn't really thought about it—reading one of his many magazines was just something he did while eating a quiet supper. Now he considered it . . . and opened up the magazine anyway. He grinned sheepishly at his sister.

"What can I tell you? I like puzzles."

She shook her head in disbelief.

LBYL stands for "look before you leap." What famous phrases are similarly abbreviated below?

1. HWHIL
2. THABTO
3. ASITSN
4. HITBP
5. IAFYDSTTA
6. BCBC
7. DJABBIC

(Answer, page 215.)

The first spoonful of soup awakened his hunger. Winston was just finishing a second bowl when the doorbell rang. His mom was upstairs, so he went to answer. He guessed it was a neighbor, come to return a borrowed item or something.

It was Zach Dilmer. Winston didn't even know who he was for a moment, so unexpected was this visit.

"Winston!" said Dilmer through the screen. "Oh, good, this is the right house. I wasn't sure."

"Uh, hi," said Winston, briefly flummoxed. "What . . . what are you doing here?"

"I found another envelope!" Dilmer said with boyish excitement. He held it up. "I took another look where I found the first ones, and I found it. It had slipped into a crack in the drawer. You didn't find the ring, did you?"

"No," said Winston, hypnotized by the envelope. "That's another puzzle piece? Are you sure?"

"Sure, I'm sure. You want to take a look?"

Winston was slowly getting over his initial shock. "We should call the others—we should let them know. Katie, come here! You're not going to believe this!"

"I brought it straight here," said Dilmer. "I heard you were the best puzzle solver in the group."

Katie came in from the kitchen, and their mother walked down the stairs saying, "Who is it?"

Something was wrong. Something was out of place. Winston felt a sensation like he was losing his balance. He said to Dilmer, in a voice that seemed to come from far away, "Who told you I was best puzzle solver in the group?"

Dilmer was marching forward into the house, and Winston, with dreamlike fascination, saw he had removed a gun from the pocket of his Windbreaker. It was small and silver. Dilmer's face had changed—he was no longer wearing a good-natured, friendly expression. He was wearing the hard expression of someone determined to take charge.

Without pointing the gun, Dilmer said, "Mrs. Breen, come on down the stairs. Don't you run back up there. Come down here and nobody will get hurt, I promise."

Claire Breen slowly descended the staircase. She seemed more angry than scared. "Who are you?"

"I'm just a guy looking for a nice piece of jewelry. Your son here is going to take me to a ring I heard about. That's all. Come down here and sit on that sofa."

There was a bad moment when Winston thought his mother might run back up the stairs. She was considering it; he could see that. Up the stairs and into the bedroom—lock the door and call the police. But her two children would be down here with this man and his gun. She couldn't do it that way. Dilmer gestured again toward the couch, this time pointing with his gun, and Mrs. Breen, defeated, descended the stairs and did as she was told.

When Winston's mother had complied, Dilmer said, "Katie, sweetie, go sit next to your mom. The two of you are going to stay there for a little while. I'm not going to tie you up or anything. You can even watch some television if you want."

Katie ran over to her mother and received an enormous, worried hug.

Dilmer called out generally, "Okay, we're good to go," and Winston had only a second to wonder who he was talking to. And then Brenda was in the doorway. She must have been just outside the door the whole time.

"Hi, Winston," she said, closing and locking the door behind her, and Winston knew who had told Dilmer he was the best puzzle solver in the group.

Dilmer peered around the room, almost as if he were sniffing the air. "Is there a Mr. Breen lurking about? Where's your dad?"

"He's not here," Winston said. He still couldn't believe this was happening.

"No, huh? Where is he?"

"He's on a business trip." Winston sorely wished he wasn't.

Dilmer nodded. "Mm-hmm. Maybe I should just check that out for myself." He handed the gun to Brenda. "Keep an eye on them."

"I will," said Brenda, with that same clever smile that had charmed Winston all day. Before, that smile had said "let's be friends." Now it said "I fooled you, and you never even suspected." It was the same smile, but now it seemed a lot colder.

Dilmer dashed up the stairs, and Winston could hear him opening and closing doors.

Winston looked at Brenda. She wasn't pointing the gun at anybody but was looking around at the three of them with a hard expression, as if daring them to try something. She still wore the same clothes she'd been wearing all day, but with that challenging expression, she seemed like an entirely different person. But no. This was the real Brenda. The nice, pretty reporter who had gone on a puzzle-filled adventure with them—that was the act.

She glanced at Winston to make sure he was behaving, and he said in a small voice, "Why are you doing this?"

"Because we want the ring," Brenda said. "Why do you think?"

Mrs. Breen spoke up from the couch. "You're breaking into my home because of some little ring? What kind of crazy idiots are you?"

Brenda didn't like that. She glared at Winston's mother. "That ring doesn't belong to anybody. It's just sitting there for whoever finds it. That dumb librarian didn't even want it for herself. She was just going to leave it there forever. Why shouldn't we take it?"

"Even if it means coming in here with guns?" Mrs. Breen looked like she was going to stand up to face Brenda, but she did not quite dare do this.

To that last question, Brenda merely shrugged, as if the point was hardly worth considering. Dilmer came downstairs then. "All clear," he said. "Let's get started. Keep an eye on the two of them. And you"—he was pointing at Winston—"come with me."

Brenda, gun in hand, settled herself into the easy chair, where she could keep an eye on Mrs. Breen and Katie. Winston looked over his shoulder as he was guided into the kitchen, and saw his mother and Katie glaring at Brenda with twin looks of peevish anger. Their identical expressions would have been funny under other circumstances.

"Sit down," said Dilmer, gesturing to the kitchen table.

Winston sat. He had felt shock when Marietta accused him of a terrible crime, but that was nothing compared to the shock he was feeling right now. He felt numb and hollowed out. Dilmer sat across from him.

"You and I are going to continue the treasure hunt," said Dilmer. "We're going to take it all the way to the end, and we're going to find that ring. I'm afraid I won't be as generous as that librarian—you're not going to get an equal share when I sell it. But my girl and I will go away, and no one in your family will be hurt, and isn't that reward enough?"

Winston nodded automatically.

"All right. Let's start." Dilmer slid the envelope across the table to Winston, who regarded it without emotion. "Go on, look inside. Let's see what we've got."

Winston picked up the envelope and shook out the contents. It was, of course, another wooden strip, inscribed with another string of numbers, like the others that Dilmer had given them:

$$20851953185209199142085215 24$$

"You didn't already look at this?" asked Winston.

"Of course I did," said Dilmer. "The second you guys left. I even solved it. But I don't know what the answer means. Now I want to see *you* solve it, and then you're going to put all the pieces together."

"How did you find out about the treasure in the first place?"

"My dad told me all about it a few years ago, after I came across these stupid puzzle pieces." Dilmer sat back in his chair. "I looked at the pieces after my father died. Didn't know what to make of them, of course. But that's okay—it's all going to work out. I've had a long time to think about getting that ring for myself. It took me a while, but I can be a pretty determined guy. I've got a good jewelry collector lined up. He'll pay me very well. The one thing I'm not, though, is good with puzzles. That's why I need you." He pointed at the strip of numbers in front of Winston. "Get cracking."

Winston closed his eyes and wished himself back in time. Just a few hours ago, he was unable to imagine who besides North and Glowacka could have broken into Mrs. Lewis's house. Now it seemed so obvious. Dilmer frightened Mrs. Lewis into looking for her father's ring and then held back a single puzzle piece so that they wouldn't be able to find it. When the treasure hunters gave up in frustration, all Dilmer had to do was take that last puzzle piece to the "best puzzle solver in the group," as determined by Dilmer's accomplice girlfriend. With the threat of a loaded gun, that solver would be forced to help Dilmer find the ring. For the first time in his life, Winston wished that he wasn't a good puzzle solver.

Winston looked at the strip and the envelope next to it. "White envelopes," he said miserably.

"What?"

"The envelopes you gave us were white. They were too new.

The ones we got from Mr. Rosetti were yellow with age. I should have noticed."

Dilmer smiled. "Very observant. But a little too late. Now, let's find my ring."

(Continue reading to see the answer.)

"Good. You got the same answer I got. But what does it mean?" Dilmer asked after Winston had solved the puzzle.

"I don't know," said Winston. He was staring at the notepad next to him, on which he had written "the secret is in the box."

"What box?" Dilmer asked. "Did you come across a box and not bother with it, because you didn't know it was important?"

Winston shook his head no. The only box he knew about was the wooden box he had bought for his sister, an impulsive birthday present he had purchased seemingly a million years ago. And while that box had a secret, it couldn't be the secret referred to by this puzzle. Could it? No. That made no sense.

"All right," said Dilmer. "You think about it. We're close, I can feel it."

Winston felt it, too. He thought the secret was the ring itself, and this was the final clue—if Dilmer had given them this last strip, before they had gone to stand uselessly on that street corner, they'd have found the ring by now. He was sure of it. Winston closed his eyes and tried to envision the corner of Cheshire and Westland. What was the box? Where was it?

There was still that last strip to work into all of this—the three numbers that Winston was now sure had to be the combination to a safe. After all, what is a safe but a great big box?

But wait a second. Say they had gotten to that street corner, and sitting right there was a large metal safe, as out of place as a herd of zebras. Would they really have needed this last puzzle to tell them to open the safe? Of course not. They would have worked that out for themselves, and mighty quickly, too. Glowacka would have thrown himself at it and opened it with his teeth, if he had to.

They wouldn't need a whole other message to tell them that the secret was in the box. It would be obvious.

And so "the box" referred to by this puzzle couldn't be something as simple as a safe. This puzzle was pointing at something else. A *different* box.

What?

Something on that street corner, Winston guessed. Maybe a mailbox had been there twenty-five years ago. But Winston couldn't envision Walter Fredericks hiding a valuable ring in a mailbox. Even twenty-five years ago, how would they have gotten it out? Wait for the mailman to come by? That was ridiculous.

Caught up in the puzzle despite his fear, Winston wondered, What other kind of box does one find on a street corner?

Well, the intersection itself was a kind of box. There were four corners, and one could draw an imaginary line connecting them. If that was the answer, what would "in the box" mean? Did Walter Fredericks hide the ring under the street? Did he expect them to arrive with jackhammers?

Winston rubbed a spot between his eyes. He thought his brain had hurt *before*. He hadn't known what thinking under pressure was.

Dilmer misread this gesture. "What? What've you got?"

Winston shook his head. "I don't know what this means."

Dilmer was frustrated. "How can you not know? Somewhere there's got to be a box. Right?"

Somehow this question flicked a tiny switch in Winston's overheated brain. The scattered elements of the whole crazy treasure hunt seemed to float together to form a single, crisp picture . . . just for a split second, before scattering again. Just long enough to give Winston the beginnings of an idea.

Somewhere. Somewhere there was a box.

Somewhere.

He thought of the intersection of Cheshire and Westland. An imaginary box—one simply needed to draw lines connecting the four corners.

Winston suddenly said, "I need a map."

"You have something?"

"I might."

"What kind of map?" Dilmer asked, ready to provide anything.

"A map of the town. There's one in the phone book." Winston pointed at a nook in the corner where phone books were piled up. Dilmer leaned over and grabbed the top one.

"Just so you know, kid," he said coolly, sliding the phone book across the table, "you better not be putting me on."

Winston nodded, barely even listening, as he flipped the book open to a map of the town. He stared at it, getting his bearings. Slowly, he began making some markings. Not even looking up at Dilmer, he said, "Your father. Where did he live?"

"My father? He lived on Swan Drive, 45 Swan Drive."

"What was the closest cross street?"

"It was right off of West Main Street. Is that important?"

Winston didn't answer. He was staring at his map. Now he turned and looked something up in the phone book itself. Satisfied, he flipped back to the map and made another pencil mark. Finally, he drew four careful, straight lines on the map. A box. Winston stared at this for just a few seconds more and then looked up.

"I know where the ring is."

(Continue reading to see the answer.)

CHAPTER THIRTEEN

DIMLY, IN THE BACK of Winston's mind, he had the idea that he would simply tell Dilmer the location of the ring, and he and Brenda would go away. But that's not what happened.

"Where is it?" said Dilmer, leaning on the table in anticipation.

"The library," said Winston. He almost couldn't believe it, but it had to be true. It *had* to be. The ring was right where they had started.

"How do you know that?"

Winston spelled it out. There were three puzzles, and each one had led to a different location: Rosetti's house, Dilmer's house, and the corner of Cheshire and Westland. What Winston had thought was that if those three locations were marked off on a map, they might form three corners of a square—or rather, a box.

"And the library is the fourth corner?" Dilmer asked.

Winston shook his head. The fourth corner, he explained, was where they were supposed to have started the treasure hunt all those years ago. Winston's father had thought it strange that Walter Fredericks hired the wrong kind of lawyer to deal with his will. But Mr. Fredericks only hired that lawyer—Gary Rogers—for one reason: His office was in the right place, and still was. Winston had looked up the address in the phone book—the lawyer's office was perfectly placed to be the fourth corner of the square. And right in the very center of the square was . . .

"The library!" Dilmer concluded. "That's good enough for me. Let's go."

Winston looked up, alarmed. "Go?"

Dilmer gave a little laugh. "Yeah! We're going to get that ring right now. You and me."

"But," said Winston, trying to catch up, "the library's closed." He realized as soon as he said it that this was probably a dumb thing to say.

Indeed, Dilmer laughed again. "Let me worry about that. You and I will go, and my girl will stay here. Nothing's going to happen to your mother or sister. We'll get the ring and come right back here. I'll have to tie the three of you up so we can get away, and that'll be the end of it. But if you try some kind of trick . . ." He let Winston's imagination fill in the rest of that sentence.

"I won't," said Winston.

"Then get up."

Dilmer led Winston back into the living room. Brenda turned her head to look at them, but the gun was still pointing in a bad direction. "He did it?" she asked.

Dilmer grinned. "You were right, baby. I thought you were putting me on when you chose the kid."

"I told you!" Brenda said with a smirk, and she looked at Winston admiringly.

"So we're going to get it. Keep watching them," said Dilmer.

Mrs. Breen said with new alarm, "You're taking Winston?"

"Just for a little while."

"No!" said his mother, and this time she did stand. "I'll go with you. Let Winston stay here."

Brenda stood also and said angrily, "Sit down!"

Dilmer shook his head. "I don't think so. I like you sitting right there on that couch. Nothing's going to happen to your son, Mrs. Breen. I like him. He's going to make me a rich man."

Brenda said again, "Sit down *now*," and Claire Breen sat.

"Don't you let down your guard, sugar," said Dilmer. "I think Mom here would rip your head off if you gave her the chance."

"She won't get the chance," Brenda said. Winston was struck by how cold she looked now. It was still so hard to believe.

"All right," said Dilmer. "Let's go."

A few minutes later, Winston was in the passenger seat of Dilmer's pickup truck. The night air was cool, and Winston hadn't thought to take a jacket, but that was the least of his worries. As Dilmer started the engine of his truck, Winston said, "How are you going to get into the library, anyway? It'll be locked tight."

Dilmer gave him a sideways grin with a nasty edge to it. "We'll work around that, believe me."

"And what if the ring isn't there?" asked Winston. "I might be wrong. Or it could have been there but somebody else got to it a long time ago."

Dilmer pulled away from the curb. "If I were you," he said, "I would think positive thoughts."

They drove through the town. Winston looked out the window at the lights in the passing houses. Was there anything he could do? Some way of contacting the police? He thought of Ray Marietta, and Officer Stokes. He had been surrounded by tough policemen all day long, but now that he needed one of them, he was stuck.

Should he jump out of the car? They weren't going that fast—it's not like they were on a highway. But it was still fast enough, and assuming Winston didn't break both legs in the attempt, what would he do next? Run? Dilmer was in a pickup truck and would be on top of him in five seconds flat.

No. That wouldn't work.

Stuck. I'm stuck. He saw no way out of this. They would go to the library. Winston had no doubt that Dilmer would get them in. They would probably find the ring—Winston didn't know if the ring would still be there, but he was absolutely sure that the library was where Fredericks had intended the treasure hunt to end. Winston found himself unable to think of what Dilmer's reaction might be if they found a safe in the library and it was empty.

He decided to take Dilmer's advice and think positive thoughts. But . . . even if they found the ring, things would end badly: Dilmer would drag him back home, tie him up along with his mother and sister, and be gone before anybody could do anything. Winston suddenly had a thought and turned to look through the back window of the pickup truck, into the large cargo area. There was a canvas sheet tied over the back, flapping in the wind.

"What are you looking at?" said Dilmer.

"Nothing," said Winston. Under that sheet, Winston guessed, were Dilmer's bags, and Brenda's, so they could make a fast getaway.

That brought up a new realization. "Brenda's not even her real name, is it?" he said.

Dilmer gave him another sharp smile. "You are a smart kid, you know? She isn't a reporter, either."

"I guess I figured that out, too," Winston said glumly.

"Good thing nobody checked the masthead in the local newspaper," said Dilmer. "That would have ended things quickly, since she's not listed there. But we couldn't think of another way to plant her with you guys. I'd say it worked out pretty well, wouldn't you?"

Winston didn't answer. He was back on his previous worrisome train of thought. Was there any way to stop Dilmer? Winston would call the police as soon as they got themselves untied. By that time, it would probably be far too late—Dilmer and Brenda (or whatever her name was) would be long gone. With the ring.

They parked away from the library. Dilmer cut the engine but made no move to get out of the car. He peered around the green. There was nobody there. All the businesses were closed down tight. There was little foot traffic at this hour, and none right now.

"All right," he said. "Let's go."

They got out of the truck. Winston folded his arms against his chest and shivered. Dilmer pulled his light jacket against himself and kept an eye out for pedestrians or policemen.

"You ever break into anything, Winston?" he asked.

What a dumb question. Winston shook his head.

"No? Well, you'll see. It's real easy, if you've got the tools and the know-how."

They walked up to the library's front doors like anybody else interested in borrowing a book. The building seemed larger than it did in the daytime, and the blackness in those windows looked inky and full.

As they approached the front doors, Dilmer gave one more hasty look around and pulled a small black case from his inside jacket pocket. He opened the case and removed a slender metal tool of some sort. He worked the lock, and as he did so, he said, "One thing you better remember, kid, is not to take more than three steps away from my side. You got that?"

"Yes."

Dilmer picked the lock with amazing speed. Winston found himself impressed, against his will. He had no idea it could be done so quickly and fluidly. They were just inside the doorway when a loud beeping sound came from their left. Winston felt a surge of relief—an alarm! Of course this place had a burglar alarm!

But Dilmer didn't seem concerned. "What have we got here? Okay . . ." he said, and he removed another tool from his case. The beeping continued while he worked. "These things usually give you thirty seconds or so to punch in a code," he explained as he removed the front panel of the alarm, revealing a small tangle of colored wires. "Obviously, I don't know the code, but I do know another way to shut this baby up." He pinched a few of the wires together and pulled another wire out entirely, and the beeping abruptly stopped.

Dilmer tossed the front panel of the busted alarm on the floor, where it made a hard plastic clatter. "That's that," he said. "Easy as pie. Now, where are we going?"

Winston was surprised at this question. "I don't know."

"What do you mean, you don't know?" Dilmer said with annoyance. "You're the one who figured out the ring has got to be here. So where is it?"

"There has to be a safe somewhere, I think."

"Well, let's go find it."

They walked into the main reading room. In the darkness, it was as creepy as a vampire's crypt. There was just barely enough light from the outside streetlamps to make out the tables and tall bookshelves. Their footsteps echoed as the two of them walked into the middle of the room, where they stopped.

"I don't know where a safe is supposed to be in here," said Dilmer. "Maybe in one of the back offices. Come on."

He opened the swinging wooden gate that led into the corral where the librarians sat during the day. Where, in fact, Mrs. Lewis had been sitting on the day she saw Winston with those first four puzzle pieces. There were a few desks and several wheeled carts loaded with books. Toward the back of the area was a door. Dilmer headed straight for it. He jiggled the doorknob.

"Locked. Can you beat that?" Dilmer took out his tool case again. "Hold this," he said, handing Winston a small, thin flashlight. "Shine it right there. Right on the lock."

Winston did so. As Dilmer worked, Winston had the notion of shining the light out the window. Would someone be passing by right at that moment, and be curious about that odd beam of light? Would that person then jump to the conclusion that a robbery was being committed, and call the police? It seemed unlikely. Winston kept the flashlight aimed properly at the lock.

Dilmer picked it as quickly as he had before. The door opened into a narrow, dark hallway. "Gimme that flashlight," Dilmer said. Winston handed it to him, and they eased into the back offices of the library.

There were three small rooms back here, including Mrs. Lewis's office. Winston had a hard time imagining that they'd find a safe here. Oh, the library might have a safe for some reason, but if so, it was probably used all the time. The ring wouldn't be there. What Walter Fredericks would have wanted was a safe that would be left undisturbed until his children had found it. A different, hidden safe.

Winston drew in a sharp breath. Dilmer turned around, quick as a cat. "What?" he said. "What's wrong?"

"I think I know where the safe is."

Dilmer smiled. "Attaboy. Where is it?"

"There's a basement downstairs, and then another basement below that. Two levels down."

"Yeah? Let's go take a look."

They reversed course. Dilmer didn't bother relocking the office door behind him. They went back through the main reading room and over to the staircase near the front door. Winston glanced through the window, again hoping that someone would be standing right there, nose to the window, investigating the strange motion he had detected from the outside. But nobody was there and nobody would be.

Dilmer opened the gate to the stairway, and he and Winston descended into truly creepy darkness. The flashlight barely cut a path through it. Dilmer stretched out one arm and swept along the wall, and Winston was startled almost to shouting when the lights in the basement hallway came on with a flickering snap.

"You turned on the lights?" Winston asked in astonishment. "Is that safe?"

Dilmer smiled. "You're looking out for me, kid? That's nice." He gestured around the hallway. "No windows down here. No one's going to see anything." Dilmer started forward to the first door. "So where is it? In one of these rooms?"

"No, no. I mean, it might be, but I think it's down one more level. I *think*." Winston pointed to the second stairway, leading to the subbasement.

Dilmer glanced down into the darkness. The light in this hallway seemed to stop abruptly at the top of the second staircase. Winston remembered how he had thought the darkness down there looked solid, and he still thought so.

"Fine," said Dilmer, a bit uneasily. "Let's go." He started down the stairs. Winston did not want to go into that darkness, but a frown from Dilmer, when he saw he wasn't being followed, got Winston's legs moving.

The beam from the flashlight showed piles of boxes and several long tables covered with all kinds of junk—books, broken toys, old clothing, and what appeared to be a whole tool kit's worth of tools. There was a fair amount of lumber lying around in odd piles. This place seemed to be used for general storage—not just by the library, but by the whole town.

Dilmer, while looking around, tripped on something—there was a solid, ringing *clang* and then the sound of something metallic rolling across the floor. Dilmer cursed and kicked out, and there was another, louder clang as a large, thick pipe rolled under one of the tables. It stopped at the wall with a dull thump.

"They should clean this place up," Dilmer said angrily. "What a mess." He again felt along the wall for a light switch, but could not immediately find one. Cursing once more, he shined his flashlight along the wall. There were cobwebs, and a lot of dust, but Dilmer couldn't find a switch. He tried the other wall and also came up empty. Grunting with annoyance, Dilmer pointed the light to the ceiling. Yes, there were light fixtures up there, with long fluorescent bulbs. Where was the switch?

There were several large wooden pallets tipped up and leaning against the wall. Dilmer tried to move the nearest of these, but it was very heavy. "Step away, Winston," Dilmer said. "Go stand there a second," he said, pointing generally. Winston moved a few steps away, and Dilmer wrestled the heavy wooden pallet to the ground—it landed with a flat, deafening crash that made Winston jump.

It seemed a while before the noise entirely faded away. Dilmer held very still and glanced up the stairs. He seemed to be holding his breath. "That was louder than I expected," he said. Winston knew he was waiting for someone to come into the library to investigate the sound. Would it even have been heard outside? Winston didn't know. They stood there, frozen, for a full minute.

Dilmer slowly exhaled and turned his light back to the wall where the pallet had been. Still no light switch! Dilmer cursed for a third time and viciously kicked the pallet three times in succession.

"Okay, okay!" Dilmer said. He stood there for a moment, getting control of himself. Finally, he announced, "I don't have time for this. The flashlight will be enough. Let's go."

They moved forward carefully. The layout of this level was exactly like the one above it—six rooms, three on each side—except none of the rooms had doors. Dilmer decided to try the first room on the right. They stood in the doorway, and Dilmer shined his flashlight around. The room was filled with long, wheeled carts, each of which held a neat row of metal folding chairs.

Dilmer carefully shined his flashlight all along the walls, looking for the safe. "Are you sure about this, kid?" he said.

"No," Winston said.

Dilmer turned around to glare at him. "Do you think it's in the library at all?"

Winston corrected himself hastily. "Oh, yes. Yes. But I don't know for sure where."

Dilmer blew out a deep breath of frustration. "All right. We're going to quickly check each of these rooms down here. If we don't find the safe, then we are going to tear this place apart. You understand?"

Winston understood.

The flashlight beam continued its scan of the room, but found only pale gray walls. Dilmer muttered something and turned around. He headed for the next room down the hall, the second on the right.

Like the hallway, this room contained a crazy assortment of junk. More metal pipes, identical to what Dilmer had tripped on. More lumber in various sizes. Two long tables were piled with computer parts— decades-old monitors and printers, and wild bouquets of colored wire.

Winston blinked in surprise as Dilmer's flashlight beam briefly played over an ancient bicycle with a banana seat and handlebars covered with orange rust. A kid on a scavenger hunt could probably spend fifteen minutes down here and win the whole thing.

"I don't see anything," Dilmer said irritably, and abruptly turned around.

He moved on to the third room on the right. This room was almost entirely devoted to one thing. A half-dozen large, skeletal bookcases—quite different from the nicer bookcases in the upstairs reading room—were haphazardly stacked with old books. Winston guessed these were out of circulation, or donations that were found to be worthless. He pulled a thick, dust-covered book from the nearest bookcase and squinted to read the title in the indirect light of Dilmer's flashlight beam. It was volume D of a very old encyclopedia.

"I can't even see the walls in here," Dilmer mumbled, and he moved slowly into the room. He focused the flashlight more slowly along the walls, trying to see past the many books.

Winston wondered once again about escape. Dilmer seemed to have momentarily forgotten about him, taking his obedience for granted. Remaining in the doorway as Dilmer moved into the room, Winston wondered if he might not just tiptoe silently backward, into the hallway. He glanced toward the stairs, illuminated in a ghostly way by the fluorescent lights on the next level up. Could he make it up there, then up the next flight to the main level, then out the gate and out the door? He didn't know. And what would he do then? Run like a madman, of course, until he found a pay phone, and then call the police.

He looked at Dilmer, who was paying no attention to him as he continued his inspection of the room. If it could be done at all, it would have to be now. Winston took stock of his courage and found the tank not entirely empty. He took a step backward and gauged Dilmer's reaction. He didn't notice. He didn't notice!

Winston glanced at the staircase again. He could see it, but not the path that led to it, which was pitch dark and covered with about fifty thousand things to trip blindly over. Winston swallowed and was about to urge himself to run when Dilmer said, "Hey, what's this?"

Dilmer was shining his flashlight on a particular bookcase. He seemed to have found something interesting. "I think I've got it," he said, and he whirled his flashlight over to Winston, who froze like a kid playing a game of statues.

Dilmer frowned. "What are you doing? You going somewhere?"

"No."

Dilmer didn't like it. "Get in here where I can see you." Winston walked into the room. He hadn't been fast enough. The opportunity, if it had been there at all, had vanished. Dilmer said, "I said not three steps away from me, didn't I?"

"Yes."

But Dilmer was too fascinated by what he had discovered to be angry for very long. "Take a look at this," he said, and swung the flashlight beam back at the bookcase. Behind the bookcase, almost entirely covered by several rows of old books, was the outer edge of something—a metal plate of some kind, embedded in the wall.

Dilmer's excitement grew. He pawed at the books, sending them tumbling to the ground, raising a cloud of ancient dust. "I think this is it! Winston, you're a damn genius! Look at this!"

Moving the books had revealed the metal plate for what it was: A small safe. Winston felt an electric surge of exhilaration. *He was right.* He had solved Walter Fredericks's puzzle. Fredericks must have arranged for a safe to be put right here in the library. And nobody who came down here knew what was in it, but everybody assumed it was somebody else's business, and it had been ignored all this time. In that moment, Winston was sure—absolutely positive—that the ring was still in there, undisturbed all these years.

"Holy cow, this is it," said Dilmer in a small, breathless voice.

One of the bookcases had to be moved, or the door to the safe wouldn't be able to open. Dilmer wrestled it away from the wall and let it drop with another enormous clatter—no longer seeming to care whether or not they made noise. Stepping between the shelves, Dilmer approached the safe.

He tugged on the handle. It was locked, unmovable.

"It's 18-25-11. Isn't that right?" Dilmer was practically giggling. The safe was embedded about six feet up on the wall, taller than Dilmer was, so he had to reach up slightly to dial the combination. He aimed the flashlight at the simple dial with one hand and with the other began to spin the combination.

As he did so, his Windbreaker rose up slightly on his body, and Winston saw something that caused the plan-making, escape-oriented part of his brain to leap into urgent action once more.

Dilmer had a cell phone clipped to his belt.

Winston's eyes darted to it, a glint of silver on Dilmer's waist, and then back up to the safe. There was a very large part of him that didn't want to leave this room. He had spent a long time on this treasure hunt and wanted to see that safe open. He wanted to see the ring inside.

"Eighteen," Dilmer said as he dialed the safe. "Twenty-five . . ." Winston's heart seemed to stop beating. He could almost see the next thirty seconds in his mind like a speeded-up movie, a prediction of the future. But he didn't know what would happen after those thirty seconds.

"Eleven," said Dilmer. He reached up for the handle. Before, it hadn't budged an inch.

Now it turned.

That was good enough for Winston. This was the safe; the combination was right; the ring was going to be in there.

The door to the safe opened with surprising smoothness, considering how rusty it must have been. Dilmer, with nearly uncontainable anticipation, stood on his tiptoes as he opened the door and aimed the flashlight inside.

Now. Winston grabbed the cell phone off Dilmer's belt. It detached with an efficient snap. Then Winston turned and ran for his life.

DILMER REACTED WITH frightening speed. Winston
had thought he would be too entranced by the contents of the safe,
but Dilmer was aware immediately of what had happened. Winston
didn't stop to consider his next move. He charged out of the room and
into the blackness of the hallway. Behind him, there was a scraping
metal sound, and he heard Dilmer stumble with an *oof!* He had probably gotten tangled trying to climb out of the metal bookcase he had
toppled. Good.

Winston kept his eyes focused keenly on the light at the top of the
stairs. He half jogged, half ran down the dark hallway, groping wildly
in front of him, and then tripped noisily over something—another
metal pipe, from the sound of it. Winston went sprawling. The floor
was cement, and there were bursts of pain like a string of firecrackers
as parts of him hit the floor—knees, elbows, ribs, shoulders. His head
bonked against the floor, and he saw a galaxy of twinkling stars.

Idiot. Idiot! he thought. He hurt in a dozen places, but he also
knew that Dilmer was about to come roaring into the hallway with

that flashlight of his. Winston would be caught. He would never make it to the stairs in time.

Winston was aware that his shoulder was brushing up against something splintery—one of the thick wooden pallets leaning against the wall. Acting entirely on impulse, Winston felt at the pallet and found there was a sizable gap between the pallet and the wall. Winston wasted no time: He crawled into the gap behind the pallet and pulled himself in.

"Get back here!" Dilmer yelled angrily. He had burst into the hallway. Winston was facing the wrong way and couldn't see what Dilmer was doing. He couldn't turn around in this narrow space. If he bumped the heavy pallet too much, it would reward him by sliding down and crushing him.

"Where are you?" Dilmer said, a bit more calmly. "There's no way you got upstairs in time. You can't see anything. No. You're still down here." Winston tried to shrink as he heard Dilmer walk right by him. Now, out the other side of his hiding spot, Winston could see Dilmer's flashlight beam sweeping the hallway. Dilmer walked slowly to the stairs and peered up, as if not entirely convinced that Winston hadn't fled. But he shook his head. "No. You're still down here. Where are you?" He turned around and began playing the flashlight beam back and forth. Dilmer peeked into the first of the rooms.

How long before he thought to look behind this pallet?

Time to use the cell phone. Winston couldn't even see it in his own hands. He felt for a hinge, opened it, and pressed randomly at buttons. He must have hit the right thing, because the keypad suddenly glowed neon green. The phone beeped loudly as it came to life. Winston winced in agony.

"I heard that," shouted Dilmer. He came out of the room he was in. "Winston, you come out here right now and I promise not to hurt you. Do you hear me?" Winston heard him, but he didn't believe him. He huddled over the phone, anxious that Dilmer not see the light. He found the antenna, lengthened it, and looked at the phone's tiny screen: NO SIGNAL AVAILABLE it informed him in cheerful blue letters. Winston was too far underground for the cell phone to be of any use. He wanted to cry in frustration and anger. Now what was he supposed to do? He had to get upstairs, but Dilmer was blocking the way. He was stuck.

"You're here in the hallway," said Dilmer, heading slowly back toward him. "Where are you hiding, Winston?"

He couldn't stay here forever. Dilmer would figure it out soon enough. He had to do something. Winston had the smallest glimmer of an idea. He put the cell phone in his pants pocket and began to feel around—carefully, carefully—the underside of the pallet. There was a wooden brace across the center of it and another up toward the top. Winston shifted into a kneeling position and held on to these braces. He tensed up, waiting for the right moment, praying he would be able to move this heavy thing when he needed to.

Dilmer said wearily, "Come on, Winston. I'll find you eventually and then we'll be right back where we started. All you're doing is wasting time." He was getting closer to Winston's hiding spot. "You think your mother and sister appreciate this? They just want this whole thing over. Believe me—"

With a strangled yell, Winston leaned with his shoulders and pushed the heavy pallet as hard as he could. It lifted forward reluctantly, over-balanced, and fell the other way. Dilmer, perfectly positioned on the other side, jumped backward, tripped, and fell. The pallet fell on one of his outstretched legs, and Dilmer screamed bloody murder.

Winston didn't think he should stick around to administer first aid. He ran for the stairs. Again he stumbled in the dark on some random piece of garbage. He didn't quite fall, though, and regained his balance right at the base of the stairs. Winston looked back briefly to see that Dilmer had freed himself from the overturned pallet and was coming straight at him.

Winston scrambled up the stairs, squinted in the fluorescent light, and turned the corner to the second staircase. He dug the cell phone out of his pants pocket as he took the stairs. Dilmer was right behind him.

The gate at the top of the stairs was shut, and Winston, panicked, could not remember how to open the thing. It was there to prevent toddlers from falling down the stairs—the latch had to be lifted up and out at the same time, and—

As he did this, Dilmer caught up to Winston and grabbed him by the shoulders. The gate swung open and the two of them tumbled to the floor just inside the main entrance.

"Help! Help!" Winston called as loud as he could, trying to untangle himself from Dilmer. But Dilmer was stronger by far, and he climbed on top of Winston, pinning him to the floor. He put both hands over Winston's mouth.

"Shut up, shut up!" he hissed. Dilmer looked angry, of course, but also confused and a little wounded, as if a good friend had betrayed him. "What is wrong with you, huh? This is a very simple thing I'm trying to do here! You are making my life very difficult. Do you understand me?"

Winston nodded. He risked a quick glance at the cell phone. It was still on. He moved his thumb to the keypad: Nine. One. One. Send. Winston was hugely relieved that the thing did not beep again in acknowledgment. A word appeared in the cell phone's tiny screen: CALLING.

"Now, I am going to get off you," said Dilmer. "And I am going to hang on to you like my hands are covered in glue. The safe is open.

There's something in there. We are going to grab it, and then we are getting out of here, and so help me, if you try one more thing—"

Dilmer started to get up, which meant taking his hands off Winston's mouth. Winston lifted the phone to his face—he didn't know if he had connected with anybody, but there was nothing to do about that now—and yelled, "The library! Come to the Glenville library!"

Dilmer was, for one second, flatly astonished at this further disobedience. It was clear he had forgotten that Winston had his cell phone. Then Dilmer recovered. He grabbed the cell phone and, in unthinking desperation, stood up and threw it against the wall. Several pieces came flying off.

Winston didn't wait to receive the same treatment. With Dilmer off him, Winston scrambled only halfway to his feet before he started running again. Winston headed for the main reading room, at full speed. Nothing to trip over up here. He went straight to the bookshelves, ran in between two of them at random, came out the other side, took a right, stepped into a particularly dark shadow, and crouched down.

He never would have dreamed that he had this much fight in him. Was there another exit from the library? He didn't know. The only door he had ever used was the main entrance. But there had to be an emergency exit somewhere, right? He tried to think, but his mind was spinning like an out-of-control merry-go-round. No. If there was another exit somewhere, he didn't know where it was. And he didn't think this was the right time to start poking around looking for it. Dilmer would get him that way for sure.

Where was Dilmer, anyway? Why wasn't he right behind him?

Maybe he was limping, because of the wooden pallet. That thing was heavy.

Winston tried to silence his breathing, which sounded as loud as a freight train. He was going to give himself away. That was probably exactly what Dilmer was doing—creeping silently around, listening for him.

There was nothing but silence in the library. If Dilmer was creeping around, he was doing an amazing job of it.

Could Winston get by him and out the main entrance?

He couldn't see anything from back here—just tall, shadowy bookshelves. But he did not want to move. Dilmer hadn't found him: This was an excellent hiding spot. To give it up seemed crazy. It seemed dangerous.

Minutes crept by. He sat there, listening to the silence, waiting for the next thing to happen, wondering how he would react when it did.

The next thing that happened was a sound like "Ugh!" Winston cringed. He didn't know what that meant or where it had come from. But the sound didn't seem to be close by and that was just fine.

The *next* thing that happened was all the lights in the library came on.

Winston nearly screamed. His hiding spot was destroyed. Now he was just a boy sitting on the floor. He scrambled backward trying to find darkness, but there was none. Dilmer would find him in seconds.

He didn't know where to go—he had to run, but the next place he ran to might be smack into Dilmer's arms. Winston crouched down low and peered around the closest bookshelf. He saw a figure standing in the doorway of the main reading room, looking around. But it wasn't Dilmer.

It was Ray Marietta.

Zach Dilmer, it seemed, had gotten greedy. Well—Winston already knew he was greedy, so this was just another example of it. Dilmer had been forced to assume that Winston's call to 911 was successful and that the cops must be on their way. Rather than chase Winston around the library, he ran back downstairs to get the ring, hoping to seize it and get away before the police arrived.

He almost made it. If he had been a little faster, he would have made it. But Dilmer was limping because of his hurt leg, and navigating the junk-filled subbasement was still a challenge in the dark. He got to the safe, grabbed the ring, and made his way back to the stairs. He got to the front door at full speed, opened it, and ran straight into the arms of the police: Marietta and two men in uniform. The "Ugh!" was Dilmer's muted shout of surprise.

Marietta recognized Dilmer immediately and understood most of what happened almost without being told. Dilmer had been the one to break into Violet Lewis's house (and a whole other bunch of houses besides). He had concocted some kind of plan to steal the ring for himself, and he had somehow discovered that the ring was in the library. That only left the question of who had made that panicked call to 911, and that received its answer when Marietta saw Winston peeking out from behind a bookcase.

Marietta peered at him. "Are you okay?"

Winston slowly stood up, still unable to believe that Dilmer might not jump out from somewhere, police or no police.

"Where is he?" Winston asked.

"Dilmer? He's in the back of a police car."

"He is?"

"Uh-huh. And we took this off of him." Marietta held it up: The ring. Winston drew closer, fascinated. When he saw it, his first thought was: Someone would wear that? It was huge and bulky, a thick gold band studded with various jewels. A person wearing that ring would have a hard time doing basic tasks with that hand—writing, opening a door, using a fork and knife. Of course, someone rich enough to own that ring probably had people to do those things for him.

The ring was odd and unwieldy, but it also seemed magical, sparkling a thousand colors in the light. Marietta handed it to Winston, who examined it with wonder and pride.

But then he looked up with a start—this wasn't over. There was more trouble to deal with. "Brenda! She's part of this, too. She's at my house right now!"

Marietta frowned. "What, that reporter?"

"She isn't a reporter! She's Dilmer's girlfriend, and she's at my house with a gun. She stayed to watch my mother and sister while I came here with Dilmer to—"

Marietta didn't need to hear anything more. He unclipped the walkie-talkie from his belt. This was a much larger walkie-talkie than the one he had worn all afternoon. This one looked like it could talk to passing airplanes. Marietta paused before speaking into it. "What's your address?" he said.

"74 Woodbridge Street."

Marietta clicked on the walkie-talkie. "Eileen, it's Ray."

A firm female voice responded immediately. "Go ahead, Ray."

"I need a car at 74 Woodbridge Street right now. Possible hostage situation, do you hear me? Proceed quiet. No sirens."

The voice responded back: "Roger that, 74 Woodbridge, quiet."

"Is Stokes on duty?" Marietta asked.

"He is," said the voice. "He checked in an hour ago for the night."

"Send him and someone else."

"Roger that," said the efficient female voice.

Marietta clicked off and looked at Winston. "Okay," he said, "Let's go." He turned and ran out of the library. Winston scrambled to keep up. He saw a police car just outside—Dilmer was in the backseat, looking sour and defeated. They made the briefest eye contact as Winston ran by, and Winston couldn't help but smile just a little. Dilmer turned his head away.

The two of them got into Marietta's SUV. Between them, on the seat, was a police light. Marietta took this and attached it somehow to the roof of his car. The world around them filled with a pulsing blue light, weird and mute without a siren to accompany it. Marietta started his car and pulled away fast.

"I heard the library call over the police scanner and I just knew it had something to do with that ring," said Marietta. "I came right over."

"I thought you were retired," Winston said.

Marietta shrugged. "There's different kinds of retirement, kid. Tell me what happened."

Winston told him—about Dilmer's arrival at their house, the last puzzle piece, Winston's being forced to solve the final puzzle. "He left Brenda to watch my mom and Katie while we went to get the ring."

Marietta shook his head. "I should have seen it. I should have seen it. And I never should have let that girl join us."

Winston said, "You didn't know."

"That's *why* I shouldn't have let her join us," Marietta said. "So then what? You figured out the ring was in the library?"

"Yes."

Marietta looked at him. "The ring was right downstairs from where we started?"

Winston nodded grimly. Marietta snorted. "Unbelievable. You still have that ring, right?"

He did. Winston was holding it tight in his fist. It'd be a remarkable thing to lose it at this point. Winston was holding it as if it might try to fly away, although he couldn't help but take glimpses at it, to prove to himself that it was real.

They neared Winston's block, and Marietta turned off the blue police light. They rounded the corner and pulled slowly up to Winston's house. Another police car, also moving in slow motion, came from the other direction at the same moment. Marietta said, "Stay here. Don't get out of the car."

Marietta got out and met the two police officers from the other car. Stokes turned and pointed at him in friendly greeting. Winston wondered what they were going to do. Marietta spoke animatedly and pointed at the house. The cops nodded respectfully.

Winston thought one of them would have a loudspeaker, so that they could call out. "The place is surrounded—come out with your hands up!" But no one seemed to be holding one of those. Did Brenda know they were here? How were they going to get her out of the house?

Marietta and the other policemen seemed to reach some kind of agreement. The policeman Winston didn't know walked up to the house. Looking like he was trying to be quiet, he slowly opened the screen door. Winston squinted, trying to see what that cop was doing. It looked like he was just standing there.

Suddenly, Marietta and Stokes ran into his field of vision. They chugged full speed up the walkway, holding some kind of long black cylinder between them. A battering ram! Marietta and Stokes hit the door with everything they had—the door flew open as if they had used dynamite. The three men rushed inside.

Even from within the closed SUV, Winston faintly heard the sounds of a scuffle. Whatever was happening in there didn't last long: Within a minute, Stokes led Brenda outside, her hands cuffed behind her back. She was looking at the ground in bitter disappointment.

Winston couldn't resist. He reached over and tooted the horn of the SUV. Brenda and Stokes both looked up. She saw him sitting there. Winston waved.

*   *   *

His mother and sister were both shaken but okay. Brenda hadn't done anything more than what she had been told—she sat there covering them with the gun. Winston hugged his sister for the second time that day—a modern record—and was himself given a huge, frightened, welcoming hug by his mother.

"You're okay?" Mrs. Breen asked. "Are you sure you're okay?"

He was sure. His head and legs and arms still hurt from the various blows they had received, and he had a nasty scrape on his forehead and a purple bruise by his eye. But he was better than okay.

"Katie," he said. "Look." He opened his hand.

She gasped and took the ring. "You found it! It's beautiful!" She immediately tried it on, although it fit around two of her fingers simultaneously.

Marietta said to their mother, "Sorry about the door." It was still on its hinges but looked twisted and beaten up, swinging tentatively back and forth as if disoriented. It was never going to close properly, and it certainly wasn't going to lock.

"Oh, of course that's all right," Mrs. Breen said. She took one of Marietta's hands and squeezed it gratefully.

"The three of you maybe should stay in a hotel tonight."

Mrs. Breen said, "Why?"

"Well," said Marietta, gesturing at the door, "the lock is broken and—"

"Oh," said their mother. "No, that's okay. You got them both, right? You got *him*, too, right?" She meant Dilmer.

Marietta nodded. "He's in a holding cell, and she's about to join him."

"Then we're fine. The screen door locks. That'll be fine until tomorrow." Winston's mom looked around. "Although, maybe I'll sleep on the couch tonight. Just to keep an eye on things down here."

"I'll also make sure a car comes by at least once an hour," said Marietta. "You'll be okay." He turned to Katie. "You okay, sweetheart?"

Katie nodded.

"Good. But I need the ring."

Katie gave a look of surprise and even looked like she might resist for a moment. Then she took the ring off her finger—fingers—and put it in Marietta's outstretched hand.

"I told the group I would see to it this got put in the evidence room," Marietta said. "Of course, now it actually *is* evidence, so that shouldn't be too difficult. Good job, kid," he said to Winston. "See you soon." He let himself out.

They locked up as best they could. Then their mom hugged them a while more and put ice and stinging medicine on Winston's bruises while he told the whole story of his remarkable escape from Dilmer.

Within an hour, Winston found himself in his bed contemplating what had been the longest day of his life. Surely it wasn't just this morning that he had woken up with the sunrise, anxious to begin solving Walter Fredericks's puzzle. That seemed like a memory so distant he had to strain to recall it. And yet, for all he had been through, he couldn't imagine falling asleep now. He thought he should at least get up and send an e-mail to his cousin Henry to let him know what had happened. Although writing that e-mail would probably take hours . . . and he'd have to include a puzzle, of course. What kind should he create? Maybe something like a crossword puzzle . . . he liked making those . . . but with some kind of extra trick to it, something he could e-mail Henry tomorrow when he told him all about the treasure hunt.

Winston thought about the possibilities and rolled them over in his mind, and fell asleep.

Write in every answer starting at the square that matches its clue number, and going clockwise. Each answer will overlap the answer in front of it and behind it by two or more letters.

1. Octopus's arm
2. Witty and smart
3. Poetry
4. Choose
5. Needing to be plugged in
6. Having more money
7. Superman, for one
8. _____ chair
9. Ancient royalty from Egypt (2 words)
10. One who gives extra help for school
11. 200 mile-per-hour wind
12. Give to charity

(Answer, page 215.)

MARIETTA CALLED LATE the next morning and requested that Winston and his family join him at the police station. When they arrived, the desk sergeant turned around and yelled, "Hey, Stokes! That kid is here."

Officer Stokes, in civilian clothes, had been chatting and laughing with a fellow policeman, but now he came up to Winston and his family.

"How are you all doing?" he said, smiling but still looking concerned.

"We're okay," said Winston.

"Thank you for your help last night," said Mrs. Breen.

"Oh, believe me, ma'am, that was my pleasure." Stokes looked at Winston. "That's some face you've got there." Winston's bruises had blossomed in the night and were now an array of reds and purples.

"Yeah, I know," said Winston. "It doesn't hurt too much."

"Good, good. Hey, I wanted to give you something," said Stokes.

"What is it?"

"Well, I felt bad about what happened yesterday, the whole thing with the fingerprints. Thinking you were the guy we were after and all that." He glanced at Winston's mother, whose expression turned grim at the memory. Stokes gave a nervous little laugh.

"Anyway, I felt awful about that, so I made you this." He gave Winston a piece of paper.

Winston unfolded it and smiled. "A puzzle. About fingerprints!"

"I got the idea you'd like that. But don't solve it now. Marietta's waiting for you all in that conference room right down the hall. Go on ahead. And I'm glad everything worked out."

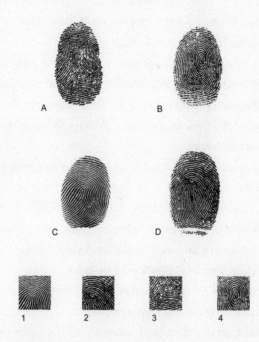

Can you match each numbered partial print to the fingerprint it came from?

(Answer, page 215.)

Everyone was already in the conference room—North and Glowacka, Mrs. Lewis, and Marietta. Winston opened the door just as Glowacka said in an amazed voice, "Are you saying they found the ring?"

"Ah, here they are," said Marietta, standing and waving Winston, Katie, and Mrs. Breen into the small room. There weren't nearly enough chairs, so Winston leaned up against the wall. Winston's mother was introduced to North and Glowacka. North delivered a polite little bow. "It's very nice to meet you," he said. "You're raising two fine children."

Glowacka, on the other hand, didn't seem to hear the introduction. He was still shaking his head in amazement. "I can't believe they found it." He looked at Winston for the first time and noticed his face. "Geez, kid. So where was it? In the gorilla cage at the zoo?"

And so Winston was called upon to tell the whole story again. Everyone was shocked, of course, when he told them how Dilmer and Brenda had showed up with another puzzle piece and a gun.

"Not Brenda," Marietta interrupted. "Beverly. Beverly Munsen."

"Who?" said Glowacka.

"She's a very sweet girl," said Marietta. "Arrest warrants in only four states."

"Ah," said North, smirking. "Why, that's hardly any."

Mrs. Lewis was shaking her head sadly. "Mrs. Breen," she said. "I am so sorry for what happened to you and your family. I promised your husband that your children would be safe!"

Winston's mother smiled sympathetically. "Everything worked out. Everybody's okay. You couldn't have known."

Winston finished the story and was interrupted again only when he revealed that the ring was hiding all along in the library. North and Glowacka were loudly appalled, of course, that they started the treasure hunt just a hundred feet away from the finish line. Only Mrs.

Lewis was silent, continuing to shake her head with a small, tired smile. Marietta must have told her all about it last night.

"So where, if I may ask, is the ring now?" said North.

"Yeah," said Glowacka. "Are we still going to sell it or what?"

Marietta nodded. "One day."

Glowacka didn't like that. "One day?"

"Well, now it's evidence in a crime. Mrs. Lewis will get it back after Dilmer and his girlfriend go to trial. I'm afraid it can't be sold until then."

North and Glowacka looked thunderstruck at this. Glowacka found his voice first. "How long are we talking?"

Marietta shrugged. "A few months. Less than a year, certainly."

"Oh, good," said North, in a dazed-sounding voice. "Less than a year."

Mrs. Lewis spoke up. "The good news is, we were allowed to photograph the ring, and I sent those pictures to my contact in Jordan. She gave me an estimate based on that."

"Really," said North, interested.

"How much?" said Glowacka.

"They valued it at sixty thousand dollars. That's fifteen thousand for each of the four of us."

Winston was awed. Fifteen thousand dollars! Katie already told him on the car ride over that she was going to split the treasure fifty-fifty with him. After all they had been through, even she couldn't manage to be as greedy as she'd originally intended. Someday, after the ring was sold, he was going to get seven thousand, five hundred dollars.

Glowacka took this news in a most unusual way: He started chuckling. Winston didn't think he knew how to chuckle. And that quickly became outright laughter. Indeed, he doubled over at the small table, banging it with his fist. "Fifteen thousand!" he said when he could breathe again.

North was staring at him, amused. "That is funny because . . . ?"

"Because I bought those damn puzzle pieces for fourteen thousand. Bruno Fredericks wanted twenty, but I bargained him down. Hey, I made a whopping thousand dollars! Hooray for me!" He snickered again and wiped the tears from his eyes.

"So that's it," said Marietta, standing. He said to North and Glowacka, "You two are free to hang around town until the trial is over and we sell the ring. Or you could actually trust Mrs. Lewis here to send you your money."

"Which I promise I will do," she said.

"Well," said North, also standing. "Those motel costs do add up. I guess I'll be heading home. I'll give you my address. I look forward to receiving the check from you."

Glowacka laughed to himself again. "A thousand dollars. I'm not much of a treasure hunter." He shook his head. "Yeah, fine. You send it to me when you get it. I trust you. Why not? If you can't trust a town librarian, who can you trust?"

"One thing, though," said North. "Can I see it?"

"Hey, yeah," said Glowacka.

Marietta considered this and then nodded. "Go see if Stokes is still out there. Tell him I said it was okay."

North smiled. "All right. I guess that's it, then. It was a pleasure working with you all." He looked around the room. "We were a good team. I'd always wanted to go on a treasure hunt, and now I have. Thank you all." As he made his way to the door, he patted Winston on the shoulder and peered at the red-and-purple bruise on his forehead. "Take care of that head of yours, Winston. It's very valuable."

"I'll go with you. I want to see it, too," said Glowacka.

"You going to the airport after that?" North asked.

"After my motel."

"You want to split a cab?"

"Sure. You eat breakfast?" Glowacka asked.

"Not yet. We'll pick something up on the way." And the two men, once enemies, left together.

Mrs. Lewis said, "What did you think of the ring, Winston?"

Winston shrugged good-naturedly. "Not the kind of thing I'd wear, I guess."

Mrs. Lewis smiled. "I want to show you something. Now that Mr. North and Mr. Glowacka are gone. I grew to like them, I have to say, but they still only care about the money. But there was something else in the safe."

Winston blinked. "There was?"

Marietta said, "I had men search the library after Dilmer was taken away. You two really had a fight down there in that subbasement, didn't you?"

"No," said Winston. "I think it just looks like that."

"Well, anyway," said Marietta. "Somebody finally thought to look in the safe, and"—he gestured to Mrs. Lewis, who brought out an envelope.

"A letter," she said. "From my father. Go ahead—you can read it. Your sister, too."

Winston took the envelope. It was made from some crisp, fancy material, as was the single piece of paper inside. He unfolded it and felt a tug at his arm as Katie urged him downward so she could see, too. The letter was written in a flowing script in a rich blue ink that somehow hadn't faded over the years.

Dear Violet, Red, Bruno, and Livia:

You found it! Somehow, you got past all of your differences, you spoke to each other, you worked together, and you found it! I knew you could. My instructions to you now are to sell the ring. It's just an item. It couldn't be less important. Sell it and split the money, and each of you buy something you want or need, or just give it away to charity. And since you're now talking to each other, continue to do so. Call each other once a week. Drop by and say hello. And if you've got to fight and argue every once in a while, well, then, go ahead and do so. You are brothers and sisters! My final command to you as your father is for you to become brothers and sisters again, in more than just name. If you've come this far, then you can go farther.

I love you all.

Your father

Winston shook his head. Poor Walter Fredericks! All his planning, and none of it worked out. Only one of his children lived long enough to see this letter. He looked up at Mrs. Lewis, somehow expecting her to be crying. She wasn't. Well, Marietta must have given her the letter soon after he found it, and she had probably read it a hundred or a thousand times already. "I'm sorry," he said. "It's a very nice letter, though."

Mrs. Lewis gave a little smile. "It's a very nice letter," she agreed. "Thank you for finding it. It's worth much more to me than the ring," she said. "All the same, though—don't make your father write one."

They all emerged from the little conference room. "So is that where you bring suspects to question them?" said Katie to Marietta.

"Mostly it's where we sit down to have coffee," he said.

For a Sunday morning, the police station seemed to be in a state of high activity. The center of it seemed to be two people, a guy and a girl, screaming at each other. They were both being held back by policemen, to keep them from tearing each other apart. Marietta glanced curiously at the chaotic scene as they walked to the exit.

"What's all this?" he asked the officer at the desk.

The policeman shrugged with boredom. "Boyfriend and girlfriend. She caught him with somebody else, so she stole his wallet and hid it. He wants her arrested, and she wants him arrested. I mostly want both of them gone."

Marietta laughed. "She hid it, huh?"

"Yeah," said the cop. "He says he's got five hundred bucks and all his credit cards in there, but she won't tell him where it is. She must have hid it good."

Ray Marietta laughed again and clapped Winston on the back. "Winston, we might have a job for you."

ANSWERS

Page 3

Page 13 The center row spells out "Gone To The Dogs."

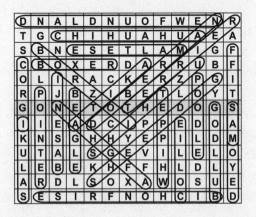

Page 21

ELK + CAT spelled backward equals TACKLE.

Page 28

BEARD does not belong. All the other words can be unscrambled into the names of fruits: MANGO, PEACH, PLUM, LIME, and GRAPE. BEARD can be unscrambled into BREAD, but this is not a fruit.

Page 36

Here are three possible answers—you may have found others:

$11 \times 11 = 121$

$(11 + 11) - 1 = 21$

$(1 + 1 + 1 + 1) - (1 + 2) = 1$

Page 39

The number on the uniforms can be turned into a letter of the alphabet by using the following simple code: $A = 1$, $B = 2$, $C = 3$, and so on. On four of the uniforms, this letter is also the first letter in the player's name. The only player for whom this does not apply is BRUNDH.

Page 50

1. NATHAN HALE (Man who said "I only regret that I have but one life to lose for my country")

2. PAUL REVERE (Man who warned Boston that the British were coming)

3. SAMUEL MORSE (Inventor of the telegraph)

4. CLARA BARTON (Famous Civil War nurse)

5. ELI WHITNEY (Inventor of the cotton gin)

6. SUSAN B. ANTHONY (Woman who agitated for women's rights)

7. JOHN HANCOCK (Famous signer of the Declaration of Independence)

Page 58

The answer is "silence."

Page 68

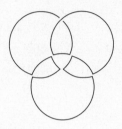

Page 73   The shaded letters can be arranged to spell ARABIC.

```
                              P
                              E                 R
T A G A L O G                 R                 O
U                 E N G L I S H                 M
R U S S I A N                 I                 A
K       W               G     A                 N
I       A     E S P E R A N T O                 I
S       H   J P   R           H                 A
H       I   A A   M A N D A R I N
        L   P N   A   O   I
        I T A L I A N     R
      U     N   S         W
      R     E   H E B R E W
  Y I D D I S H           G
      U     E   P O L I S H
      U           A
          C A N T O N E S E
```

Page 82

574	483	786
+ 9664	+ 9773	+ 9556
10238	10256	10342

458	367	548
+ 9778	+ 9887	+ 9778
10236	10254	10326

873	872	752
+ 9553	+ 9662	+ 9882
10426	10534	10634

876	637
+ 9556	+ 9887
10432	10524

Page 85

All the items Marisa likes are described by words made up of alternating consonants and vowels. Marisa would play the TUBA.

Page 89

All three have CHIPS (potato chips at the sandwich shop, a memory chip in the computer, and poker chips at the casino).

Page 116

These are the first letters in each of the words ONE, TWO, THREE . . . and so on. The next letter should be *E*, for EIGHT.

Page 120

The four strips can be rearranged to spell BENJAMIN FRANKLIN.

Page 140

To divide up the toppings equally, give one person slices 1 and 5, another person slices 2 and 4, the third person slices 3 and 8, and the last person slices 6 and 7.

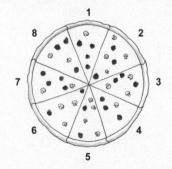

Page 166

1. He who hesitates is lost.

2. Two heads are better than one.

3. A stitch in time saves nine.

4. Honesty is the best policy.

5. If at first you don't succeed, try, try again.

6. Beggars can't be choosers.

7. Don't judge a book by its cover.

Page 201

T	E	N	T	A	C	L	E	V	E	R
A										S
N										E
O										L
D										E
A										C
N										T
R										R
O										I
T										C
U	T	G	N	I	K	C	O	R	E	H

Page 203

1—C; 2—D; 3—A; 4—B

Turn the page for a preview of the next adventure
in **THE PUZZLING WORLD OF WINSTON BREEN,**

THE POTATO CHIP PUZZLES

C
H
A
P
T
E
R

O N E

WINSTON BREEN DIDN'T know why it was called "study hall." They weren't in a hall, and hardly anyone studied. Sometimes you'd find kids finishing homework due the next period. You could tell that's what they were doing—they had a wide-eyed, racing-the-clock air to them, and they gripped their pens so hard that blood stopped flowing to their fingertips. But this was the last week of school, and there was no more homework. Kids sat in little clusters, talking semi-quietly, occasionally bursting into laughter, which would attract a glare from Mrs. Livetta, the study hall monitor. A couple of kids were reading, and one girl, with hypnotic concentration, was covering her desktop with elaborate graffiti.

Winston, of course, was solving a puzzle. He kept a couple of puzzle books in his schoolbag at all times. There had been a day earlier in the year when he found himself puzzleless in study hall, and Mrs. Livetta refused to let him go to his locker. With nothing to read and nothing to solve, he sat there for a while in utter boredom. In fact, that was the day he discovered that the letters of BOREDOM can be scrambled to make the word BEDROOM. That was a pleasing discovery, at least.

Now he was always prepared. He clicked a few times on his mechanical pencil and doodled in the margin while he thought.

In a word square, words read the same both across and down. In the following two puzzles, solve the clues to create the word square.

1	2	3	4
2			
3			
4			

1. Badly behaved child

2. Competition for runners

3. There are four of them in a deck

4. Pop quiz, for example

1	2	3	4
2			
3			
4			

1. Secret way of writing

2. Kitchen appliance

3. Card in Monopoly

4. Odds and _____

This last word square has five letters in each word . . . and the clues aren't given in order, so you'll have to figure out which word goes where.

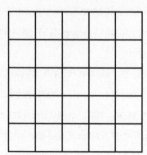

• "Great White" fish

• What's in the fireplace after a fire

• Questioned

• Abruptly to the point

• Spaghetti or ziti

"Winston!" Mrs. Livetta all but screamed in his ear.

Winston jerked like a freshly caught fish, nearly falling out of his chair. The other kids in the study hall laughed. Mrs. Livetta was standing in front of him, hands on hips.

"Wh-what? Yes?" Winston tried to regain his wits. He knew what had happened. Sometimes he became so absorbed in a puzzle that the world around him simply faded away. Mrs. Livetta must have called him once or twice from the comfort of her chair and then, when Winston didn't answer, said his name louder, and then louder still, and then she finally came over and yelled at him. The next step might have been to hit him with a textbook.

The kids laughed again, but Mrs. Livetta wasn't laughing. "You are wanted down at the principal's office. Didn't you hear the announcement?" She pointed at the loudspeaker on the wall.

Winston reddened. It was worse than he thought. The loudspeaker, which was indeed loud, had barked his name, and he hadn't heard it at all. Wow. That had to be some kind of record.

Wait a minute—the principal's office wanted to see him?

"Why does the principal want to see me?" he asked.

"I don't know," Mrs. Livetta said. "It's a loudspeaker—you can't have a conversation with it. Ask when you get down there. Now go!"

Was he in trouble? He couldn't see how. Was something wrong at home? His mind reached in every direction at once as he walked through the empty hallways down to the main office. As he rounded the corner to the school's large central lobby, the intercom system crackled and chirped. The school secretary said once again, in the voice of an old lady robot: "Winston Breen, please report to the principal's office. Winston Breen, to the principal's office." Boy, whatever the reason was, they sure wanted to see him. He bit his lower lip and tried to prepare himself.

When he reached the main office, Mrs. Lembo was still returning to her desk from the PA system. "Ah, there you are," she said.

"Yes, sorry," said Winston.

"Well, go right in. Mr. Unger's expecting you."

The principal's office was down a short hallway, ending in a door you never wanted to open. Winston had never had a reason to knock on this door, and that was fine with him. He was still trying to figure out some way he might be in trouble. He took a deep breath and knocked softly. "Come in," said a brusque voice. Winston creaked the door open.

Mr. Unger was not behind his desk. He was up and pacing. "Ah, Winston. Good. Thought maybe you were absent today. Or cutting class!"

Winston recognized that as a joke but had no idea how to respond. "Yes, no, um, I was—"

But Mr. Unger wasn't looking for any explanations. "You're still the puzzle person, right?"

"Sure. . . ." Winston had shuffled entirely into the room now. He watched the principal pace back and forth, glancing occasionally at a piece of paper in his hand. When Mr. Unger walked the halls in his gray suit and shiny shoes, he was a severe, frowning authority. Now he didn't look stern at all. In fact, he looked rather like—Winston could hardly believe it—an excited little kid.

"All right. All right. Good," he said. "I want you to look at this. Here." Mr. Unger thrust the paper into Winston's hands.

It was quite fancy—stiff and crackly, and the color of rich cream. On it were a bunch of letters and numbers, written in ink:

C3	J5	S2	Q1	W3
A4	P2	L3	D1	E4
B5	F2	S1	O4	C2
Q5	D1	L2	B4	N1
R3	N4	B3	H1	E2
D4	R2	N5	F3	W1

(Continue reading to see the answer to this puzzle.)

This was not at all what he had expected from a visit to the principal's office. "What is this?" asked Winston.

"I was hoping you could tell me."

"It looks like a code of some kind. Where did it come from?"

Unger shook his head. "Don't know. It was in my mailbox this morning, but there was no return address."

"Was there a postmark?"

Mr. Unger stopped pacing. "The postmark! I didn't think of that. I knew you were the right person to call on this." He sat down in his chair, leaned over, and dug through his garbage pail, looking for the right envelope. "Aha, here we go," he said. The envelope was fancy, too. Mr. Unger brushed it off and looked at it, frowning.

"What does it say?" said Winston.

Mr. Unger didn't respond. He just handed the envelope over.

Winston looked at the front. There was no postmark. There was no stamp. "Oh," he said. He decided to sit in one of the two chairs in front of the principal's desk.

"Someone must have come in and slipped it into my mailbox," said Mr. Unger.

"I guess that means it's from someone nearby," said Winston.

Unger nodded his head. "I guess so. I guess so. I'll ask if any of the secretaries saw anything. But the main office is busy all morning. Anybody could have come in and put something in my mailbox. Can you figure out what it is?"

"I don't know," said Winston. "It could mean anything. Maybe it has something to do with a map."

"A map," the principal repeated, not understanding.

"You know how maps have letters across the top and numbers down the side? So you can find locations on them?"

"Ah, yes," said Mr. Unger, sitting back in his chair. "Coordinates. So we need a map . . . a map of what? The town?"

"I don't know," Winston said again. "Maybe."

"I can have Mrs. Lembo bring one in."

Winston shook his head. "The problem is, which map? The map in the phone book, the map in the road atlas? They're all different."

"Hmm," said Mr. Unger, frowning.

Winston added, "And do we need a map of the town or the state or the country? We could be staring at maps the rest of our life."

"All right," said the principal. "Then what do you suggest? Maybe it's not a code. Maybe it's something else."

"What?"

"Another kind of puzzle, maybe. A connect the dots."

Winston blinked. "What?"

The principal leaned forward. "Can you connect these letters and numbers in some way? Draw lines between them? Start at A1 then go to A2 . . . ?"

Winston thought about it. It didn't sound right, but it was more than he'd come up with. But then he noticed something. "There *is* no A1," he said. "Or A2. The first pair alphabetically is"—he scanned the paper—"A4. And then there's no A5."

"Hmm," said Mr. Unger.

Winston said, "I still think it's a code." He stood up and started pacing, just as the principal had been when he arrived. "Each letter and number pair is going to stand for a letter. Or a bunch of letters. Or . . ." He drifted off, staring at the paper. A wisp of an idea had breezed through his mind, fluttering just out of reach. "There's no A5," he said again.

Mr. Unger said, "Do you think that's important?"

"Maybe," said Winston, rubbing his forehead. The first pair was C3. If that represented some other letter, what letter could it be? Maybe it was three letters past C . . . which meant F.

Winston's eyes widened.

Mr. Unger saw that. "You have an idea, don't you? Did you just solve it?"

"I think so," Winston said, and told him his idea.

The principal took the paper back. "So then J plus five is the letter O . . . S plus two is the letter U . . . and Q plus one is R."

"That spells FOUR," Winston said, getting more and more excited.

They went through the whole code, counting out the alphabet again and again like students in a very strange nursery school. When they were done, they sat back and looked at what they had written:

FOUR ZERO EIGHT SEVEN FOUR EIGHT SIX

Winston was elated, but the principal was frowning at the answer. "Seven numbers," said Mr. Unger. "That's not a very satisfying solution. What does it mean?"

Winston said, "Maybe it's a phone number."

Mr. Unger rubbed the top of his balding head. "What *is* this? If somebody wanted me to call them, why not just give me the number? Or, heck, why not call *me*? What's with all this spy movie stuff?"

"I don't know," said Winston. "Let's call it and see."

A look of bewilderment on his face, Mr. Unger reached over and hit the speaker button on his sleek black telephone. A dial tone filled the room. The principal booped in the seven digits. There was a long, tense pause as the phone rang several times, and then a gentle click, followed by a booming megaphone of a voice. Mr. Unger hastily lowered the volume a couple of notches.

"You did it!" said the voice. "You, my friends, have broken the code! And now I would like to warmly invite you to a very special contest. I am Dmitri Simon, the president of Simon's Snack Foods. And I am going to give fifty thousand dollars to one lucky school." Mr. Unger's jaw dropped open. "You've solved the first puzzle, but there will be many more puzzles to solve. On this Friday, May 18, at ten A.M., send three students and one teacher to Simon's Snack Foods, 1 Livingston Avenue, in Maplewood. At the tone, please tell me the name of your school, so that I know who to expect. And congratulations on making it this far. I will see you soon!"

There was a sudden beep, and the principal leaned in and said quickly, "Walter Fredericks Junior High, Glenville. Bernard Unger, principal."

Mr. Unger turned off the phone. His eyes were wide open and dazzled. "Fifty thousand dollars. Did he say fifty thousand dollars? If we solve a puzzle contest?" He gripped his armrests as if he thought his chair might suddenly fly. "Can this be real?" he said.

"You can call the company and find out," Winston said.

The principal nodded. "I will. I definitely will."

A slow smile crept to Winston's face. "If it *is* real, I volunteer to be one of those students," he said.

"What? Of course you do. You *better*," said Mr. Unger. "Get two more kids. Whoever you want. Fifty thousand dollars!" The principal stood up, his eyes full of wonder. He looked like he had just seen a magician do the most amazing trick ever. "I'll find a teacher to go with you," he said. "It's the day after school ends, and technically, everyone will be on vacation. But I know a few of them won't mind. Yes. Let me think. . . ." He gazed thoughtfully up at the ceiling. After a moment, he began pacing again.

Winston got the feeling his meeting with the principal was over. Mr. Unger now looked positively giddy, like a man who has just arrived at his own surprise birthday party. "We can't lose, can we? We just can't lose!"

"I don't know," said Winston. "I don't want to *promise* anything—"

"Oh, I know, I know," said the principal. "But I can feel it. Go! Get your team together! We don't have much time! Just a couple of days! We're going to win!"

Winston nodded enthusiastically and backed out of the office. He didn't tell the principal that he didn't need to get his team together— he knew exactly who his teammates were going to be. All he had to do now was tell them. Winston took off running down the hallway.

Turn the page for a peek at another adventure in
THE PUZZLING WORLD OF WINSTON BREEN,

THE PUZZLER'S MANSION

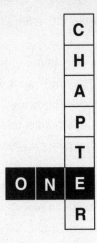

WINSTON BREEN HAD never been in trouble before—
not *this* much trouble. Winston's father shook his head. He looked
tired and disappointed. Somehow that was worse than angry.

They were sitting together on the sofa. Winston's mom and his
sister, Katie, were in the kitchen playing a board game and taking
turns glancing over to the living room. His mom looked worried,
while Katie's expression combined sisterly concern with smug satisfaction that she was not the one in trouble.

Unfortunately, Winston had been summoned to the living room
sofa quite a few times lately.

The problem was this: Winston's social studies teacher, Mr.
Burke, was a walking, talking sleeping pill. Winston had never fully
appreciated the way other teachers made their lessons interesting,
even entertaining. Mr. Burke was not there to entertain them. The
man had said as much on the first day of school: he was there to
teach American history, not to amuse them. And from that day forward, Mr. Burke stood at the front of the room, rocking on his heels
and droning about Lewis and Clark or Plymouth Rock or whatever,

occasionally referring to his notes but otherwise not moving an inch.

Paying attention to this man was impossible. Impossible! The mind was forced to wander, and Winston's mind, as usual, wandered to puzzles. His notebook contained the occasional scribble about the lesson, but mostly it was filled with attempts to anagram Lewis and Clark or Plymouth Rock into funny new phrases. (War Dance Kills! Pluck Thy Room!)

Mr. Burke soon figured out that his students weren't hanging on his every word. He would call on kids to repeat what he'd just said, and when the unfortunate victim could not, he would send a note home to be signed by that kid's parents. Totally unfair.

Winston had received three notes in five weeks. His mother and father were not happy. He tried explaining that Mr. Burke was the most boring teacher on earth, that he *had* to think about more interesting things in order to stay awake. His parents didn't want to hear it. They warned him that his love of puzzles was interfering with his schoolwork, and if it continued, there would be a price to pay.

For a while, everything was fine. Winston paid attention in class and resisted sketching out puzzle ideas. He planted his elbow on his desk, fastened his chin to the palm of his hand, and stared at Mr. Burke, determined not to receive another aggravating note.

And then, after all that, it was *science* class where Winston had his big downfall. Like a boxer who's too focused on an opponent's left jab, Winston got hit with a right hook that he never saw coming.

Science was a perfectly fine class. Mrs. Haider was a short, energetic woman who made her subject seem pretty interesting—way more than Mr. Burke managed, anyway. And twice a week there were labs, which Winston always enjoyed.

His lab partner, by virtue of alphabetical order, was a girl named Pamela Cassetti. She was absent on the day Winston landed in the vice principal's office, and that was probably half the problem right there. If Pamela had been around, Winston might have paid more attention to that day's experiment, which involved pendulums. But, no. Winston's eyes settled on some glass beakers, rinsed out and drying by the sink, close to his lab station. They reminded him of a puzzle he had seen some time ago, and he wondered if could re-create it.

There was plenty of time left to get his experiment done, so he took the three beakers to his table and examined them.

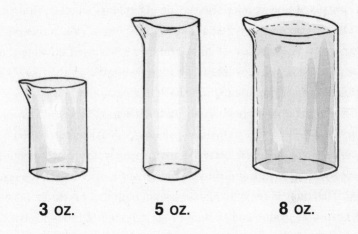

3 oz.   **5 oz.**   **8 oz.**

There are three beakers. One holds 8 ounces and is full of water. The others are empty. One can hold 3 ounces, and the other can hold 5 ounces. None of the beakers have measurements marked on them, so unless a beaker is full, you can't accurately determine how much water is in it. Nonetheless, can you figure out how to measure out exactly 4 ounces of water?

*　　*　　*

He was setting one of the beakers down when Mrs. Haider called out, "Winston, *what* are you doing?" Winston's reaction was to try to hide the beakers, which was dumb, since Mrs. Haider had already seen them. And it was even dumber than *that*, because in his haste to get the beakers back to the sink, he dropped two of them. They seemed to almost float downward, giving Winston plenty of time to gasp and wish himself back in time thirty seconds or so. Then they shattered on the floor.

Mrs. Haider was on him at once, a screaming typhoon of a lady. She asked very loudly why Winston was playing with the beakers in the first place. She wondered at the top of her lungs whether Winston had lost his mind. She yelled at him to grab a broom and a dustpan, clean up every last shard of glass, and then get himself down to the vice principal's office, where he would become Mr. Rothenberger's problem and she would no longer have to look at him.

Winston had never been in Mr. Rothenberger's "hot seat," an orange plastic chair next to the vice principal's desk, and he hoped to never be there again. He received a withering lecture about school property and respect and values, and all sorts of related subjects, until Winston was ready to sign a solemn oath that he would never get in trouble again—not in junior high school, not in high school, not in college. Never. And then Mr. Rothenberger said, "I am going to have to call your parents about this, you understand." Winston slumped in his chair. He had survived Mrs. Haider's screaming and Mr. Rothenberger's lecture, but there were more surprises ahead on this miserable obstacle course.

His father, thankfully, wasn't much for yelling. This evening he didn't seem to have a lecture in him, either. He only shook his head and thought for a long time before saying, "Well, Winston . . . what are we going to do about this?"

"I don't know," Winston replied honestly.

"That makes two of us," said Nathan Breen. "I mean, you'll be paying the school back for the equipment you broke. That much is clear. And there will be a punishment. No video games or television during the week until further notice."

Winston's eyes flicked down. *During the week* was an important concession. That meant he could still have these things over the weekend.

His father continued, "I don't know what to say about your puzzles. I know you love doing them. I know you love creating them. I have always encouraged that. I'm very proud of you, and I'm proud of this ability you have developed." He paused long enough to sigh and shake his head again. "But it is becoming a distraction. Do you see that?"

It would have been hard to miss. "Yes," Winston said.

"What do you plan to do about it?"

"I'm not going to do puzzles as much," he said. That sounded incredible even to him. He looked at his father's face and sensed that more was needed. "And I won't do them in school anymore." That wasn't very convincing, either, so he added, "Not during classes, anyway."

His father stared at him as if trying to decide how much of this to believe. Finally he allowed himself a rueful little smile. "You have to decide who you're going to be, Winston. Your grades aren't as good this year, you're getting these notes home from your teachers—"

Just one teacher, Winston thought but did not say.

"—and now this thing in science class. That brain of yours is everywhere but where it's supposed to be." He gave a final, frustrated toss of his hands. "Only you can change that. Go do your homework." And with that, Nathan Breen got up and went to his office.

Katie, in the kitchen, made a disgusted sound. She must have thought Winston would be grounded, or possibly banished from the house. "Oh, you got so *lucky*," she called out.

She was probably right, but Winston didn't feel lucky.

The dreadful week ended and then it was Saturday. At last, Winston was allowed to watch television and play video games, but he found he didn't want to. He didn't want to solve anything in his puzzle books, either. He was trying to keep puzzles on a low simmer instead of a raging boil.

He wished he could get together with Mal and Jake, his two best friends, but Winston hadn't seen much of them since the start of school. Winston had shared classes with one or both of his friends since first grade—but this year, Mal and Jake had three classes together, while Winston's schedule didn't overlap with theirs at all. Not even for lunch! Worse, his two friends were off in their own orbits. Jake had joined the swim team and was over at the high school for practice almost every afternoon. And Mal had gotten a role in the school play and was busy with rehearsals. Winston was starting to feel like he'd been exiled to a desert island somewhere.

Summer had decided to put its feet up and linger into October. Katie was watching cartoons, and his parents were busy in their own grown-up worlds, his father doing paperwork in his office and his mother sorting clothes in the bedroom. Winston felt restless. He had to get out of here, even if he had nowhere to go.

A few minutes later, he was on his bicycle, pedaling into a warm morning breeze. Aimless, he headed toward the town green, and from there he supposed he would go see Mr. Penrose. The last few times he had visited Penrose's Curio Shop, Penrose had taught him a few things about chess. Maybe he could get another lesson, or maybe he would just explore the shop's crowded shelves and its endless supply of fascinating bric-a-brac. At least he'd be able to talk to somebody.

Penrose greeted him like an old friend, and the two of them chatted about this and that. Winston, intending to ask for a chess lesson, impulsively asked for a game instead. Penrose brought out the board, and soon they were sitting quietly together, Winston with a cold soda nearby.

It didn't take long for Winston to realize this was a mistake. Penrose's black pieces performed in elegant harmony, while Winston's white pieces were like sixteen kittens tangled in a ball of yarn. Winston's army was soon shredded, and every possible move looked like it would only lead to further disaster. Penrose wasn't even paying attention to the board at this point. He read a magazine and occasionally rose from his chair to help a customer. Hardly a word had passed over the chessboard in the last hour, except when one man, holding a brass lamp he had just purchased, looked at the game, patted Winston on the shoulder, and said, "Good luck, kid."

Winston shook his head. What had made him think he could win this game, or even be competitive, after five brief chess lessons? He extended a finger and knocked his king over, officially resigning the game.

Mr. Penrose offered a hand. "A good game."

Winston shook it but said, "No, it wasn't."

"Oh, now. Don't be hard on yourself," Mr. Penrose said. "You handled the opening moves reasonably well. You tried to control the middle of the board. It's clear that you understand the basics. You see when an opponent's piece is about to make a threat, but you don't always see when two pieces are working in tandem. And that's fine. It's early days, Winston. With practice, you will improve. I can give you some books if you wish to study on your own."

"Maybe," Winston said with a shrug.

Penrose understood that he had been politely rebuffed. "Or perhaps you would prefer this." He reached under his counter and came up with a second chessboard—a smaller one, just six by six.

"What's that, chess for beginners?" Winston asked.

Mr. Penrose smiled and said, "Some people prefer to teach the game on a smaller board. I'm not of that mind myself. But I thought you might like a little chess puzzle." He placed the board on the countertop, reached underneath again, and came back with a handful of chess pieces, all queens. Winston found himself intrigued.

"All you have to do," Mr. Penrose said, "is put these six queens on the chessboard so that none of them are attacking each other. Which means, of course, that none can be in the same row or column, or on the same diagonal. Can you do it?"

So much for not doing puzzles today. Winston took a few minutes to try out Penrose's challenge and was soon absorbed, sliding queens this way and that around the board. He'd been working for a while when the bell over the door rang and the mailman came in. A moment later, Mr. Penrose, flipping through the junk mail and catalogs, made a little sound, not quite a gasp.

"Are you okay?" Winston asked.

"Oh, yes," Penrose said in a faraway voice. "Everything is fine." He was gazing at a small red envelope. Now he reached for a letter opener.

Winston watched as Penrose became engrossed by the contents of the envelope. After a moment, he began sliding queens around the chessboard again, pretending to be interested in the puzzle even when Mr. Penrose said, "Huh!" as if some wonderful mystery had just deepened. Winston looked up again to find his old friend smiling cryptically at him.

"What?" Winston said.

Mr. Penrose raised a finger: *Wait a minute—I'm thinking.* After a moment, he went behind the counter and paged through a small, leather-bound book. Finding what he wanted, he picked up the phone and dialed.

Someone on the other end answered, and Mr. Penrose said, "Norma! It's good to hear your voice. It's Arthur Penrose. Yes, quite well. Thank you. Is he in?" There was a brief silence, and then Penrose said, "Richard! How are you. Yes? Oh, here, too. I'm glad to hear it. I wanted to ask about this invitation. Does it mean what it says? It's quite a departure from the usual thing. . . ." There was a pause, then Penrose laughed and said, "Well, I'm wondering if the guests strictly need to be relations." He looked at Winston and said, "I have somebody I would like to bring along. Oh, yes. Someone who will truly appreciate what you do. That's okay, then? Excellent. I shall see you in a couple of weeks. Of course, I wouldn't miss it. All right, then. Bye."

Penrose hung up and sat down, as pleased as Winston had ever seen him. Winston had forgotten all about the chessboard. Mr. Penrose wanted to take him somewhere?

"A few weeks ago," Penrose said, "you mentioned how you don't get to see those two friends of yours as frequently anymore. Those two boys."

"Mal and Jake. Yeah," Winston said.

"We haven't really spoken about it since then. But if I may say so, Winston, you seemed rather down about it. And you don't seem all that much improved even today."

Winston frowned, and his eyes dropped to the chessboard. "It hasn't been a good time, I guess. Mal and Jake are busy. . . . School has been hard. . . ." He concluded with a shrug.

"Well, then," said Mr. Penrose, "I may have just the ticket."

"The ticket for what?"

"The ticket to distract you from your current raft of problems, of course." He slid the red envelope across the counter.

Winston was amazed that his curiosity about Penrose's letter was going to be satisfied so soon. He picked up the envelope. It unfolded to reveal a single ornately printed card at its center:

You are invited to a weekend
of games, puzzles, and amusements
at the home of Richard Overton.
You know where that is, right?
Arrive October 21.
The games start October 22.
Bring the family this time, if you like!
But either way, show up.
Don't make me ask you twice.

Winston read the invitation three times before saying to Mr. Penrose, "You want me to go to a party with you? A party that lasts all *weekend*?"

Mr. Penrose said, "Normally these events are restricted to invitees only, but you are in luck. For some reason, he's decided to let guests bring their children along. I have no children, so instead I am offering this to you. I think you would find Richard's weekend gatherings to be a lot of fun. And you look like you could use some fun right about now."

"Who is this guy?"

Penrose said, "You've never heard of Richard Overton?"

Winston shook his head.

"He's a musician. He plays the piano," Mr. Penrose said.

"Oh," said Winston. "Is he good?"

Penrose smiled. Winston had the feeling he had just asked a stupid question. "Let me give you a CD," Penrose said. "Take it home and listen to it. You can judge for yourself."

Winston thought, The answer to the question is yes. Richard Overton is a good piano player. But he said, "Okay, sure."

Penrose had a small shelf dedicated to old music. He moved his finger along this, searching, and came up with a particular compact disc.

"Oh, hey," said Winston. "I don't want to take something you're supposed to sell."

Penrose waved a hand. "I don't sell much music, and I have numerous copies of this album. It's my gift to you. I'm sure you'll like it. But whether you like it or not, I *know* you'll enjoy a weekend at Richard's estate."

"His . . . estate?" Winston was starting to get intrigued.

Penrose nodded. "He has a large, beautiful house a couple of hours upstate. And every once in a while, he invites a number of his friends to visit, and he challenges us with puzzles and games that he has created."

"What kind of puzzles?" Winston asked.

"Oh, they're different every time," Penrose said. "My friend Richard is a clever fellow. I think the two of you would get along very well."

Winston looked at the CD. It seemed no different than the handful of classical albums his parents owned. The cover showed a close-up of a pair of hands hovering over a piano keyboard, fingers arched as if about to play something complicated and dramatic.

"How do you know this guy?" he asked.

"My wife was a musician," Penrose said.

"Your wife?"

"She died some years ago."

"Oh," Winston said. He didn't know Mr. Penrose had been married.

"They performed a series of concerts together. This was quite a while back, you understand. In fact, it's probably close to fifty years now. My goodness." Penrose wore a faint and dreamy smile, as if he could still hear the music. "Anyway," he said, "I stayed friendly with Richard even after Rebecca passed away. He knows I've always enjoyed his games." He became more clear-eyed and said, "So will you, Winston, I guarantee it. Ask your parents if you can go. If they have any questions, they can call me."

The whole idea that he might try to walk away from puzzles—even for a day—suddenly seemed ridiculous. A weekend of puzzly games at some famous person's mansion? How could Winston not jump at this?

"Okay. I'll go ask them right now." He thanked his friend for the invitation.

ANSWERS

Page 3.

You can measure out 4 ounces of water in six moves:

1. Fill the 5-ounce beaker from the 8-ounce beaker.
2. Fill the 3-ounce beaker from the 5-ounce beaker. This will leave 2 ounces in the 5-ounce beaker.
3. Pour the 3-ounce beaker back into the 8-ounce beaker.
4. Pour the 2 ounces left in the 5-ounce beaker into the 3-ounce beaker.
5. Again fill the 5-ounce beaker from the 8-ounce beaker.
6. Fill the 3-ounce beaker from the 5-ounce beaker. Since there are 2 ounces already in the smallest beaker, you will need to add only 1 ounce to fill it, and this will leave you with 4 ounces in the 5-ounce beaker.

Page 8.

There are a number of possible answers, but here's one:

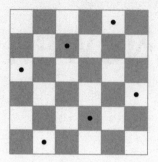